I0690474

SHAKESPEARE'S CUTHBERT

#1

by

Patrick Barrett

A Wild Wolf Publication

Published by Wild Wolf Publishing in 2016
Copyright © 2016 Patrick Barrett

First print

All characters appearing in this work are fictitious. Any resemblance to real persons, living or dead, is purely coincidental.

ISBN: 978-1-907954-50-4
Also available as an e-book

www.wildwolfpublishing.com

Chapter 1

The crow tilted one wing and rode the thermals diagonally across the valley. He could see it all from here- scattered houses and a farm nestled in a fold of the earth below him.

Whoever designed him had been truly inspired. The way his head stuck out in front gave a panoramic view without his wings obscuring threats or danger.

However, the colour wasn't perfect and it made formation flying at night an absolute bugger.

Some birds covered miles every day in search of food, or at least the chance of something interesting to stare at. The crow was content with the valley. The occupants and their habits kept him riveted as he tried to fathom why humans made life so complicated. They built houses and didn't leave the roofs open for a start. How would a crow take flight in emergency with a roof over its nest? And doors? Why shut something behind you when it would only be in the way again next time you came out?

The crow glided closer to the farm and watched someone head into a barn with an empty bucket. He recognised this one. He was about to feed the chickens and, by association, supply the crow with breakfast.

The chap who ran the farm seemed to be the same one who dealt with dead people. He made a huge job of wrapping them in cloth, fastening them into a box and then burying the lot on top of the hill.

Even a crow knows that bodies are best left out at night for the local fox. Spreading his wings and fluttering a few feathers to adjust his trim, the crow landed gracefully on top of a fence. One wing caught a rake propped carelessly nearby and the implement slid sideways, hitting the barn door and opening the latch. The door creaked open ominously.

Cuthbert watched the crow land, he watched the rake fall and he watched the barn door as it finished creaking and crashed open.

Four angry tons of bow-legged malevolence faced him. He stared. The bull stared back.

Cuthbert wasn't prone to panicking. The messages didn't usually get there in time for his reactions to get their boots on, so he continued to cross the farmyard, nonchalantly swinging the bucket of chicken feed.

This was the first time the bull had experienced apathy. Sheer abject terror was the norm and it paused. The bull pawed the ground in anger, playing for time to allow this idiot in front of him to recognise him and scream.

The chickens bobbed about as if one of them had lost a contact lens before they spotted Cuthbert, and appeared from everywhere like demented snowflakes.

The bull ponderously swung its mighty head to watch the distraction, his horns gleaming with intent. When the head swung back, Cuthbert was gone. The bull charged into the middle of the farmyard skidding to a halt as if 'El Cordobes' himself was out there.

The expression 'Bull Market' was a bit of a mystery because bulls were not the fastest thinkers around, and when they found themselves in any type of market, it was pretty much 'game over.' This one swung his head from side to side and gradually wondered why the chickens congregated around the horse trough. Not wanting to appear slow compared to a chicken, the bull ambled over.

Cuthbert gibbered silently. He could feel the ground shake. "Think, Cuthbert," he urged himself. "Analyse your resources." Cuthbert looked around. He was behind a horse trough and he had a metal bucket and a flock of chickens. Briefly he wondered how badly a bucketful of chickens would hurt a bull. Perhaps it was best not to annoy it.

The bull had met chickens before. They did not share social skills with each other and he usually just walked all over them. He sneezed as a sudden burst of feathers appeared under his hooves.

Cuthbert had a plan. He would suddenly jump up and strike the metal bucket against the iron water pump on the trough. If he shouted at the same time, the noise should startle the bull and he could run for the house.

The chickens clacked and chattered as he swept them away from the bucket.

Leaping up, Cuthbert bellowed and swung the bucket, missing the pump and striking the bull right on the nose. Both man and bull went cross-eyed and gasped- one at the realisation of what had happened, and the other at the realisation of what was about to happen.

Cuthbert ran.

4

The bull roared. Nobody was allowed to embarrass him in front of a chicken. He charged. One horn snapped the pump clean off and a geyser of water shot into the air. He firmly stamped one hoof into the metal bucket and was enveloped by a cloud of corn chips. The deluge from the pump turned the corn into a paste almost immediately and he ran blindly, clumping across the yard in search of Cuthbert.

Cuthbert had managed to reach his washing line. He now had rope and a set of signal flags. Was it 'red rag to a bull' and 'white to surrender? It didn't really matter- a bachelor farmer's clothing usually ceased to be white the second it came out of the packaging. Cuthbert advanced steadily towards the bull holding out a red flannel shirt.

The bull snorted out two jets of super-heated steam as it peered through the congealed mess all over its face. Was this clown coming to wipe his eyes, he thought in disbelief.

Cuthbert struck a pose and shook the garment. The bull tensed and charged and the clanking increased rapidly as the bull picked up speed. Cuthbert stepped nimbly to one side, allowing the creature to crash into the huge stone gate-post. The bull was stunned. Cuthbert smiled, made a mental note to buy a new bucket, and went to put the kettle on. The bull slowly clanked back to the barn for a lie down.

Chapter 2

The old thatched house finally stopped its night-time creaking and now the farmyard noises began.

It was time for Cuthbert to take his place in the world- his place was at the head of the 'one-man-band' shambles he had inherited.

The undertaking business vied for attention with the family theatre tradition and both clamoured for attention with the farm animals.

Cuthbert's farm was at the centre of the valley.

The valley was a beautiful place and seemed to have a secret identity, that of an open prison.

No-one left if they could avoid it. Anybody who did returned with a vague uneasiness about the outside world. Cuthbert swung his unremarkable legs over the edge of the bed. This was followed by his ordinary body attached to his average head. Cuthbert was the living embodiment of neutral- if he stood amongst the bodies, he would probably be the first to be buried.

He didn't shave, partly because he didn't need to, and partly because his reflection didn't always bother to show up. Cuthbert threw open the bedroom shutters and the daylight reluctantly explored the gloom.

Everything in the house was inherited: the four poster bed, the dark, crouching cupboards and the unpredictable long-case clock in the hall. Electricity was a scarce visitor to the valley and was easily scared away.

Cuthbert peered beneath the beetling brows of the thatch and watched a crow sit upon his stile.

The crow tilted its head first one way and then the next- this was to give the appearance of nature's constant hunt for food. However, this was all a theatrical performance because as soon as the kitchen door opened, the crow would steal Cuthbert's bacon.

Cuthbert's morning ritual was a routine of opening up ready for business. He unfastened the shutters, he undid all the doors.

His father always used to say, "Be ready for business, Cuthbert. It's no good a corpse turning up if it can't get through the door." His father also said, "Get out of that hole and stop snivelling, Cuthbert," repeatedly.

Cuthbert's memory was quite fragmented at times.

Chapter 3

Making his way across to the old barn and flinging open the big doors, Cuthbert stood and inhaled the atmosphere along with the dust and pigeon droppings.

The barn was used as a theatre. It was a valley tradition to stage a play by William Shakespeare once a year.

Cuthbert's mother had been an actress. Everybody could remember her either before she began to act or later when she couldn't really expect the good roles any more. Oddly enough no-one seemed to remember her at her prime.

Walking slowly between the rows of chairs, he watched the dust motes dance in the shafts of light beaming through cracks and gaps in the old wooden walls. His mind began to fill with the thunder of the chariot race, the clash of sword on shield, the roar of jets and helicopters, car chases and men running down tunnels being chased by stone balls. He sighed. This was provincial theatre and anyway Shakespeare wasn't too well up on helicopters.

Still, as he stood on the stage and looked over the rows, sometimes he could feel … something, a vibration left from the past or perhaps a building passion that could explode into the future?

Shaking his head, Cuthbert stepped down from the stage and automatically straightened the aisle seat on the front row. If he came in late at night, he sometimes caught a badger sat there. It never left the seat how it found it. *Must be a male*, thought Cuthbert.

Back outside, Cuthbert surveyed his domain. The house was much envied in the village – it was ancient and the thatch was neglected. It looked like an old man peering through bushy eyebrows and the ivy seemed to think that not paying rent entitled it to smother everything.

Stone outbuildings were scattered around like a child's building set. Cuthbert ran the undertaking business from one of them. It was not much different from applying make-up to a corpse that was desperately trying to look alive, and doing the same for an actor with a similar motivation. Cuthbert had no real sense of identity or ambition. Whenever there was a void, something came along and filled it.

It was usually preceded by comments like, "I suppose you'll be taking over the Dad's business, then?" or "I suppose the house is yours now, even though you'll never be man enough to fill it."

The alterations to enlarge the barn- sorry, theatre- over the years had kept the pub gossip going single-handed. Three-legged pigs had come and gone without comment, but it was deemed necessary. The theatre tradition ran deep in the valley and so did the dedication to the Bard. Local children were inducted into the performances at an early age, just to guarantee that things stayed truly awful.

Chapter 4

Cuthbert looked up at the clear blue sky and watched the crow circling high above.

What does he think about, thought Cuthbert. *With a view like that, he must constantly re-appraise life and all its meanings.*

The crow looked down at Cuthbert and thought, *Doesn't he actually do anything?*

Cuthbert went back into the barn and swept the stage. This was a weekly ritual and somehow made him feel closer to the boards. It was at these moments when he thought he heard the whisper of a dramatic line or the rustle of silk as a leading lady entered 'stage left'. These thoughts could be quite daunting for someone with no imagination, like Cuthbert. Another problem with having no imagination was that reactions were hard to come by.

He stepped out from the theatre and at that precise moment he was assailed by a vision of teeth, eyes, hooves and the breath of Beelzebub.

It wasn't the milkman's horse- a guaranteed smack in the face with a warm wet flannel of a tongue announced that one. Cuthbert froze as this image whirled maniacally before him, generating its own dust storm. Two tails seemed to be whipping about at different heights and a shrill whinnying came from two places at once. Cuthbert's senses and reactions had retreated to that dark warm place where they felt safe, so he simply stood there as things settled down before him.

Something shrilled, "How dare you startle Bunny like that. You almost had us orff."

Cuthbert stared as the double-vision slowly settled into the vision of a double. The horse was a foaming, grimacing, brown thing with a flowing tail. The rider was almost identical. Cuthbert still stared. He had sorted out the double vision, now he only had to handle the idea of three tons of horse flesh being called 'Bunny' and spot the other person in the equation that equalled 'Us'.

The horse whirled around again and the rider's ponytail whipped around in synchrony with the horse's tail.

"Good grief", shrilled the rider, "I assume you can read." The voice came from the middle of the dust storm like a biblical warning. Then, the vision was gone, re-arranging his path and jumping his gate.

The dust cloud slowly settled and Cuthbert's senses returned in time to see a letter on the ground.

Chapter 5

Sitting at his kitchen table, Cuthbert re-read the letter. The farm and all its out-buildings had once belonged to the old Manor house just over the hill. The house, Mandrake Hall, had recently been sold and this was an invitation for him to visit.

Cuthbert shuddered- he didn't like meeting people. He preferred it when they met on his slab and there was no need for courtesy or pretence. And the old hall seemed to lurk. He was sure he could hear the ancient stones creak as it turned to watch him on the rare occasions he approached it.

Sticking the letter upright in a crack in the huge old table was the equivalent to filing it as 'Urgent'.

Cuthbert went over to the cooking range which spat malevolently as he approached. Pouring a mug of tea, he wandered outside to one of his out-buildings.

On the slab today was his nemesis. This man before him had terrorised generations of schoolchildren in the valley and Cuthbert was to prepare him for that great tutorial in the sky. The moustache still seemed to bristle indignantly even though the spite and venom no longer flowed.

Briefly Cuthbert considered shaving it off, thus sending him to his maker with nothing to hide behind, but that would be unprofessional … whereas carving 'Skool Stinkz.' on the inside of the coffin lid right before the teacher's eyes seemed really, really appropriate.

Let him stare at that for eternity without being able to correct it, thought Cuthbert. With the lid firmly screwed down and all grievances aired, Cuthbert turned his mind to visiting the Hall.

Clothes were always a problem. He couldn't really borrow a suit from a corpse- they never seemed to fit. There was the theatre wardrobe. Let's face it, it was his wardrobe.

Sighing, and giving the coffin one last kick, Cuthbert went to wrestle with the water pump over his kitchen sink. This rusty old hand-pump had a perfectly adequate supply of fresh clean water from the well, but it somehow preferred to emit a brown splatter and only coughed out intermittently whenever it was needed in a hurry.

Cuthbert tugged nervously at someone else's collar. The suit had been left by the relative of a corpse, but had never been used. He walked as if to his own funeral and his chief mourner's expression was absolutely genuine.

Chapter 6

The Old Hall appeared slowly as Cuthbert rounded the hill. Evening sun glinted from its windows giving the impression that it had just winked at him.

Watched by two stone lions flanking the steps, Cuthbert followed his shadow as it marched towards a door as old as the Hall. It had withstood civil wars, feuds and demands for paternity suits in its time and it wore the scars proudly. It was Cuthbert's last chance. Perhaps it would stick. Perhaps no-one would hear his feeble knock.

The door opened. Cuthbert never knowingly hated anyone, but the man who opened the door had just reserved himself a very cold slab indeed.

Cuthbert was greeted by a nod, a smile and a slight sideways turn of the body. These calculated actions resulted in Cuthbert having to return the nod and smile back whilst simultaneously twisting into too small a gap without falling over his own feet.

After negotiating the butler and staggering into the Hall like an ungainly duckling, Cuthbert was kept off balance by a booming voice and a crushing hand-shake.

"Welcome, welcome. Come on in, come on in."

Cuthbert was steered deeper into the building by an arm around his shoulder. People always seemed to steer Cuthbert when they met him. If they were so frightened of losing him, why did they invite him?

The man slapped his hand onto Cuthbert's shoulder. A cloud of formaldehyde burst out of the material.

"Ah, mothballs," boomed the man. "Same problem here. Keep putting ducks in my pockets and they fall straight through. No point shooting them if you lose the damn things, eh?"

The entrance hall mostly consisted of a staircase disappearing into the darkness somewhere above. Marching up the walls were the past owners of the Hall and several startled looking stags' heads who were probably not too thrilled by their career choice.

The man manoeuvred Cuthbert into a long room fitted with floor length windows down one side and mirrors all the way down the other. He turned to Cuthbert and introduced himself.

"Henry Chisolm," he announced, pumping Cuthbert's hand. "We moved in some weeks ago."

There's that 'we' again, thought Cuthbert, looking around.

"What do you think? Think?"

Cuthbert concentrated- did the man repeat the last word?

Henry Chisolm seemed to be building up to something and he continued, "Thought this might be just what you are looking for. For."

Cuthbert blinked. He had done it again.

Henry stared at Cuthbert impatiently, "The ballroom. Do you want to stage some plays here or not? Not?"

Cuthbert caught up, partly. "Oh, no, thank you. The echo would be quite unsuitable."

Henry took a step backwards. "Echo, what echo? Echo?" He continued, "Daughter said you were strange, didn't she, Ronald?"

Now, confusion to the confused is like oxygen to the living, so Cuthbert's face betrayed nothing as he realised that he hadn't caught up at all. It seemed that 'we' was now referred to as 'Ronald'.

Someone stepped out from behind Henry. He was shorter than Henry and he was slimmer than Henry. In fact he fitted behind Henry perfectly and he seemed to always be one word behind him.

Cuthbert relaxed. So that was it.

Henry introduced his brother Ronald.

Ronald studied Cuthbert carefully as if calculating which calibre bullet would do the job quickly, before leaving the room without a word.

Cuthbert studied him in turn and decided that he may have a use for that stunted coffin in his barn after all.

He walks just like a penguin, thought Cuthbert.

Henry guided Cuthbert gently along the mirrored ballroom.

Cuthbert noticed that every time they passed a support wall, they disappeared. Then at the next mirror, they reappeared. *Just like a nun on a zebra crossing. Now you see her, now you don't.*

Henry had stopped and was looking at him strangely. One eyebrow rose and he asked, "Well?"

Cuthbert was caught out. He had drifted; perhaps that's why people held onto him.

Clearing his throat, Cuthbert made the best of it. "Can you repeat one little part of that, please?"

Henry prepared himself. "Which little part?"

"All of it," said Cuthbert.

Henry sighed- his daughter hadn't exaggerated at all. He began again. "I have heard all about your theatre company. My family and friends are fascinated by Shakespeare and would like to help in any way we can. We also like local history, so anything you could tell us about the Hall or its land or any … .tunnels perhaps?"

Cuthbert's mind stalled. This was one of those moments when he remembered being entrusted with the mysteries of the valley and his parents had sworn him to secrecy. It was the time to construct a plausible alibi and throw these strangers completely off the scent. "Er, tunnels?" he asked, his face betraying exactly what was going on behind it- nothing.

Henry's eyebrow rose again and Cuthbert discovered that there was a back door to the Hall.

As Cuthbert stammered the usual guff about being a working farmer and undertaker- therefore he didn't have much time for tales and rumours- Henry shook his hand and closed the door so that each of them was on a different side of it.

He followed the path around the Hall musing over his visit. Others had asked about the tunnels.

Cuthbert's one serious love affair had been with Geraldine, the local museum curator. She had asked about the tunnels and was even rumoured to have done some excavating.

Of course, there were tunnels- the valley was riddled with them. It had all begun with the river suddenly changing course many years ago. The then owner of the Hall started a project to ensure a regular supply of water to the valley.

A reservoir was dug at the top of the hill and tunnels delivered the rainwater through them into the village, through the water mill and out to the lake. Everyone was involved and the system was the valley's pride and joy. What interest these tunnels would be to others was beyond Cuthbert. Their purpose was obvious, unless, of course, they meant the really early tunnels.

Cuthbert was distracted by a sound he recognised. It came from the site of the old family crypt. It was the scrape of a stone lid being moved.

As established, confusion is Cuthbert's natural state, but sometimes confusion needs company and this time it invited panic.

Cuthbert ran. As an undertaker, he knew that the dead were dead, but he always sewed the shroud to the coffin lining just in case.

If he had stayed for a moment longer, he may have seen someone with a lamp and a shovel amble across the grounds. He walked just like a penguin.

After washing his hands and changing his clothes, Ronald took his place on the club fender beside the roaring fire. Arranged in a semi-circle were several old winged armchairs crouching on ball and claw feet, each armchair holding a newcomer to the valley.

"Find anything yet, Ronald?" asked Henry.

Ronald glanced up and answered belligerently, "Course not; this place is riddled with tunnels and passageways. It could be anywhere. If there really is an unknown manuscript by Shakespeare hidden down there, it could have rotted away years ago."

Henry opened his mouth to speak, but Ronald hadn't finished. "I gave up a good contract in a civil war to come on this angry duck hunt with you."

Henry sighed. "That's 'wild goose chase', Ronald, and I'm sure that your victims will be happy to postpone the massacre for a week or two."

Ronald sulked quietly as the fire took the chill of the tunnels out of his bones and Henry addressed another member of the group.

"Geraldine, has the museum given us any clues yet?"

She shrugged. "There are definite references to a William Shakespeare being employed as a teacher here at Mandrake Hall, and he was known to have been writing at that time. He started the tradition of the valley dwellers performing plays for him, so that he could see a rough performance before trying to sell it in London. The locals have followed this every year since then, and Cuthbert's family have always organised it. The parents are both dead and he is in sole charge of things now." She steepled her fingers and continued, "If anyone knows the whereabouts of a manuscript, it is Cuthbert, but I have never heard a word from him about it."

The Captain leaned forward from his chair and suggested, "Torture, that's the ticket. Works every time. Even got a cheap ride down here after I shoved the clerk's fingers into a light fitting."

"That was me," exploded Ronald. "You just stood and watched as usual."

"Each to his own," snapped the Captain. "Officer and a gentleman, you know. We have people for the messy bits."

Henry raised both hands and appealed for calm. His experience as a war correspondent had taught him that everyone had an opinion and, by and large, they were all useless.

"Ronald," he said, "keep checking the tunnels. Captain, you live in the old mill house now. Check it thoroughly and, Geraldine, scour the museum for any clue." He scratched his chin before adding, "We may have to infiltrate this year's play to catch everyone off guard. Who knows, that clown Cuthbert may even perform it for us, eh?"

Chapter 7

Rehearsals were scheduled for tonight and Cuthbert threw open the doors to the theatre. He was still pondering the visit to the Hall, but the rehearsals would take his mind off it. Valley rehearsals would take Drake's mind off the Armada.

Walking down the centre aisle, he automatically put the aisle seat back upright on his way past. The play this year was 'The Tempest'.

Cuthbert's new neighbour was a chap called Captain Edgar and he had moved into the old mill. No-one knew whether Edgar was his first or last name, or even what he had been the Captain of. He was certainly keen. He had supplied shovels, ropes and crowbars as props and he had promised a real surprise for tonight.

Once the village gossip could have supplied all the inside knowledge about these outsiders, but they didn't lean on the same five-bar gate or queue up in the Post Office, where Mrs Biggle could delay them as the gossip to work her magic. In fact, the village gossip was threatening to leave the valley.

Cuthbert wondered impishly how anyone would know she made noise about going.

The Captain called out from the doorway, "Come on, young Cuthbert, front and centre. Give a hand here."

Cuthbert idly dusted a few chair backs on his way to the door again. He stopped suddenly, rooted to the spot as the bronze barrel of a huge cannon inched its way into the theatre. "Good grief, Captain," exclaimed Cuthbert, "have you dragged that thing all the way from the mill on your own?"

The Captain looked up from his labours and replied, "Good heavens, no. Mrs Edgar is back there somewhere."

Cuthbert peered around the door. Sure enough, a red face appeared behind one of the spoked wheels and a set of fingers waggled towards him.

Mrs Edgar had probably dressed up for this visit and the effort showed vaguely in the wreckage. Her hair had started out in a bun, but was now more of a soufflé. No-one had ever heard her speak, presumably so she could save her breath for pushing cannons.

Before the cannon fully entered the theatre, the twins exploded into being. If they had names, no-one knew what they were. They were simply 'The Twins'. It was all in the tone, depending upon whatever they had just been accused of. "Look out, it's the twins" was a real attention grabber in the valley.

Now they just stood and gaped at the long bronze barrel, the dangerously open hole at the end, and the spoked wheels. Best of all was the bag of black powder and the round shiny cannon ball. For the twins, it proved that if there was a God, it wasn't who everybody else thought it was.

They were followed by Margery, universally known as 'The Twins' Mum.' She had been the beauty of the valley in her day, but her husband's marital promises hadn't survived the twins. Giving Cuthbert a weary smile, she ushered her offspring out of the way as the cannon crept all the way in.

Mrs Edgar seemed close to fainting, so Margery sat her down and fussed around her.

Cuthbert and the Captain checked the floor and the ceiling in the manner of men out of their depth everywhere.

One of the twins opened the bag of powder and the other one tossed the ball from hand to hand.

The Captain caught Cuthbert's horrified look and assured him, "Don't worry, no-one remembers how to fire one of these things these days."

Several things seemed to happen simultaneously. The world disappeared in a cloud of smoke, the aisle seat disintegrated, a hole appeared in the far wall, a bright ray of sunshine hit Cuthbert full in the face, and the Captain's eyebrows evaporated. If anyone heard anything at the time, they certainly didn't for some time afterwards.

Cuthbert awoke slowly to a vision. His Geraldine was back. She was leaning over him with her hair swaying and lips pursed. The whole effect was of heaven. Was this how people felt just before Cuthbert met them?

The reverie was interrupted by a voice saying, "Nah, he ain't dead, watch this ..."

The pain in Cuthbert's shin made him sit bolt upright very quickly and the twins slid away into the smoke.

The smoke was knee high and the cannon lay on its side suspiciously like the 'smoking gun' at the scene of the crime.

20

Mrs Edgar's hair had become *très chic* in a style never before seen in the valley and, without his eyebrows, the Captain was forever startled.

Cuthbert was only slightly confused, which made him the most lucid one present. He had known that there were only two things missing from the scene when the twins spotted the cannon. The loud bang and the destruction fitted the bill nicely. As the ringing in his ears made him look around for the reason, he spotted a figure seemingly rising up from the ground and disappearing behind the stage curtain. It walked just like a penguin.

Chapter 8

Over Cuthbert's kitchen table, Geraldine explained that she had left the valley to further her archaeological career.

Apparently whilst Cuthbert put bodies into the ground, Geraldine had been pulling them out. They laughed easily as Geraldine tried to avoid drinking Cuthbert's tea, and gradually she revealed that she had taken a job at the local museum. Not only was she back in the valley, she would also take part in the annual plays.

Cuthbert was elated. Now he had a real reason to get up in the morning. Emptying buckets from under the leaks in the roof was more of a necessity.

The evening found Cuthbert back in the theatre re-arranging the debris. Anyone watching would have seen him pick up a cushion, do a little waltz, and put it back in exactly the same place. Love really was the fuel to fire the engine of confusion.

The front row of seats was loose as usual, but now the aisle seat was missing completely.

Cuthbert peered down into a dark hole. The cannon ball must have hit this one and ricocheted through the wall. Fetching the back-stage lantern, he sank it into the cavity below. Impulsively, Cuthbert lowered himself into the hole until his feet met a solid, rounded surface. He knew every inch of the valley and had been banned from all its secret places as a child, but this was a new one.

Holding the lantern aloft, he gazed around. It was the crypt belonging to the Hall. This must be the last resting place of the Mandrake family.

From his own career, Cuthbert knew that there was nothing to fear from the dead, but the footprints were from the very much alive. He was standing on a stone sarcophagus and the dust around him was scuffed with footprints. They entered from a hole in the wall, visited every sarcophagus and niche, and then they left the same way. Cuthbert slipped on the curved lid and raised a lazy cloud of dust when he hit the floor. He was committed now; he couldn't climb back out, he would have to follow the footprints.

This is why Cuthbert did not have adventures. Even as a child, they seemed to end with his father saying, "You did what?" or "And does it sound like a good idea now, Cuthbert?" or the all-time favourite, "Tell your mother Cuthbert. She's responsible."

Squeezing through the hole in the bricks, Cuthbert pushed the lantern through and entered a tunnel leading slightly uphill.

Geraldine had asked about tunnels when she first appeared in the valley. Somehow the thought bothered him.

Having absolutely no choice, he followed the tunnel. The stone walls were ancient and the roof curved into an arch. He was definitely heading for the Hall, so when a flight of stone steps appeared, he climbed even higher.

The arched door at the top had been left unlocked and the hinges ran with fresh oil. Someone intended coming back. The only way was forward and Cuthbert entered a long passageway. The lantern light crept ahead of him and showed ancestral portraits spaced out at regular intervals. He heard the muted rumble of voices.

Cuthbert consulted his reflexes, but for some reason they prompted him to blow out the lantern, 'so that no-one would hear him.' Trying to figure out the logic of that one stopped the terror from gaining a foothold, and he moved forward with arms outstretched.

Cuthbert's hands met the back of a hanging tapestry. A join in the canvas moved apart as Cuthbert steadied himself. He could see into a large living room. There were more paintings and a blazing log fire.

Ronald Chisolm sat on the padded seat of a club fender with his back to the fire. His face was black and his hair was sparse and spiky. He was obviously still deaf from the cannon shot as he was shouting.

"He knew," he exclaimed. "I tell you, he knew I was there. He aimed the thing straight at me. As soon as I lifted the trap-door, he fired."

His brother Henry waved a hand dismissively. "He didn't know at all, Ronald. He didn't even know that the cannon would be there, did he, Captain?"

Cuthbert looked towards the row of high backed armchairs facing the fire. He recognised Captain Edgar as he leant into the fire-light.

"Sorry about that, old boy," he apologised to Ronald, "That was my little wheeze to get explosives, tools and rope into the theatre ready for the dig." He ruefully rubbed the soot from his face and caressed a missing eyebrow. "I must admit it was a close one, though." He leant back in his chair again.

Henry addressed the room. "Does anyone think that he knows?"

The Captain humphed. "Fool doesn't know a single thing and he has lived on top of it for years, hasn't he?"

Henry raised an eyebrow at another chair.

Geraldine leant forward and spoke. "He is harmless. Anything he does know, he gets it wrong. Nobody would have trusted him with any secrets, he just doesn't know."

"Try looking down a cannon and saying that," shouted Ronald.

The group stood and ambled out of the room together.

Cuthbert was deep in thought. He had no idea who they were talking about, but he sounded really dim.

It had been a shock to see Geraldine there. They were all newcomers to the valley- they all arrived separately and yet they all knew each other.

Cuthbert was suddenly aware of a draught, so he moved into the empty room. Sitting on the same padded seat Ronald had used, Cuthbert felt the heat on his back. He didn't need the lantern for the moment, so he set it down behind him.

There was a whooompf as the last of the paraffin ignited, setting fire to two flags flanking the fire-place. The sudden extra heat forced Cuthbert to his feet. He stared in horror at the conflagration.

Cuthbert suffered from 'panic induced selective vision'. This meant that in times of stress he only saw part of the solution. This was apparent as he raced across the room upon seeing a fire extinguisher in the corner, but not the lion skin rug. Jamming one foot firmly between its teeth, he skidded over to the red cylinder, avidly pursued by the two-dimensional predator. The resulting collision caused the fire extinguisher to erupt and send up a cascade of white foamy bubbles, coating Cuthbert and the lion with a slimy porridge. Rubber hosing had wrapped around his neck and they were all entwined.

The ground shook as the daughter of the house crashed into the room, roaring for an explanation. Cuthbert had christened her Arkle because he didn't know her name, but he knew what she looked like. Hearing her voice, he was now convinced that it hadn't been the horse talking outside his barn that day.

The daughter saw the flames and immediately turned for the fire extinguisher. She was prepared to battle a raging inferno, but she wasn't prepared for the sight in the corner.

Cuthbert, his attached lion and tangled extinguisher, had become a twelve foot long, slimy, undulating slug that clonked every time it moved, but the extinguisher tried to stay where it was.

The daughter seemed to have an overload of happy thoughts. Swooning, she landed in the spot vacated by the lion.

Cuthbert dragged his burden swishing and clunking across the room.

Progress improved when he reached the outdoors. He picked up speed as the clanking became more rapid and then fell down the front steps and out into the night.

Chapter 9

The next day found Cuthbert chopping off the carapace of dried foam and having violent negotiations with his water pump.

The extinguisher was bubbling away at the bottom of the milkman's well and the lion skin had been put in with Mrs Higgins and the lid firmly screwed down. If they ever excavated the grave and found those teeth, the newspapers would have a field day.

The next day Cuthbert found several notes pushed under his door. They were all from members of the cast asking for a new rehearsal date. Whatever they lacked in ability, they certainly made up for it in spelling mistakes.

Cuthbert scavenged around until he found something to cover the hole and replace the missing seat. An old iron tractor seat welded to a piece of plate fitted the bill nicely. By Cuthbert's standards, this was a professional solution. Standing back and admiring his handiwork, Cuthbert again imagined the audience rising for a standing ovation and saw flowers being thrown onto the stage, instead of pigeon droppings.

He returned to the main doors and opened them cautiously as he stepped back into the valley's approximation of the real world. His meeting with Bunny was fresh in his mind, as well as the hoof print on his shoe. No Bunny, he thought with relief.

This time the effect was actually that of being hit with a wet, warm mop.

Cuthbert absorbed the shock as the tongue struck him in one direction, but he ducked before the back swing. This one didn't worry him- he recognised this one, it was the milkman's horse.

Cuthbert did not hate the milkman, but his resentment was so close to hatred that it would be hard to pull them apart in a scuffle.

The man had movie star looks, he rode his milk wagon like Ben Hur on the winning lap, and his teeth actually flashed.

"Morning, sport," boomed the man, leaping down and landing like a cat.

Putting an arm around Cuthbert's shoulder, he steered him away from the barn.

Once again everyone seemed to hold onto Cuthbert when they talked to him. They seemed to think that he was so insignificant he would disappear mid-sentence. He really must give it a try.

"I was worried about you, Cuthbert," the milkman continued. "Heard about the twins' assassination attempt." He threw his head back and laughed.

Even his laugh was that of a matinee idol. He was Cuthbert's leading man. What else could he be? Muscles rippling, teeth glinting and the retention span of a mackerel. He could sword fight, shoot, swing from ropes and do a forward roll with a dagger between his teeth. However, the spoken lines had to be kept to a minimum and the leading lady had to swoon.

After reassuring his leading man that, yes, the lead actor carried a sword and, yes, he was the strong silent type and, yes, the damsel would swoon into his arms, Cuthbert was released.

Watching the milkman vault back into his cart, Cuthbert noted his skill as he balanced perfectly whilst speeding away. Cuthbert realised that he could never stage 'The Merchant of Venice'. The only part for his leading man would be to hack off the pound of flesh for Shylock and catch a spectator as the leading lady swooned.

Chapter 10

Leaning against the stile in misery, Cuthbert had caused the crow to perk up in case there was a suicide in the offing, but he waddled off as Cuthbert's face became a shade that definitely wasn't deathly pale.

Cuthbert was having an epiphany. He could clearly see himself in the queue waiting politely as the others rushed to be born. "Oh, excuse me," he'd say as he stepped back, or, "No, of course I don't mind. Be my guest."

The milkman, of course, was at the front of the queue and by the time Cuthbert reached the front, the quartermaster angel would bleakly survey the empty shelves and scratch his head.

That is another thing, thought Cuthbert. *What sort of name is Cuthbert?* He didn't feel like a Cuthbert. He didn't think he looked like a Cuthbert, but he had never met another one to find out. His mirror image didn't seem to be Cuthbert, but sometimes it was just too timid to appear.

All these things reached a pinnacle of emotions. Cuthbert clenched his fists. *This is it,* he thought. *I'm going to smash this stile and wreck this wall with my bare hands.*

Looking around, he wondered where the crow had gone to. All that actually happened was a mildly explosive "Damn."

Cuthbert began to lock up for the night. Somehow, this lonely ritual seemed to be forced upon him by the rest of the world's insistence on closing down for eight hours.

Lying on his inherited four poster bed, Cuthbert gazed up at the canopy. Once, his ambitions had included marriage to a ravishing starlet and going global with his undertaking business. Now, though, he considered it enough just to get through another production of 'The Awful Theatre Company'.

The night established itself silkily around the arthritic old house. The usual creaks and groans were interspersed by random chimes from the haunted long case clock in the hall. It was labelled 'haunted' because it would explain all the ridiculous combinations of bings and bongs emanating from it … and also saved paying anyone to repair it.

The problem of the leading lady was at the front of Cuthbert's thinking at the moment. He always used the front of his brain for the important stuff- anything else could be filed at the back. It was tempting to use Geraldine for the lead, but Cuthbert couldn't face seeing her admire her reflection in the milkman's teeth.

Belinda, the barmaid, was good looking enough, but tended to have a fit of the giggles at any odd expressions. If the leading man was to 'plight his troth' or refer to her as a 'comely wench', the audience might as well go home.

Actually, the audience usually consisted of the badger, a duck and anyone waiting to take the players home.

Cuthbert remembered that the newcomers were keen to get involved, but there was something holding him back from asking them. Perhaps it was the mention of explosives that had bothered him.

It was then that the night threw a different sound at him. It was one of those noises that took you by surprise, unless you were listening for it. Of course, then it wouldn't be a revelation and you wouldn't notice it.

Cuthbert eased himself out of bed and tried to peer beneath the beetling brows of the thatch. Nothing moved in the dark- perhaps it was the badger coming to complain about the tractor seat.

The distinct rattle of a door latch echoed up the stairs, causing Cuthbert's heartbeat to intimidate him with its bumping. Cuthbert reached under the bed for the item of last resort. Somehow he couldn't hold it in the two-handed way his father had shown him. After a quick analysis in the dark, he returned the chamber pot and pulled out the gun.

The gun was another legacy, an old, heavy blunderbuss. It was always kept loaded and primed. Cuthbert had no idea since when.

Anytime his father had needed some moral support, he would look at Cuthbert, wink repeatedly and nod upwards towards the bedroom to indicate that his son should fetch the weapon.

This had caused some confusion when his father had a stroke and Cuthbert appeared with the gun, causing a massive heart attack and thus elevating himself to 'master of the house' status.

Moving stealthily, Cuthbert descended one step at a time. He had asked his father several times why they kept a gun loaded and the answer was always the same. "The Russians are coming."

Cuthbert never asked why. He presumed they didn't have funeral parlours of their own. Surely, they weren't coming to watch the plays?

This thought struck him as he reached the bend in the stairs and he began to laugh. Now, when Cuthbert laughed it sounded like a machine gun firing marbles interspersed with hail on a tin roof. It was particularly startling when it happened at a funeral. However, in the dark on a staircase it was apocalyptic. The intruder lost his nerve, the trigger lost its grip and the newel post lost its finial.

The clock erupted with the sound of two skeletons making love inside a galvanised dustbin and the house no longer had two occupants. The smoke cleared and the clock gave a last nervous cough.

Was it Cuthbert's imagination or did life get more exciting as you got older?

Checking the yard outside and seeing nothing, Cuthbert checked inside. The cellar door was swinging open.

Footprints in the dust showed that the intruder hadn't gone down, but he had certainly come up.

Cuthbert held the gun as if it could actually fire again without twenty minutes of loading and prayers, and entered the cellar.

Someone had disturbed the Halloween cobwebs by brushing past them.

Cuthbert tutted. The clumsy burglar had destroyed whole council estates of spiders, whole families had been made homeless. The hole in the brickwork gaped at him. The man had come through the tunnels.

Lamps and lanterns were part of the furniture of the valley, where electricity was a coincidence unless it happened along when you needed it. Even then it was treated with great suspicion.

Choosing a hurricane lamp with enough fluid sloshing about to investigate a tunnel, Cuthbert lit the wick that glowed humbly, though it had ambitions to become a raging inferno some day, and stepped through the hole.

These tunnels were well known in the valley. They were part of a water system supplied by a reservoir on the top of the hill to feed the old mill and turn the wheel. They split off in several directions because the water source could suddenly 'spring-up' somewhere else. No-one had ever seen evidence from above and Cuthbert could see why now. The arched tunnels could last forever, especially now they were not needed.

Cuthbert advanced down the tunnel accompanied by a low moaning sound. It was unsettling, so he stopped doing it.

The draught up his night-shirt reminded him that he was not well equipped for an adventure, but he worked on the theory that 'If you are not expecting trouble and it comes along, it can't be your fault, can it?'

*

As Cuthbert plodded ahead, an irate little man was building up a head of steam before a log fire.

"He was expecting me, I tell you. The man is prepared for Armageddon- every time I appear, he shoots at me."

He could see his temporary insanity reflected in the stares of those occupying the chairs- it was like facing the Spanish Inquisition. The flames at his back only reinforced the impression.

Henry was always the first to defuse a situation. He leaned forward. "We know more about this twerp than he does about himself," he said. "The guns are just relics of a farming past."

"Farming past," spluttered Ronald. "Why does a farmer need a cannon? Is it for ploughing fields at a distance?" Any other time he would have been quite pleased with that one, but he was beyond reason at the moment. His temper wasn't helped by splinters of wood from the newel post embedded about his person.

Henry spoke again. "Geraldine?"

She answered. "He knows nothing, and I mean that literally. He only notices things of absolutely no importance to others. He could walk through a riot and think there was a sale on."

"Well, he damn well knows a target when he sees one," muttered Ronald darkly.

The conspirators lapsed into silence and Ronald tugged at his splinters.

*

The tunnel was becoming monotonous. Even arched brickwork becomes boring after a while.

Cuthbert thought of turning back, but it was easier to carry on than it was to get co-operation from a one-track mind.

The set of steps leading up to the left relieved the monotony somewhat and he climbed them.

The door at the top had been roughly opened and a large cupboard pushed away from the wall.

Cuthbert didn't recognise the room. This was odd. He had visited everywhere in the valley at some time or another, usually to apologise and offer restitution. There were several books strewn along a table and Cuthbert moved over to one that had a sausage as a bookmark. The large kitchen was still unfamiliar. It was like finally meeting Mrs Strident without her hat. It had been a real surprise. Of course, he hadn't known that she was bald either.

Cuthbert gently moved the sausage and focused on a ketchup fingerprint. It was a local history book written by a man called Clithero. Cuthbert remembered him. It was during Cuthbert's 'modernise the business phase'.

Most of his father's methods had been cribbed from the Pharaoh Tutankhamen's G.P.. After reading a free copy of the 'Morticians Mirror', he had sent for loads of new-fangled chemicals, all designed to either speed some things up or slow other things down.

He had just been getting to grips with the tamper-proof lids when someone knocked at the door. Not noticing the liquid seeping down his hand and into his coffee, Cuthbert took a sip and answered the summons.

The man at the door seemed to think that 'Local Historian' was a qualification and expected access to all areas just because he wanted to have a look.

Trying desperately to look taller by sheer self-importance alone, he explained that he was fully entitled to explore the historic tunnels. Instead of showing any authority, he stuck out his goatee beard to prove that he looked the part. Talking in rapid fire bursts like a machine gun fed on dirty ammunition, the man's attention seemed to wander.

He had noticed that Cuthbert's mouth moved in strange ways as if he was practising before he spoke. The historian also noticed that Cuthbert's eyes occasionally rolled up in his head for no apparent reason. The clincher was when Cuthbert threw his coffee over him.

Cuthbert closed the door. 'That was strange,' he thought. He was never knowingly rude to anyone, ever.

The truth was that Cuthbert had accidentally embalmed his jaw. When he went to shake the man's hand, his thumb had got stuck in a buttonhole and he had still been holding his cup.

Cuthbert turned the pages. So, the funny little man had written his book after all.

One passage caught Cuthbert's eye, 'The flow of water was so unpredictable into the valley that several tunnels led to the water mill. When one tunnel remained constantly in use, the water wheel was taken off the old mill and fitted to the new mill. The old mill simply continued as a farm.'

This passage had been underlined several times, but it didn't mean anything to Cuthbert. He had a sneaking feeling that he had just discovered something, but he shrugged and closed the book. The pages settled with a puff of dust to show their disgust.

On the way back through the tunnel, Cuthbert was drawn back to the passage he had read.

Born and brought up in the valley, he knew all the buildings. There was only one farm and only one water mill.

Cuthbert's brain grew weary and simply caused him to bang his head on a low point in the roof.

This had the desired effect and Cuthbert said aloud whilst rubbing his head, "My farm must have been the original mill."

This was a new sensation for Cuthbert. It was a pity that original thinking really hurt.

Cuthbert barricaded the hole in his cellar wall and went upstairs. It was nice to have the tunnels explained, but why were people popping up out of them like demented moles?

He made himself a cup of tea while the cooking range took a nap. It was much safer to be near it then.

Chapter 11

Life had always been complicated for Cuthbert- not by Cuthbert, only for him. He couldn't answer the door without circumstances spinning out of control.

Constable Beeching once brought him the corpse of a vagrant found in the bottom of a hedge. Because the tramp was a stranger to both the valley and hygiene, no-one bothered to see if he was capable of waking up.

Cuthbert had rigged up the apparatus with all its drips and rubber tubes and begun to infuse the man with the embalming fluids when he heard a knock at the door.

Two very neat people promptly asked him whether he had been saved.

Part of this was lost as the door creaked and Cuthbert thought they had said "Have you been saving?"

Now Cuthbert was very proud of his saving discipline and launched into a description of the various empty jars he used for the purpose. He told the bemused couple about his 'swear-jar' and his 'late-jar' and even his 'wicked thoughts-jar'.

The man at the door made an attempt at humour by asking, "Will you form a rock band and have a 'jam-jar?"

Cuthbert ignored this as he was distracted by the man's wife. Her eyes were huge and she was tugging on her husband's sleeve as she looked over Cuthbert's shoulder.

Apparently, the naked tramp had been revived by the alcoholic content of Cuthbert's fluids and had stood up and stretched.

Seeing a woman watching him, the beggar made a run for it, only to be pulled back at high speed by the rubber tubing.

The man at the door had now seen this vision and he too stared wildly over Cuthbert's shoulder. With a last shout of "The Lord shall set you free", the couple fled.

At the same time, the tramp banged his head on the apparatus and fell back on the table exactly where Cuthbert had left him.

Cuthbert closed the door thinking, 'How nice of them to come and warn me that the ford was blocked by a tree.' He then carried on with completely messing up the tramp's day.

Chapter 12

As he unlocked and opened all the doors the next day, Cuthbert thought, *If people keep knocking holes in my house I won't need to do this for much longer.*

A thought had sidled into Cuthbert's brain during the night- what if the Captain had bought the mill thinking it was the original mill? Now that he knew the difference, perhaps that's why the attention had shifted to *his* house. What was everyone looking for?

If there was treasure here, it had certainly kept itself from Cuthbert's family. Owning the farm had never seemed like going up in the world, more like sinking further into it.

Cuthbert stared into the mirror. This was something he tried to avoid ever since he had got into a conversation with his reflection. It was easily done; Cuthbert considered that as the lips were moving and the face seemed interested, it would be rude to ignore him, so they chatted. They were both so polite that it went on until they both fell asleep.

After a breakfast of cereal invaded by nuts, Cuthbert climbed to the top of the hill. After pushing through nature's jumble made up of anything that fancied growing in a lump, he reached the summit.

The old reservoir was a grass covered mound that had partly collapsed under the weight of nature's responsibilities. The access doors were chained and locked, but the twins had taught everyone how to pick the padlock long ago.

Several craters had appeared where the ground had subsided and a man sat fishing at one of these. He was hunched over the hole with a hood pulled up over his head and looked like an Eskimo checking his freezer.

"Morning, Whistle," said Cuthbert cheerily as he sat next to him.

The hood dipped slightly in acknowledgement. Whistle was a man after Cuthbert's own heart, the perfect companion. They could spend all day together without anything complicated passing between them. He was from an old valley family of 'Entwhistles' and his nickname was partly a contraction of this, but mostly due to the curious habit of including the word 'whistle' in most of his sentences.

'This must be really difficult,' thought Cuthbert. 'Perhaps that's why he doesn't say much.'

"Going to be a nice day," began Cuthbert.

"Whistle see," said the fisherman.

Cuthbert nodded wisely, "Difficult to predict really."

Whistle tapped the side of his nose, which was meant to convey secret inner knowledge, but usually just meant sinus trouble. "Whistle know when whistle know, Cuthbert. Then whistle all know, lad."

Cuthbert nodded sagely again; it was his favourite way of playing for time.

The reservoir had been dry for years, but if Cuthbert mentioned it, Whistle would sulk and mutter, "Just because there is none in there now, doesn't mean that there won't be soon, whistle see."

Watching Whistle glare into the hole, defying the fish to ignore him, Cuthbert asked, "Has anyone else been up here lately?"

There was a long silence before Whistle replied. "Strange goings-on, Cuthbert lad. Whistle not see the like again. Whistle all perish."

Cuthbert studied the ground before him. The hood of doom had been joined by the blanket of despair. They only needed the cloak of darkness and Whistle would have a whole new outfit.

What on earth do you mean?" asked Cuthbert incredulously. He'd never had to think about anything Whistle said before. They were both in uncharted waters here.

The hood turned towards Cuthbert ominously. "Remember, Cuthbert lad," it said, "you can whistle while you work and you can whistle while you whittle, but if you whistle while you whittle you'll have blood on your hands."

Cuthbert looked into the hole and wondered if fumes were escaping from his workshop and getting into the tunnels. He then looked around for any half-eaten magic mushrooms, but all seemed normal except that Whistle had gone.

There was an indent in the grass, but no sign of anyone. Cuthbert could see for miles around- no-one. Shouting into the hole only produced that mocking silence that always seemed to know something you didn't. He was alone.

Chapter 13

Cuthbert came out of his reverie to find himself outside the Mandrake Arms, the one place in the village everyone came to eventually. It was similar to his chapel of rest, except they served crisps.

Entering into the gloom, Cuthbert noted all the usual shapes in the customary places. Hands wrapped protectively around a glass, in case the angel of death should tap on someone's shoulder. Wouldn't want to spill any, would they?

Belinda was in her place behind the bar. A true professional, she had even carried on serving when the roof blew off and, in turn, had become known as 'The barmaid to the stars'. She saw Cuthbert, sighed, pulled a pint and prepared for a doom-laden farmer conversation.

When Belinda settled her bosom on the bar, Cuthbert entered a safe, warm place where he could talk. It was like confiding in an old settee; it absorbed the sound and didn't correct his grammar.

Taking Cuthbert by surprise, Belinda interrupted his wandering tale by asking, "Who is Whistle?"

Cuthbert stared and began to describe him.

Belinda saw the old Cuthbert returning, so she quickly said, "Yes, yes, I know all that, but who is he?" Cuthbert still stared, so Belinda continued, "If he came into the bar now without his hood, would you recognise him?"

Cuthbert shook his head. "No, probably not," he admitted.

"So, how do you know it was him?" she persisted.

Cuthbert scoffed. "He would have to be a terrific actor to fool me."

No shortage of actors around here lately, Belinda thought as she walked away.

Chapter 14

Cuthbert wandered into the street. Other people were noticing something strange. This could be one of those times when a man had to discover his 'inner-self' or his 'inner-strength'. Cuthbert didn't like the sound of that. He liked his inners to stay where they were. When a man's inners became his outers, that's when they didn't wake up on Cuthbert's slab.

Lost in thought, Cuthbert stumbled on something. Someone had left a catapult lying on the ground. Tutting, he picked it up before someone tripped over it.

Vaguely he remembered the twins once catching him with something similar, except there had been super-glue on the handle.

Trying to throw the thing away from him, he thought *I won't fall for that one again. Besides, it was loaded last time.* Then he saw the glass marble stuck into the leather pouch. *Uh-oh.*

Furious with himself for falling for it once more, Cuthbert went over to the old well, leant over the stonework and fired the marble harmlessly into its depths.

At least the Post Office window was safe this time, he thought.

At the bottom of the well, Mrs Edgar was trying to count all the pretty flashes of light as her husband tried to revive her.

"Ye gods," the Captain muttered, "all she had to do was hold the lantern. How did she manage to spill paraffin all over Ronald and then faint?"

Ronald meanwhile was screaming down the tunnel like a blazing meteor demonstrating the Doppler effect of receding sound, whilst trying to run fast enough to keep the flames behind him.

Cuthbert was free of the catapult.

After ten minutes of licking by Daisy the cow, it had transferred itself to her tongue. It was her problem now. In this rare moment of peace, Cuthbert reflected upon how lonely it could be trying to solve a problem alone. He hadn't always been alone.

Once he had an imaginary friend named Chester. He was there whenever he was needed, never interrupted and he didn't correct Cuthbert's grammar either.

This was the first thing Cuthbert ascertained when interviewing new friends or acquaintances. Things had been perfect for several years until Chester stopped believing in him.

Around the fire at Mandrake Hall, Ronald was ranting as he kept well away from the flames. "It was him again. I saw his silhouette against the sky. I'd recognise those ears anywhere. He leaned over and shot me."

The Captain snapped, "It wasn't you he shot, it was Elspeth."

"Who?" chorused the whole room.

"Elspeth," spluttered the Captain. "My wife, Mrs Edgar."

"Oh," said everyone.

Henry asked wearily, "So what did he shoot you with this time?"

Ronald stopped pacing and chuckled. "Oh, he's a crafty one all right," he said. "It must have had a flash arrester, a silencer and a night sight. I didn't hear it or see it. If I hadn't ducked behind that woman, he would have got me."

"What?" shrieked the Captain, "you hid behind a defenceless woman?" Spluttering, he continued, "You risked the life of my beloved …?"

"Elspeth," supplied the room, really getting into this now.

Ronald ignored him. He was re-living the moment. "It was the snap-shot of a lifetime," he conceded. "I thought I was good, but this chap must be a master assassin."

Someone commented, "For a master assassin, he doesn't leave many bodies."

Henry took the floor. He owned the house anyway. "All right, Ronald, you would have us believe that this man Cuthbert has accumulated several state of the art weapons and is adept at using them. He is also capable of outwitting us at every turn and he knows our plans before we do?"

"Er, yes," replied Ronald in the tone of one about to be ridiculed.

"Then why hasn't he solved the mystery?" asked Henry. "Why is there still a secret? Why is the greatest actor the world has never seen living on a farm and appearing to be a complete ninny?"

They all looked around as Elspeth, dumped and forgotten in a corner, moaned, "He is the guardian."

Ronald scoffed. "I don't care if he's the Daily Male. He's real trouble."

Geraldine spoke. "Perhaps they are both right. Maybe he is here to protect the secret from the likes of us." She allowed them to absorb this, before adding, "Why don't we set some traps and see how he deals with them?"

Heads nodded around the room.

"Hmmm," said Henry, wishing he had thought of it.

"Hmmm," said Geraldine. planning ahead.

"Hmmm", said the Captain because everyone else had.

"Hmmm", said Ronald, wondering which bit of him would ache tomorrow.

Chapter 15

The next morning Cuthbert threw back the shutters and welcomed the day. He was greeted in return by a cow giving him a baleful look.

"Oh come on, Daisy," said Cuthbert. "The glue will wear off. It did last time."

Daisy heaved herself around and went in search of something to floss with.

Spotting a wire across Cuthbert's doorway, she clamped her jaws down on it and threw her head from side to side. *Just the job,* she thought. *Whoever said bovines were stupid?*

A movement behind caught her eye. A man had appeared from beyond the horse trough and was backing away nervously. Cows don't get many visitors, so Daisy ambled over to play.

Ignoring the strange things dangling from each end of the wire, and the hissing noise, her last thought was, *He runs just like a cartoon penguin.*

Ronald turned towards the cow just as it disappeared in a blinding flash. Thrown backwards, he was pinned to the barn door by a pair of horns still warm from their last owner. He dangled there, mesmerised by the glare of a crow that had just seen three tons of beef blown to smithereens before its very beak.

Cuthbert crossed the yard. He had been so tired last night that he didn't remember making the hot chocolate beside his bed. Cuthbert didn't remember owning any either. He had been so tired that he knocked the cup over and the contents had eaten through to the room below.

Distracted by a column of ants carrying unidentifiable bits of cow, he didn't even look up as he slammed the barn door back, knocking Ronald out cold in the process.

Cuthbert swept the stage methodically and whistled while he worked. It wasn't a tune as such, more the kind of shriek made by a keening wind. It was the type of wind that howled across the Arctic tundra for months on end and drove men to the brink of insanity with its endless tuneless persistence.

Cuthbert's whistling was having an effect upon the Captain. He hadn't expected to be involved in this because the bomb was supposed to be fool proof. *Obviously this chap is no fool,* thought the Captain. He ground his teeth together to try and drown out the siren song of monotony as Cuthbert came closer.

Knuckles white from holding the rope, the Captain watched for Cuthbert to reach a certain point on the stage. The heavy sand bags above him were to help open the curtains by utilising gravity. This sand bag was going to neutralise Cuthbert.

The Captain's brain was desperately sending survival hints to his ears. *Must stop the whistling and must cover ears up. Need hands to cover ears up.*

Cuthbert was very close to the spot when he saw the sleeping badger about to slide off the tractor seat. Leaning out over the stage, Cuthbert used the brush handle to push the overhanging badger bits back into place.

He never noticed the sand bag hurtle towards him, which stopped dead about twelve inches above the stage where he would have been.

The Captain, dangling thirty feet above, decided that the old army trick of wrapping the rope around one's arm could have been ignored this time.

The badger had awoken, so Cuthbert escorted it grumpily to the door and showed it out. Stumbling as his eyes adjusted to the gloom, Cuthbert bent to retrieve his brush. An arrow whirred past above his head and left silently through the open door. Cuthbert paused to listen. A pigeon clattered away in the rafters and he could hear sand trickling onto the stage from a dangling sand bag that he hadn't noticed. Tutting, he gripped his brush and climbed onto the stage to sweep the sand away.

The Captain slid down the rope with murder in his heart. Geraldine took up the first pressure on her bowstring, the new arrow glinted wickedly.

Cuthbert was having a moment of 'stage memory'. It was similar to stage fright, but didn't involve remembering how frightened you were.

He was re-living the moment when he received a standing ovation as a child. While playing Cinderella and, throwing away the broom, he had back-flipped across the stage to rapturous applause. Could he still do it?

Cuthbert tap danced sideways, threw away the broom and back-flipped across the stage, triggering the old trapdoor mechanism and disappearing in a cloud of dust.

The broom hit Geraldine and the arrow smashed through the barn wall, piercing Ronald's buttock and freeing him from the horns of a dilemma. The Captain landed on the spilled sand and skidded into Geraldine, propelling them both off the stage just as Henry lifted the iron plate under the tractor seat with a wicked dagger in his teeth. The tangle that was the Captain and Geraldine rolled into Henry, knocking them all into the tunnel and causing the iron plate to fall back down again.

Cuthbert appeared from the trap door in the stage, dusting himself down and blushing furiously. *Good grief,* he thought, *thank goodness there was no-one around.* Still brushing himself, he picked up a discarded bow to return it to the props room. *Blessed twins, they could have had someone's eye out with that,* he thought.

Chapter 16

It was a solemn meeting at the old Hall that evening. Each of the conspirators kept to their own chair, wrapped in their own thoughts.

Even when Henry's huge daughter sneered at them and announced, "Well, you lot have failed. I suppose I'll have to seduce him, then," not one comment was heard in reply.

Henry was regretting the decision to hold the dagger in his teeth as it had widened his smile by about two inches. Ronald sat on a rubber ring with a 'thousand yard stare'. He simply could not articulate the things he had experienced. The enforced close contact between Geraldine and the Captain kept them quiet for entirely different reasons. Gradually, they began to speak.

"That man has had special training," said one.

"A Ninja, at least," agreed another.

Geraldine said, "That wasn't the Cuthbert I know."

Henry leaned forward. "Do you shink he'sh an imposhter?" he asked, trying to come to terms with his mouth being wider than his moustache.

"He is the Guardian," intoned a forgotten Elspeth.

The silence descended again, to be broken when the Captain tremulously asked, "What if he attacks us here?"

"Here?" echoed several chairs at once.

The Captain said, "Back in the Troubles, we used to say that if a snake has a toothache, don't poke it with a stick."

"Do snakes have teeth?" asked Geraldine.

"It's a metaphor," snapped the Captain.

"I don't care what it's for," said Ronald. "Why would he attack us here?"

The Captain replied, "Well, we've rather started it, haven't we?" and added, "and he knows where we live."

Heads appeared from the depths of the old wing back chairs as people assessed the room and realised that there were five of them and only four corners to hide in.

"The doors," said someone.

"The windows," said someone else.

"Thoshe shodding tunnelsh," grimaced Henry.

The room emptied rapidly to cries of "Need wood", "Need nails", and "To the barricadesh."

As piles of wood and heaps of nails appeared underneath the windows, Ronald paced up and down. "This is our best chance yet." He tried to raise a finger in spite of his injuries and said, "One, we barricade the doors and windows. Two, we set traps everywhere with sharp spikes. Three, we pour boiling oil off the roof."

Geraldine interrupted, "And then we invade Poland, I suppose."

Ronald glared and tried to ease aches and pains he couldn't even remember getting.

The butler coughed politely, startling everyone. "The local undertaker is here. Shall I let him in?"

His eyes widened as everyone screamed "No," and the problem of five people and four corners reappeared.

"I'll say that you are unavailable then, shall I?" The butler smoothly left the room.

When the door closed, Geraldine asked, "Who hired the butler. Can we trust him?"

Henry waved for Ronald to answer.

How can a man be taken seriously when he sounds like Donald Duck? Ronald thought. "He came with the Hall. We don't know what half of the rooms are for, but he seems to know where everything is."

Geraldine made a note to keep an eye on the man.

Cuthbert was surprised and disappointed when the butler turned him away; typical of these newcomers to offer help and then back out.

Now he had all these roles to fill.

Chapter 17

Wandering along the front of the house, Cuthbert heard banging. He moved over to one of the large windows and peered through a crack in the shutters. *Huh,* he thought. *They are in all right and very busy hammering something to something else.*

Suddenly, he remembered Henry's words about the Hall being perfect for performing the plays ...

That was it. They were building a stage. They were going to steal his production.

The hammering increased in tempo as Cuthbert stormed down the drive. A large offending thistle leaned out over the path and Cuthbert took out his frustrations on it. Swinging a fist at it simply got him prickled, so he aimed a kick at it instead. Missing completely, he spun in a circle and tried with the other foot.

Ronald was watching him leave from an upstairs window. "Incredible," he shouted downstairs. "He even practises his skills when he's walking. This chap is a real killing machine."

The hammering came even faster. They were preparing for a siege of medieval proportions.

Cuthbert sat at home nursing his hand. He didn't ask for much out of life. In fact he didn't ask for anything. All his troubles came free of charge and unsolicited. How dare they try to steal his play and entice away his audience? Actually he had no idea how they would entice a duck, a crow and a badger, but he was certain they had a plan. Cuthbert also had a plan. Well, in truth it was basically to see what their plan was, in the hope that this would inspire his. The trick then was to activate his plan before theirs. He realised that there was always a danger that they would decide on the same plan, in which case they would cancel each other out and nothing would happen. Cuthbert's head hurt as much as his hand did now, so he decided to simply go and have a look.

The night was dark until the clouds were whisked away like a faulty curtain mechanism. The moonlight revealed the dips in the ground as dark places where only imagination lurked.

Cuthbert headed for the crypt under the theatre. In his job he wasn't afraid of the dead, but film scripts had to come from somewhere.

On the way, Cuthbert remembered another crypt from his apprentice days.

The valley had been filled with gossip about men with briefcases banging on the door of the old Hall. Soon after, the owner had passed away and the visitors stopped coming, Cuthbert had fallen through a broken slab and found a tunnel into the Hall. He discovered a coffin whose lid had never been screwed shut. Perhaps the owner had never passed away at all.

Cuthbert dropped down into the same crypt he had discovered all those years ago and lit a candle stub. Steadying himself against the slimy wall, he rubbed the cobwebs off his face. Then he pushed his hair out of his eyes and scratched his nose. The result of all this was that he was soon covered in the green slimy moss from the walls.

He followed the passage until he came to a wooden wall. It was the back of the panelling in the Hall. The crafty old devil must have slipped back in after the fuss died down. Cuthbert explored the panelling by touch, feeling for a catch to open the door.

Inside the Hall, various shapes lurked in the shadows behind some wicked looking devices. Geraldine had raided the museum and had proved herself to be quite an expert on ways to reduce the human form to pulp.

She had fashioned a culverin from an old cooking pot and filled it with scrap metal. Ronald crouched behind it now, listening intently. He had organised a torch for everyone and arranged a series of coded flashes to communicate with. Hearing a noise behind the panelling, he flashed an alert, shifting slightly so that one of his lesser injuries was in contact with the floor. Torches flashed from different places in acknowledgement.

They waited.

Cuthbert slid open a panel, only to find himself behind a huge tapestry. The Hall seemed threateningly silent. His house always had some strange noise to compensate for the lack of a heartbeat.

Reaching into his pocket, Cuthbert withdrew a box of soggy matches and his candle stub. The slime had covered him from head to foot now and the match was reluctant to perform.

Scratch, flash. Scratch, flash. Scratch, flash.

Cuthbert inadvertently gave the signal to 'Open fire at the front door.'

The roar of the culverin could only be felt from within- it was too much for a set of ears to comprehend. The blizzard of candlesticks, pokers, butcher's weights and nails reduced the solid oak door to a layer of splinters strewn across the drive. One stone lion was turned by the blast so that it could see the other lion's head bouncing merrily down the drive.

Inside the Hall, the smoke cleared rapidly, but the air continued to vibrate. Ronald stared at an indistinct, slimy figure standing by the tapestry several feet away from where the door used to be, looking at a match in amazement. The once Grade I listed hallway was now in a different category altogether. In fact it was in the garden.

The culverin had faithfully obeyed every one of Newton's laws of motion and, having obliterated everything in front of it, had flown backwards, taking the Captain with it. An old wine cellar had been uncovered in the process.

The slimy creature turned slowly and its eyes flashed at Ronald, who shrieked soundlessly and ran for it. Bursting through a door into a corridor, he completely forgot about the web of trip-wires and booby traps lying in wait. As he ran, some strings pulled tight, others snapped. Huge candle stands rocked and then fell towards him. Portraits of ancestors framed by half a ton of gilding fell forward and a patch of oil on the floor accelerated him into this gauntlet of destruction, where suits of armour stood patiently waiting for him.

Henry looked down through from the galleried landing. Above him, the glass cupola on the roof illuminated the scene. He sighed. *All those hours of entwining rope, string and fishing line and that clot wrecks it in seconds,* he thought to himself.

The intruder was obviously inside now, and Henry had seen the flash, but not actually heard anything since the house shook all around him. *Patience,* thought Henry. *My turn will come.*

He looked up to the glass roof above him where the ancient bell cast a shadow over the glass, smiled and took up the strain on the rope. Below him, the cold night air rushed in to do battle with the central heating.

Cuthbert looked around. He wasn't sure what he had done, but the devastation seemed to be the type that followed him around. Sidling along past what was left of the panelling, he moved deeper into the house. The sounds of hammering had come from the ballroom, which would be where they were building the stage and the set. Cuthbert moved towards the suspect area.

Geraldine stared in rapture at the bars of moonlight slanting across the floor from the windows only to be reflected back by the wall of mirrors all along the opposite side. She could imagine the swish of the long dresses and laughter as couples met, flirted and danced the night away.

Something moved at the other end of the long room, Geraldine tensed. She had heard the blast, but not seen any signal flashes or been updated. Assuming the worst, she prepared to drop the first foreign body to enter. With a shudder at the recent close contact, she almost hoped that it was the Captain. She took up the first pressure on the bow string.

Cuthbert entered the ballroom. The silvery light reminded him of being in a goldfish bowl, not that he had spent that long in the bowl. It had been his welcome on his first day at school when the others elected him 'spaceman'. Cuthbert would never forget the strange greenish luminescence. *They could have emptied it first,* he thought ruefully.

Geraldine's senses were fully attuned and her nerves were as taut as her bow string.

Something indistinct was coming along the mirrored wall towards her. It was upright, but blurred, and it seemed to be leaving a trail. This was it- the defining moment. It was the instant when the hunter faces his prey, usually, a helpless animal about to be dispatched with thousands of pounds worth of technology.

The strange bouncing moonlight, added to the slime in Cuthbert's eyes, meant that he didn't actually see Geraldine. What he did see was Ronald flinging open a mirrored door, screaming across the dance floor and crashing through the glass windows out into the night.

Geraldine, however, had a defining moment, but not the one she had expected. As the mirrored door flew open, she was faced by her own reflection. She fired and shot herself. The sight of her own arrow hitting her between the eyes and then the vision shattering and falling at her feet was too much for a trained archaeologist to cope with. She dropped the bow and sleep-walked across the floor to follow Ronald through the cartoon hole in the window.

Cuthbert was suddenly faced with the plain back of the mirrored door. He knew that the ballroom was a dead-end, so he turned into the new passage and carried on along his way.

The long passageway was littered with dismembered suits of armour, punctured paintings and fallen candle-stands. *Why do rich folk have to be fashionably untidy?* he asked himself. Himself answered, "Hark who's talking."

The slime was hardening on Cuthbert now and pieces kept falling off him. Feeling a draught to one side, Cuthbert started to climb upwards using a narrow staircase.

Henry had heard a crash and an ear-splitting scream, but stayed where he was. If he was to be the last man standing, so be it. He stared up at the reassuring shape of the bell and again tested the tension in the rope. The assailant had to exit by the front door because they had nailed everything else shut. That would be his moment, when the invincible assassin appeared below him.

"For whom the bell tolls," whispered Henry. "For whom the bell tolls."

Cuthbert emerged on the roof. He was insulated from the chill night air by his coating of mud and fungi. Taking stock of the situation, he realised he had found no evidence of any stage building or seat installation. He thought that the banging must have been these people nailing all the doors and windows shut, but he had no idea why, as he had no idea why there was smoke billowing out of the doorway behind him, but suspected that it was his fault and the stairs were acting as a chimney.

In fact, the reluctant match dropped by Cuthbert had become a raging inferno and it was chasing combustible material through the house because its life depended on it.

Cuthbert saw the glow of flames through the domed glass cupola in the roof. The situation, whatever it was, was now serious. Cuthbert headed for the bell. He must raise the alarm.

The last owner of the Hall had shared Cuthbert's father's conviction that 'The Russians are coming'. When the old church fell into disrepair, he had one of the bells dragged up onto the roof so that he could keep watch. Quite how he would spot the invasion fleet from this far inland was anybody's guess. No-one dared ask, in case he needed another bell.

Cuthbert tried to reach the bell, but it was suspended on a wooden frame just out of reach. There was a rope attached to it, but when Cuthbert tugged on it, it tugged back. Finding a discarded plank, Cuthbert pushed against the bell to start it swinging. He knew it wouldn't clang straight away, not until the clapper could hit the sides, so he kept pushing.

Henry felt a tug on the bell rope and thought that the wind must be getting up. He withdrew his double-barrelled shotgun from its case. It was his favourite weapon. His father used to say, "Why fire one bullet when you can chuck a handful with one of these?" Sporting chance had always raised a snigger in their family.

His plan was to tug on the bell rope as soon as his quarry appeared below him. This would ring the bell, the target would look up and see both barrels coming, and it would be 'Game over'. He looked up at the night sky. The clouds seemed to be crossing the moon and coming back again. Something was moving up there. He calmed himself. There was nothing above except the huge bell on its mouldy, worm-eaten frame. Even as Henry ordered his cramped muscles to move, the frame collapsed due to the sudden change in its load-bearing requirements. Wood, glass and bronze cascaded downwards and Henry's last curse was muffled as he travelled inside the bell on its journey into the cellar.

Cuthbert wasted no more time as a huge gout of flames shot through the hole where the cupola had been. Racing down the fire escape, he left the carnage behind him, finally convinced that there would be no rival plays staged at the Hall.

Chapter 18

Over the next few days, people came to stare at the sombre remains of Mandrake Hall. The four corners stood like blackened teeth and rafters stuck up like the remains of a huge barbecued animal.

Cuthbert wandered around the ruin, kicking at pieces outside that used to be inside.

For Cuthbert, it was like visiting the scene of the crime. He wasn't sure how much of it had been his fault, but, with his track record, he would be in the credits somewhere.

He was startled by a voice nearby. "Good for business, was it?"

Cuthbert turned, but the wind changed and he was enveloped in smoke. Coughing his way towards the voice, he was confronted by a scruffy little chap with rampant red hair flattened down by an old tweed cap. His Wellington boots were obviously too big for him and he had turned the tops down like the old pictures of 'Puss-in-boots'.

"Pardon?" coughed Cuthbert.

The little chap sighed. "You're the undertaker, aren't you? I thought bodies were good for business?" he stated, nodding towards the ruin.

Cuthbert adopted a professional expression and said soberly, "No death is good news. We have but a short time to live and some are cut down too soon." It sounded pompous to even Cuthbert, but guilt was getting in the way.

The little chap was not to be put off. "Yes, we know all that, but the bodies all come to you, don't they?"

Cuthbert was suddenly alert. Now he came to think of it, the house had seemed full of incident, but he hadn't actually seen anyone.

He thought that he saw Ronald smash through the window, but with the slime in his eyes he couldn't be sure. If it had been him, he certainly hadn't run like a penguin. Someone had blown up the entrance door and someone had smashed some glass in the ballroom. Someone else definitely vandalised the corridor. Then there was that muffled howling when the bell fell. None of those things had been caused directly by him, but he hadn't seen anyone else.

Studying the newcomer in front of him, Cuthbert went on the offensive. "Who are you?"

The man had the sun behind him and it turned his hair into a red halo around his ears.

"Percy Plumm." replied the man promptly. "Gardener to the big house, man and boy," he added proudly.

Cuthbert was astonished. "I've lived in the valley all my life and I've never seen you."

"That's because I was gardening," replied Percy emphatically.

"I've never seen you in the village," pressed Cuthbert.

"Busy gardening," stated Percy.

"Or at school ..." tried Cuthbert.

"Learning gardening," said Percy.

Cuthbert thought for a moment. "What about the big house garden party then?" he asked triumphantly.

Percy didn't miss a beat. "Who supplied the strawberries, then?" he retorted.

Cuthbert took a breath, and tried, "Family from around here?"

"Oh yes," replied Percy, "always been a Plumm gardening at the Hall. Always had the plum job, all the way down the family tree."

"That'll be a Plumm tree then," quipped Cuthbert. Percy stared and remained silent. Cuthbert tried another tack. "I don't remember a garden. Even the goats don't bother to sneak in."

Percy retorted, "They know better. They wouldn't be allowed near my Dahlia vines."

"Aha," cried Cuthbert, "even I know that Dahlia's don't grow on vines."

Percy glared. "They do in my garden."

Cuthbert felt his sanity packing its bags and preparing to leave. Percy was built like a prop-forward and he wasn't going to shift, so he tried, "Where do you live then?"

"Gardener's cottage," replied Percy promptly.

"There isn't one," wailed Cuthbert.

"Yes, there is," insisted Percy, but his tone seemed unsure now.

Cuthbert pounced, "Show me, then."

Percy turned reluctantly and led the way, shoulders sagging slightly.

Pushing through a pile of brambles, Cuthbert sarcastically commented, "Nice and tidy, this garden."

"Do I tell you how to plant bodies?" snapped Percy.

Turning a corner, Cuthbert saw that the old collapsed greenhouses were still in the same state they had been in years ago.

Percy led the way into an old shed. Sweeping his arm around in mock pride, he announced, "Here we are."

Cuthbert looked around. There was barely enough room for the two of them. The one old chair was supported by up-turned plant-pots and one wall was covered in shelves. The shelves were groaning under the weight of trophies.

"What are those for?" asked Cuthbert politely.

"Gardening trophies," beamed Percy proudly.

Cuthbert moved closer. One of the figures seemed to be a golfer putting with the head of his club snapped off. "Is he playing golf?" asked Cuthbert.

"No," replied Percy, "he's dibbing, ready for planting."

Cuthbert shifted his gaze. "Is he playing darts?"

"No," snapped Percy, "he's picking grapes."

Cuthbert focused on another trophy. "Is he playing bowls?"

"No," muttered Percy, "he's turnip rolling."

Cuthbert had to admit that this chap was good. It was obvious that he had bought the trophies from a charity shop and snapped bits off. Cuthbert picked out the one least likely to have an explanation and tried one last time.

"Is he on a bicycle?"

"It's the annual planting cycle," sighed Percy as if addressing an imbecile.

Cuthbert backed off. "Perhaps some kids got in and broke some of them?" he suggested.

"While I was gardening?" asked Percy like a man being thrown a life-line. "Yes, that's it. Flaming kids."

*

Cuthbert and Percy actually parted friends. The best type of friends too. They promised to 'look each other up' and 'the kettle was always on' and of course, 'should you ever need anything …'

Also, as Percy pointed out, "My gardening takes up an awful lot of time."

Cuthbert hadn't meant a word of it either.

Chapter 19

The next day, a crowd outside the Post Office attracted Cuthbert's attention. Apparently people had begun re-appearing.

That nice Captain Edgar had awoken with a crashing hangover after discovering a lost wine cellar. Henry Chisolm was trapped under a bell down in the produce cellar and dug his way out with a spoon, and Ronald had come back sheepishly to see why no-one came looking for him. Mrs Biggle from the Post Office received a postcard from Geraldine, who wished everyone a 'Merry Bonfire Thursday' and hoped they enjoyed their Easter Eggs. Apparently, she had found an apartment on the moon. The address of the local asylum seemed to explain most of it adequately.

To round it all off nicely for the women, that nice Mrs Edgar (Elspeth) had wandered out of a long lost crypt and gone home to catch up on her dusting.

The lack of bodies gave Cuthbert some spare time and he began to carry out repairs around the farmhouse. With spare wood from the ruins of the Hall, he spent hours whittling out a new acorn newel post. Unfortunately, they all came out looking like squirrels. Now he had a collection of cross-eyed squirrels and no newel post.

The bricks in the cellar wall were of a particularly spiteful type and they insisted on falling back into the tunnel. Feeling the draught, Cuthbert left them there and decided that he had in fact installed air conditioning.

The only success seemed to be the long case clock in the hall that now timidly ticked away and seemed to chime in all the right places. Cuthbert's father had sworn by the ancient sun dial in the yard, but it hadn't worked properly since Cuthbert brought it inside to save himself getting wet.

Cuthbert was actually avoiding something. It was time to announce the annual performance of one of Shakespeare's plays. He would have to choose his players and decide who was destroying what this year. This could set off a round of feuds lasting until next year.

Cuthbert still remembered passing over someone from the next valley and the man had spent ages pouring powdered cement down

Cuthbert's well. Cuthbert never noticed because he didn't have a well, but apparently the village sewers backed up something awful.

Cuthbert jolted awake as someone hammered on his door. He had nodded off with his feet on the bucket of cement from repairing his cellar wall. Actually, he had fallen asleep with his feet inside the bucket and, when he came to stand up, he rocked like one of those toys no-one could knock over. The visitor was becoming impatient as Cuthbert dragged himself along firmly stuck in the bucket. When he managed to open the door, he was surprised to see Henry, Ronald and the Captain standing there.

Henry had been studying his feet as he waited, but then Cuthbert's bucket-clad ones came into view and he re-focused. The Captain spotted it too and slipped his mind into neutral until someone could explain it to him.

Cuthbert asked, "Has there been a passing?" The visitors stared at his feet. Cuthbert tried, "Has someone passed away?" Still no reply. With a sigh, Cuthbert tried, "Has someone kicked the bucket?"

This jolted them and Henry said, "Oh no, this is a social call, mind if we come in?" and moved forward. Cuthbert held out an arm to bar them entrance, but Henry brushed past, turning Cuthbert through three hundred and sixty degrees like a turnstile. The Captain did the same, but Ronald simply walked under his arm. Cuthbert leaned casually in the doorway as they looked around and muttered together. This stance strained Cuthbert's ankles, so he settled for standing upright with his hands on his hips like a totem pole. He looked just like the giant syringe that frightened Daisy the cow when the vet came.

"Look," began Henry in a conciliatory tone, "we got off to a bad start. No-one knows what happened up at the Hall. Probably rats in the wiring, eh?"

Heads nodded all around the room and Cuthbert remembered the butchers' hooks set in the beams above his head. *If I could jump up and grab one of them, I could swing my feet against the heavy table and knock the bucket off*, he thought.

The clock chimed dramatically and the Captain remarked, "I say, what a beautiful specimen. Is it a Tompion?"

Cuthbert neither knew nor cared. Everyone was going around the corner to look and this was his chance. Cuthbert jumped up and began to swing, just as Ronald reappeared and raised an arm holding a throwing knife. "Right, Mister Ninja," he sneered and threw it.

The bucket caught the underside of the table, flipping it over, catching the knife and banging Ronald against the wall. The bucket came off and Ronald stepped into it as he staggered across the room. When the other two men returned to the room, Ronald was standing dazed in a bucket and Cuthbert was putting the kettle on.

Trying desperately not to stare at Ronald, Henry asked whether the clock had always been there. They assured Cuthbert they were all keen to take part in one of his plays. Picking Ronald up between them, they left as if it was the usual way to say farewell.

Cuthbert watched them go. *Strangers are certainly strange,* he thought, *especially that Ronald. He seems to think I'm someone else.* Briefly, Cuthbert wondered if Ronald was 'in his cups'. His father had always said that about old McGuiness and it always puzzled Cuthbert as a child.

"He sees the world through the bottom of a beer glass. When the glass is half empty, his world is less blurred," his father would say. Or, on another occasion, "Old McGuiness has beer on his beard, his tie and his birth certificate."

This led the child Cuthbert to conclude that it was all right to drink until (a) his father said it was enough or (b) his father started tutting or (c) his father wasn't watching. However, this left Cuthbert with a problem. *How do the villagers know when they have drunk enough now that my father has gone?*

Cuthbert had never seen his father's body, not after he'd shot him anyway. Tradition dictated that he must be prepared by another master undertaker. Cuthbert had been quite hurt. All that practise on gerbils and hamsters wasted, until the relatives began to stack up and the valley needed him. Oh, the secrets Cuthbert had, having to ask the relatives to leave while he tackled fourteen hours of rigor-mortis with only his wits and a coal hammer.

Then there was the time that an inspector had visited and used an embalmed ear as blotting paper.

He had somehow avoided being inundated after the great epidemic. Rumour had it that people had emigrated to avoid being buried by him. Cuthbert knew this was just coincidence. It had been a holiday period.

The question about the clock had seemed strange. Cuthbert never wondered why anything was where it was. His main concern was why things weren't there- like the bodies he misplaced from time to time.

Cuthbert thought about the clock; he remembered it from all the way back. He had always been fascinated by the shiny brass weights swinging and the phases of the moon slowly turning behind the painted clouds on the clock face. One clear night he stood outside for hours waiting for the sky to behave in the same way. He had given up and concluded that the universe needed winding up.

Henry seemed to think that the clock might be worth something. Cuthbert sniffed. Wealth wasn't welcome in the valley. An extra cow was an extra job, two tractors broke down twice as often, and foreign travel didn't appeal either. You could see the next valley from the top of this one, so why bother to walk all the way over there?

Chapter 20

It seemed to Cuthbert that outsiders made their own problems. He remembered some chap visiting while he was repairing a dry stone wall on a red hot day. It was so hot that Cuthbert had taken his boots off and the wall promptly collapsed and buried them.

"Do you have any old furniture?" asked the visitor.

"Oh, yes," replied Cuthbert and carried on working.

"Well, do you want to sell it?" persisted, the man.

"Whatever for?" asked Cuthbert without looking around.

Martin Hepplewhite sighed. This wasn't the first valley he had dealt with. They always acted dumb at first and then demanded a price to make Sotheby's blush. Martin had a history of making great finds. He had called himself Chippendale at first, but changed it when women demanded that he take his clothes off. He had Cuthbert's measure all right. He had already spotted the three-hundred year old coffer full of potatoes in the barn. The trick was to fool the customer into thinking that something else was valuable and then buy the coffer cheaply as a 'compensation prize'.

Let the games begin, thought Martin. "Nice old chair you've got there."

"Where?" asked Cuthbert without looking up.

"Over by the door, under the chicken," said Martin, indicating a rickety and wormy old specimen.

"Oh, you can have that," said Cuthbert.

Martin hesitated. "Oh, er, no I probably couldn't afford it. A sharp lad like you would want a good bit for it," he stammered.

Cuthbert stopped work and looked at him. "Course you can afford it- it's free."

Martin scratched his head- it wasn't supposed to go like this. His thoughts were interrupted by a clatter of rocks and he saw a boot poking out from under the wall. "Er," he tried, "I could probably only afford that old box over there blocking the barn door."

Cuthbert looked at the barn, then looked at Martin. "You want to go in the barn?" he asked slowly and smiled. Martin really didn't want to, but he wasn't sure why. The sweat trickled down his back.

The chair in question had been left there by Angus, the local manic depressive. He had tried to hang himself several times and failed, so he dumped it at Cuthbert's and declared it 'broken'. He kept the rope, in case he found a new chair. Mrs Biggle tried to help by giving him an old armchair, but he kept falling asleep in it. No wonder he was depressed.

Martin shook himself mentally. He had been trained by his father and had been taught to 'never give up'. When he was an apprentice he had been amazed at how many people gave up furniture for 'a goldfish and a balloon'. It had been his job to keep the goldfish alive or, on a busy day, slice up a carrot and shake the plastic bag to make it wiggle. He rummaged in his pocket and came out with a wristwatch on an expanding strap. With a flourish borrowed from Barnum and Bailey's Circus, he dangled it before Cuthbert in the mistaken hope that hypnotism would speed things up a bit. "Tells the time in Hong Kong, this does," Martin gloated.

"Why?" asked Cuthbert.

"Why what?" asked Martin.

"Why does it tell the time in Hong Kong if it's different from here? Don't they have clocks in Hong Kong?"

Martin spluttered, "Of course they have clocks in Hong Kong."

Cuthbert persisted, "Well, they won't have for long if they keep sending them over here." He watched Martin changing colour in the heat. He continued, "Do they want mine so they can tell the time in the valley?" he offered.

Martin exploded, "Who wants to tell the time in this dump?"

Cuthbert grinned, "Precisely."

Martin was not going to leave an early oak coffer in the hands of a buffoon. His face was red and one flap of his deerstalker hat hung down like 'Wily Coyote' after a brush with 'Road-Runner'. "I expect you could do with some extra cash," he tried. "That old box over there, tool box is it? I could run to a few bob for that as a favour to you."

Another rattle of stone revealed another boot, close to the other one.

"Er, do you do this for a living?" asked Martin nervously.

Cuthbert gazed back at him. "No, I'm the undertaker," he stated.

Martin managed to absorb the words, half smile and even swivel one eye to the boots before Cuthbert added, "There's something in the house I would like to show you."

Martin lost his last reserves and fled. Diving into his deliberately filthy van, he roared off with the back doors flapping like petticoats.

Cuthbert picked up his boots and clapped them together as he neared the farmhouse door. The chicken took off in a panic and the chair collapsed into dust. "Shucks," muttered Cuthbert with a smile. "Another fortune lost."

Chapter 21

Cuthbert didn't have much time. Traditionally, the valley staged the play somewhere between 'The Turnip Fair' and 'All Souls' Benefit'.

The Turnip Fair was self-explanatory. What village didn't have a day when everyone dressed as a turnip and tried to guess what his neighbour had come as?

The All Souls' Benefit was a little more complicated. Newcomers soon discovered that there wasn't a church called 'All Souls'. It was actually an ancient ritual that involved pouring ale onto the graves of all relatives so that all dead souls received a drink. It was a shared responsibility to ensure that all live souls could have a drink as well as toasting their relatives by the graveside.

Cuthbert always struggled with this one because he was the son of a teetotal undertaker. His compromise was to wander through the cemetery with an open can in his hand. He would then 'stumble' near his father's grave and 'accidentally' spill the contents. That way, honour and the village were satisfied. If he hadn't taken part, he would have got the blame for all the ills visited upon them for the next year. He was never far away from the blame for most things anyway.

Another unique quirk of the valley was the bus service. Basically, there wasn't one. The owner of the bus company had fought hard to gain all the local routes and he was determined to keep them. The trouble was that 'things happened' in this particular valley and the owner wouldn't allow his buses to stop until at least two of the missing ones were returned. This meant that Mrs Biggle's pigs would be homeless and the valley Mafia would need a new club house. The owner was forced by the *Open Highways and Bus Routes Act, 1902* to maintain the route and he did this by sending a bus through the valley once a year. It didn't stop; the driver actually shut his eyes and flew through the village as fast as he could, horn blaring and good luck charms jangling.

Unfortunately this coincided with the shepherd sending his flock to the annual market. The horn on the bus sounded just like the horn on the market truck. In any other community, a simple 'mark one eyeball' would spot the difference every time, but this was the valley, and the sheep were in the capable paws of 'Blind-Pugh'.

He was the black and white sheep dog with semaphore ears and absolutely no forward vision at all. Attack him from behind, and you would soon realise how far away the accident and emergency department was.

The world in front of 'Blind Pugh' was unknown territory. The sequence always unfolded in the same way. The sheep were put into the pinfold and Blind-Pugh snoozed outside.

The approaching bus driver sounded his horn as per regulations and closed his eyes.

Blind-Pugh woke up, opened the gate and herded the protesting sheep into the road. As soon as the bleating stopped, Blind-Pugh assumed that the lorry was loaded and went back to sleep.

The driver opened his eyes after the village, and continued on his way. The shepherd was left to moan about slow payment from the cattle market and the bus owner shook his head, wondering why someone threw wet sheepskins at one of his buses every year.

Cuthbert was watched very carefully by everyone except Blind-Pugh on All Souls' Night, but a quick stumble and an empty can left on the gravestone settled everyone again.

Chapter 22

Cuthbert's theatre was full of mumbling people. They all held sheets of notes in front of them. Some sat with their backs to everyone and some paced about. The milkman practised his sword swing; most of the lines he forgot could be replaced by a grunt anyway.

The twins giggled together over the script as one tried to read the funny names and the other looked for swear words.

Marjorie was surprised to find herself in the role of the heroine, complete with heaving bosom. She peered over the script, looking from the milkman and back to Cuthbert, watching for signs of collusion.

Henry was the Ship's Captain and the Captain was the Gunner. This piece of easily avoidable confusion ran through the play like the words in Blackpool rock. Every time someone shouted "Captain" two people answered, one of whom was a Gunner. In the end, the fake Captain accused the real Captain of mutiny and threatened to "hang him from the yard-arm". He didn't actually know where that was, but no-one called his bluff.

Mrs Edgar had a non-speaking part as a Crewman, partly to hide her frazzled hair under a bandana and partly to stop her dusting the Ship's rail. The cobwebs were for authenticity.

Ronald flicked furiously through the script for the fourth time looking for his part. Cuthbert had thought of building a deep water tank and using him for the anchor, but this one should keep him out of the way.

Catching Ronald's eye, Cuthbert announced, "First look-out, crows' nest."

Ronald found his lines. Muttering in disbelief, he read, "Reef ahead [came a small voice]" followed by "The yards are creaking. Captain. They need a little squirt." He glared at Cuthbert and read out the final line allocated to him, "Aye-aye, Captain, I will be down shortly."

Malice gleamed in Ronald's eyes, as he suspected the lines he was given all contained references to his height.

Cuthbert innocently asked, "Any problem with the size of your parts, Ronald?"

Belinda shrieked, "Her eyes flashed as his hand lingered over his weapon," and promptly collapsed into a fit of giggles.

Cuthbert under-lined this in pencil and chided himself for not making it 'Belinda proof'.

Cuthbert felt a tugging on his sleeve and turned to deal with Percy Plumm. Whenever he looked at Percy, Cuthbert was forced to think of Halloween. Perhaps it was the halo of wild red hair around the grinning turnip face, or the scruffy old hat keeping everything in place.

Percy was playing the Bosun, mostly because his turned down wellies looked like sea boots. The trouble was he suffered from stage-fright. Under pressure, and hot lights, he would revert to his other identity.

For instance, when Henry shouted, "Where the devil have you been, Bosun?" Percy panicked and stammered, "Gardening."

Trying to be professional, Henry ad-libbed, "Where, in the crows' nest, Bosun?"

"Nah," snapped Percy, "bird muck is no good for rhubarb."

Handing Percy a script to replace the third one he had lost, Cuthbert resisted the urge to pat his Bosun on the head, and checked on the twins. They were originally put in charge of lighting and stage effects, but when one of them operated the flying harness unexpectedly, Mrs Biggle flashed into the wings so fast that her dentures stayed behind to take the encore.

They were now two stunted crewmen who would dig up the treasure. Cuthbert even allowed them to polish the cannon after the Captain assured him that the only cannon ball in the valley had disappeared somewhere over the copse. No-one had noticed yet that one of the stone balls from the gate posts at Mandrake Hall was missing.

The treasure chest was an old trunk from Cuthbert's attic full of costume jewellery and discarded ring pulls from the metal detecting club, and bits of unclaimed jewellery he lady who ran the Library van sent when she had a spring clean.

Mrs Page ran the library van. She was very strict about returning a book on time and would scold a miscreant by showing them an appropriate passage from one of her books. The relevant book would appear in a flash, and the accused was expected to read the passage out loud. If you couldn't read, then you had no business being on the library van.

Cuthbert had been late returning 'Embalming for Dummies'. He had wondered how many bereaved ventriloquists he might have to deal with in future. In answer to Mrs Page's scowl, he stammered that he had been "Tied up".

She quickly produced a Bible and indicated the relevant passage. Cuthbert read, "The truth shall set you free." This was scary stuff as Cuthbert had been fibbing.

Their next encounter was when Cuthbert returned a stained copy of 'Invisible stitching for cosmetic purposes'. Mrs Page had thrust a 'Singer sewing machine manual' under his nose, which apparently recommended 'Stuffing the body under the machine and working the treadle with both feet.'

Tonight, Mrs Page rehearsed for the part of Marjorie's maid servant. This was pure mischief on Cuthbert's part. He wanted to see if she would carry a load of books onto the stage and keep holding them up for the audience to read.

The village gossip had done a superb job rallying the cast with carefully dropped comments like "Cuthbert doesn't think that anyone could play this part properly you know" or "Cuthbert was hoping you would be ill after you stole the show last year". Her reward was to be allowed to hang around pretending to tune the piano.

Now, the piano was like no other. For a start, it was only there because no-one else wanted it. The keyboard sagged in the middle and a rousing chorus became 'clog dancing on the floor above' because all the little felt hammers had rotted. The brass candle holders swayed hypnotically to the rhythm and bits of inlay fell out and got wedged in the keys, producing chords Beethoven could have only dreamt of.

It sat at the front now in sullen silence, but the keys were moving. Gradually everyone began to notice and the murmur of rehearsals died. The keys undulated dramatically and occasionally a note sounded. Some of the braver souls edged forward.

The leading man tried to appear heroic without getting too close. Cuthbert was mildly interested, and Marjorie seemed to have deep suspicions. Percy was carrying out a pincer movement and came up behind the piano. The keys were engaged in a frenzied dance now and the disparate notes were tumbling out and trying to catch up. Percy put something to his lips and blew. A deafening "Paaarp" rented the air and the twins were ejected from the top of the piano in a cloud of dust and mouse droppings

Margery pounced and grabbed them, dragging them off towards home, apologising until she was out of earshot. Everyone began to clear away and say goodnight.

Cuthbert approached Percy. "What's that?"

"Mole Whistle," replied Percy.

"How did you know?" Cuthbert enquired.

Percy took a breath and explained. "Well, you probably noticed that the note sounded slightly before the key moved. That meant that the impetus for the hammer to strike the wire came from inside, not outside. After a quick scan of the room, it was obvious the only two people who could fit inside were actually missing."

He beamed proudly at Cuthbert, who commented, "And you learnt all that when you were …"

"Gardening," said Percy.

Cuthbert said, "Yes, I bet it is quite musical out there, what with all those blue-bells and daffodil trumpets."

Percy was regretting his display of intuition and snapped, "There you go again. I don't tell you which way up to plant yours, do I?" With a self-justified flounce, he left.

Cuthbert watched him go and thought to himself, *Well, mate, if you are going to make life-long enemies, you may as well start with the twins.*

Shaking his head, Cuthbert began to tidy up.

Chapter 23

Henry and Ronald had taken rooms at the Mandrake Arms Inn. They sat near the log fire and Ronald said, "You're enjoying this, aren't you?"

Henry squirmed. "I don't know what you mean."

Ronald continued, "All this showing off. Ever since you went to that fancy school, you've enjoyed dressing in tights and poncing about."

Henry sat up. "I resent that," he snapped. "I was introduced to the arts and learning while you chose burglary and lurking with intent."

Ronald sneered. "Paid for all the poncing though, didn't it?" He paused and then continued, "Tell me again, why are we still in the valley that time forgot?"

Henry sighed. "That clot must know about the secret. The only way now is to gain his trust and have a good look around. It's my job to find it and your job to steal it."

"Then can I have him?" asked Ronald eagerly, leaning forward like a gun dog waiting for the shot.

Henry glared at his brother. "I suppose so. You seem to be behind on points." With that, he stood and went to bed.

Ronald stared into the fire for a long time. His had not been an easy life; it would be easy to sit and feel sorry for himself, so he did.

Chapter 24

Cuthbert sat at his kitchen table with the script. He removed all temptations for Belinda's giggling fits and any long words that might tax his leading man.

At this rate, he will be communicating by the flashing of his teeth, thought Cuthbert. Oddly enough, he had detected some chemistry between the milkman and Margery. This made him smile- his heroic leading man handling the twins? That could cause sleepless nights.

His thoughts then turned to Percy, strange little chap. He seemed to have hidden depths, but would anyone want to explore them? Bit like a stagnant pond, really.

Cuthbert followed his locking up ritual and sank into his feather mattress. Wrapped in the heat of feathers and the prose of Shakespeare, he drifted off to a place where only a Cuthbert could be a King.

He never stirred when the fox chased the duck onto the thatched roof and slid down the other side. His eyes didn't flicker when the fox crashed into a pile of galvanised watering cans under his window, or when it stomped off with one stuck on each of its front feet.

But when the chicken gave a gasp of surprise, he was awake immediately. Cuthbert was country born and bred. He could sleep through all of nature's turf-wars and attempted late suppers, but this was an anomaly. Chickens didn't think fast enough to gasp. They pecked, they paused, and they were supper. Not much surprised a chicken. They were the classic example of 'underestimating the obvious'. After all, they were just background, weren't they? Few outside of the true country folk had experience of a 'rogue-chicken'.

At one stage peacocks had been introduced to give the alarm, much to the delight of the foxes. When the mummy fox heard the alarm cries of the peacock, she put the kettle on. She knew that supper was on its way.

Everyone knew about alarms and security lights, but who feared the humble chicken? It was not the chap creeping across the farmyard, for certain. The chickens clucked all day and slept all night, didn't they? The man scanned the ground around him and noted a single chicken. *Huh,* he thought, *that one is even too gormless to sleep* and carried on along his way. The 'Rogue-Chicken' watched.

Cuthbert had been plagued by a particularly nasty wild cat. He had tried everything to catch it and stop it attacking his chicks, but nothing worked. Then, one day, it ran straight in front of his combined harvester. Cuthbert had stopped and looked around.

The only other thing in sight was a chicken. It bobbed away discreetly, but Cuthbert knew it wasn't one of his. Then, some days later, Cuthbert had been charged by an escaped bull that skidded on the mud and slid into the lake in a cloud of steam and fury. Again, the only thing in sight was the chicken. Finally, when Cuthbert set off in his tractor for the village, he almost ran over the thing. It wandered straight out in front of him. Then Cuthbert realised that he had forgotten the letter he meant to post.

That was it. This chicken was special- countrymen spoke of them in whispers. Cuthbert had himself a 'Rogue-Chicken'. When the creature appeared to be too stupid to enter the hen-house at night, Cuthbert just winked and left it to its nocturnal wanderings. It was their secret.

Cuthbert peered out from under the thatch as a flash of lightning lit the yard. Someone had entered the barn and the chicken was closing in. Night-shirt flapping, Cuthbert raced out of the house and grabbed a scythe from against the wall. He headed for the barn as the heavens flashed above him.

Martin Hepplewhite was not used to stooping this low, but it was the only way to lift the coffer. The legs came out of the mud with a 'gloop'. Tipping the coffer sideways, he allowed the potatoes to rumble out across the floor.

Gripping the sides firmly, he lifted his prize, and then he froze. There, in the doorway, back-lit by a flash of lightning, was the figure of death. The skinny arms and legs, the flapping robes and the scythe.

The chicken on the apparition's shoulder didn't seem to fit, but this was no time for betting his life on it. Martin screamed and dropped the object of his desire. Running on the spot as he fired potatoes behind him, he gained some purchase and fled.

Cuthbert leaned the scythe against the barn wall and lifted the chicken from his shoulder. Stroking its feathers, he said, "It's a good job I came along. Goodness knows what you would have done to him."

Cuthbert went back to bed and the chicken approached the hen-house door. He did this every night. He tripped up the little ramp and raised one claw to the latch. Then, as usual, he forgot why he was standing there and wandered off again.

The next morning, Cuthbert answered a knock at his door. He paused. Having experienced some very odd encounters at this door, he opened it carefully.

A young lady with a wide smile stood there. As an experiment, Cuthbert closed the door for a moment and then opened it again. The young lady was still there, but the smile was not as wide now.

"Good morning," she said, "My name is Avril and I am from the Triple Echo."

"What, what, what?" asked Cuthbert in an attempt at humour.

Apparently having heard that one before, the young lady's smile disappeared altogether. She produced a notebook with a shiny spiral running along the top. "Can I interview you for the paper?"

Cuthbert was distracted- he had always been fascinated by the shiny spiral on these notebooks. Even as a child he imagined himself being tiny and running along the spiral, on the bottom, on the top, on the bottom, on the top, and always getting closer to the end. His eyes glazed over and he smiled as he imagined his tiny figure running madly along.

Avril, however, regarded his attention as being somewhere else entirely and she quickly buttoned her blouse, jerking the notebook and shaking Cuthbert out of his reverie.

"Sorry," he said, "I can never take my eyes off them." The reporter slapped his face and stormed off. Cuthbert went back inside rubbing his face. Now he remembered why he never answered the door.

A strange tittering brought him back to the door, and he peered around the corner. Percy sat on the log pile like a gnome. "Shouldn't upset that one," he said. "Lots of influence."

Cuthbert rubbed his cheek, "Oh, know her, do you?"

"Course I do," said Percy jumping down and yet not seeming any taller. "We meet when I'm writing my column."

Cuthbert looked at him. "You have a column?" he asked incredulously.

"Oh yes," said Percy proudly, "read by millions."

Cuthbert chanced, "Would it be about …?"

"Gardening," interrupted Percy, trying to see into the kitchen.

Cuthbert barred the way. "Read by millions, eh?"

"That's right, thousands," said Percy bobbing up and down trying to see in.

"Thousands, eh?" said Cuthbert.

Percy replied, "Oh yes, hundreds at least. Is the kettle on?"

Cuthbert sighed and stepped aside. Somehow his day was being decided for him. Percy clomped into the kitchen and took a seat at the table. "My advice is all over the place," he said.

Just like horse muck, thought Cuthbert, but actually said, "Tea?" and "What can I do for you, Percy?"

Percy became rather bashful. Cuthbert suspected that, over time, he would resemble every one of the dwarves by stages.

Percy was saying "… glad it wasn't just me, then."

Cuthbert supplied, "Oh no, it was obvious. It's a perfect match, except for the twins.

"Why, do they fancy her?" asked Percy.

"No, no," said Cuthbert, "just the milkman."

"The twins fancy the milkman?" asked Percy appalled.

"No," shrieked Cuthbert, "the twins fancy world domination. Margery fancies the milkman."

Percy paused, "Don't you mean the gardener?" he asked puzzled.

An equally puzzled Cuthbert said, "What gardener? It's set on board a ship. We're all at sea."

"We certainly are, mate," snapped Percy. "I thought I could discuss this with you, man to undertaker, but you seem to be jealous of my charisma."

Cuthbert looked at him, "Do you mean Chrysanthemum?"

There was a tiny light at the end of the tunnel that might just become a solution in Cuthbert's fevered brain, but Percy stormed off in a huff.

The tiny light became an express train bearing down rapidly on Cuthbert. "Oh ye gods," muttered Cuthbert, "he thinks Margery fancies him."

Cuthbert was left with more flashing images than a projectionist with a broken film, so he dashed outside to try to repair some damage, but Percy was halfway back to his arboreal fantasy world. Cuthbert passed a chicken that seemed to have mislaid a chair and briefly wondered why he no longer had a cow. This was typical. When real life visited Cuthbert, it came like the seventh cavalry with the whole Sioux nation screaming behind it.

The trick was to step out of the way.

Chapter 25

Cuthbert left Percy to it and, spotting the potatoes scattered about the yard, he began to replace and refill the coffer.

He ran his fingers over the carving and wondered at the patience of the old craftsmen. *It must have taken ages,* he thought. Then he realised. It was just like him with his dry-stone wall.

Perfection took time, especially when it kept falling back down. Looking closer at the carving, he saw that the lock-plate was surrounded by writhing dragons and part of the carving showed a feather in a pot. He had never noticed it before.

Closing the lid, he brushed the soil from his hands. Cuthbert sluggishly applied himself. Broken nights didn't suit him. He had tried once before to go without sleep when he attended Mortuary College. It was an evening class and he was exhausted. He woke up laid out on a desk with his arms folded and his lips sewn together. Assuming that it was a prank, the Principal threw him out. He would have explained, but no-one had bothered to cut the stitches.

Cuthbert was trying to feed the duck oranges to cut out extra ingredients later, when a car pulled into the farmyard. A huge shadow fell across Cuthbert, followed by a wheezing sound.

"Morning, Constable Beeching," said Cuthbert without looking up.

The constable stood panting. "I've got a complaint, Cuthbert," he wheezed.

"Doctors in the village," said Cuthbert tonelessly. Cuthbert and the constable had clashed professionally after PC Beeching left his truncheon in with a body he had interrogated and Cuthbert buried it and then refused to dig it up again. The amount had been docked from Beeching's next pay cheque and there had been bad blood between them ever since.

"Several complaints, actually," panted the officer.

"Same address," retorted Cuthbert.

The constable's feet were hurting and he was in no mood for yokels trying to get the better of him.

"I could always take you in, you know", he threatened. Cuthbert sighed. Trying to fit into a police car with Beeching and seventy-six discarded pizza cartons was a real threat.

"Sit down, officer," said Cuthbert politely.

"That's more like it," gloated the Constable as he sat on the mound indicated. He didn't notice the swarm of flies displaced by this as he sank down into the manure heap.

Constable Beeching had come to be a country Copper by a round-a-bout route. He could fire up the siren and give chase with the best of them, but he couldn't get out of the car to complete the arrest when he got there. Once, he had trapped a car full of villains in a cul-de-sac, but it took him so long to free himself from the seat belt, steering wheel, pedals and gear stick that the gang had shared out the loot, changed their clothing and torched the car. They had even cheekily left him a tip under his windscreen wiper.

Constable Beeching wriggled his ample rear and sank lower. The flies were circling like spitfires over Biggin Hill. "A young lady reporter says that you were staring at her ... ahem."

"Oh, is that what you call it?" asked Cuthbert, always keen to learn the proper name for anything.

"You don't deny it, then?" asked the officer. He wasn't used to it being this easy. "What part of it interested you the most?" he asked, producing his notebook.

Cuthbert paid attention for a second, but it was just a basic pencil-licker variety.

"Oh, the curves I suppose," said Cuthbert, before adding, "and the way she let them catch the sun."

The constable was looking rather flushed at this point, "Curves? Let them catch the sun?" he spluttered.

Turning the page, he changed the subject. "What can you tell me about the Hall?"

Cuthbert thought for a moment. "Big place," he began. "Lots of windows."

The constable interrupted, "Not that," he snapped, crossing things out, "What happened to it?"

Cuthbert began again, "Somebody built it. Somebody else lived in it, and then another somebody burned it down."

The constable stared at him. He was beginning to suspect that this was psychology. *Well, two can play at that game,* he thought. "Shut up." he said.

Cuthbert returned the stare and asked politely, "Do I shut up before or during the statement?"

The constable squirmed. "What is that smell?" he demanded.

"The country?" suggested Cuthbert enjoying himself immensely.

They glared at each other until Cuthbert broke the impasse. "Could have been an act of God, I suppose?"

Constable Beeching snapped his notebook shut and pointed at Cuthbert. "Don't try that one with me, young-feller-me-lad," he said. "Myrtle Beeching tried that one on me once," he declared. "Claimed that lightning hit a tree making it fall on her roof causing the house to catch fire. Then she claimed that a helicopter mistook it for an illuminated landing pad and crashed on top blowing the house up completely." He took a breath. "I didn't fall for that one. I know a put-up job when I see it."

Cuthbert contributed, "Well she was ninety-six, and she was your mother."

"What are you suggesting?" asked Beeching suspiciously. Cuthbert shrugged.

The constable was now peering between his own knees and surrounded by enraged insects. "What have you done, Cuthbert? I'll have you arrested."

Cuthbert watched him struggle before asking, "Did they ever ask where that truncheon actually went?" The constable wriggled and ignored him. Cuthbert continued, "Then there was that suicide I buried, the one with a hole in his back." The constable was paying attention now. "Then there was the pair of legs that didn't match the torso. Her legs were far too nice for him."

Beeching flopped sideways like a landed whale and crawled towards his car. "I'll get you, Cuthbert," he vowed.

The police car drove slowly away with all its windows open and a swarm of blue-bottle flies wondering where this giant 'blue-bottle' was taking them.

*

Cuthbert sat on the stile and watched Henry approach. He was swinging his stick and whistling. "Afternoon, Cuthbert. In trouble with the Law, are we?"

Cuthbert remained silent. He knew when talk was just noise and he waited for Henry to get to the point. It came soon enough. "Just wanted to thank you for including me in the play, Cuthbert. Good bit of fun.

Er, your leading lady, Margery is it? Is there a husband at all? A man could settle with a woman like that. Buy his little piece of England and look for treasure, eh, Cuthbert?"

Cuthbert hoped for a careless word, so he asked, "Would you find anything around here?"

Henry looked at him shrewdly. "Oh yes, it's here all right. I heard it from the undertaker himself."

Cuthbert felt himself gawp. He hadn't given away any secrets; he didn't know any- none that he could remember anyway.

Henry smiled, "No, not you Cuthbert, not you," and he walked on whistling.

Cuthbert was speechless. Had Henry met his father? Then something occurred to him. Strangers always came to the farm to ask the way to Mandrake Hall because you could not see it from the road. Henry had arrived with a fleet of trucks and gone straight there. So he already knew it was there. Had Cuthbert's father known something and not passed it on just because Cuthbert shot him? Perhaps it was time to look into the family papers.

This meant the desk. As a child Cuthbert had been terrified of the desk. It seemed to crouch in the dark recess waiting for an opportunity to pounce. As a child he had avoided it. As an adult he was mature enough to give it a wide berth.

His father had called it a 'roll-top' desk- it was slatted and rolled up and disappeared around the back somewhere. Cuthbert explored drawers full of stiff old papers that crackled arthritically when he opened them. The fascinating little drawers held nothing but paper clips and strange rubber thumbs covered in ink.

Cuthbert had asked his father about secret drawers, but the reply had been, "If I told you, they wouldn't be a secret, would they?" It had been quite amusing at the time, but pretty annoying now.

Many years ago, Cuthbert overheard a row between his parents. His mum had shouted that she could spend as much as she liked because "Her fortune would cover it."

His father had laughed and scoffed at her 'paper fortune'. If there was wealth, Cuthbert had never seen any evidence of it. Like most farms, if something new appeared, it usually meant that one of the animals was missing. As the undertaker, Cuthbert's father always seemed pleased to hear of a death in the valley; it paid the bills.

Cuthbert never thought about money. His parents had always told him that he would never have to worry about money, so he didn't.

The pile of 'treasures' from the desk was pitiful. Cuthbert tried to slam the lid shut in disgust, but the mechanism seemed to be caught in its own complications and it stuck. Finally, shutting it with a muffled thump, Cuthbert found the secret drawer. The impact had sprung it open in the side of the desk, knocking over his lantern and setting fire to the curtains. Cuthbert could see an old scroll lying in the drawer, but he could also see flames leaping upwards.

Several trips to the kitchen and many thrown bowls of water later, Cuthbert took out the scroll. Around him, disappointed flames hissed angrily and sputtered out.

He took the scroll into the kitchen and laid it out on the table. Behind him, a duck looked through the window with a strange glassy stare. The scroll had been rolled for so long that it had an inbuilt resistance to lying flat. Cuthbert had once had a corpse like that, but garden rollers have many uses.

The document was finally pinned down at each corner and Cuthbert began to read. Then he realised that simply being able to read was no use at all. A dying spider wandering through an inkwell and staggering across the page would have made a neater job of it. Cuthbert struggled for ages, but only learned that Elizabeth the First insisted upon all her titles being quoted in every document and the scribe had slavishly written them down as if she might actually read it and catch him out.

Rubbing his eyes, Cuthbert rolled the scroll back up. He needed a secret place for this tonight, and scratched his head. All the nooks and crannies were known to him, so they were no longer secret.

He needed some new ones. Of course, he might spend all night finding new ones that could be no longer used because they were no longer secret. Cuthbert sighed. Logic was a terrible burden. He carried the scroll upstairs with him.

The duck slowly sank out of sight, taking its glassy stare with it.

Chapter 26

Sitting on the bed, Cuthbert gazed once again at the scroll. He recognised that the impression in the wax seal was that of Mandrake Hall.

It was also on the pub sign of the Mandrake Arms. The Old Hall would have been a good place to look for clues, if he hadn't just burnt it down. Amongst the letters Cuthbert could make out some of the words. All the 'I's were 'J's and all the 'S's' were 'F's. He was amazed that a dyslexic lawyer could find work in those days.

Staring sleeplessly around, Cuthbert's eye traced the carving on his huge inherited four poster bed. He spotted the same symbol as the one on the coffer- a pot with a feather in it.

Staring at the canopy above him, Cuthbert mentally ran through the architecture of the village. He had seen that symbol somewhere else.

The village had appeared gradually over the years. Whoever could build would build, and those who couldn't propped something up and lived underneath it.

Mandrake Hall, the farm, the old mill and the derelict church were the oldest survivors. There had been some innovative designs in the last few generations, but not all survived.

The Baker had combined his trade with the need to put a roof above his head. His mother had read him Hansel and Gretel and he thought that 'cottage loaf' was a specification. He had heard about advertising back when having your name on a bus meant seeing it several times a day.

He had built his house out of hand baked brick-loaves, using flapjacks for the roof tiles and marzipan for the twiddly bits. He used coloured icing to outline everything and it attracted sightseers from all over the world. It also attracted a plague of mice, a flock of crows and a herd of goats who, putting aside their differences, simply enjoyed the feast.

A spell of pretty awful weather turned the foundations into sludge and the baker and his menagerie moved on. On a really hot day, the locals say that you can still smell freshly baked bread.

Cuthbert also remembered the blacksmith building his own house. He had travelled and seen some fancy iron bridges somewhere, so he made his own iron house. He had forged and hammered and hammered and forged until a truly unique house stood before him.

What appeared to be mullioned windows were made from horse shoes, and the walls were an intricate lattice work. It was even musical, as the wind picked up and gained in speed to graduate from a moan throughout the framework into a full banshee scream.

As the storm clouds boiled overhead, the crowds dispersed, but the blacksmith stood his ground and proudly leant against his doorframe as the lightning struck. Cuthbert remembered it as ashes to ashes, dust to dust.

Cuthbert was distracting himself. It would have been one of the older buildings like the Hall. Then he remembered, The Hall, it was on the gate-posts. He would never sleep now, so he dressed and decided to go and explore. No-one would see him in the middle of the night.

The night sky was crystal clear as Cuthbert made his way up the hill. Now that the Hall had gone and wasn't watching him, it was simply a nice walk. Cuthbert stared up at the timeless patterns of the stars. Born into country life, he could never see the mystery of the night sky. Try telling a farmer that the thing up there was a plough. Orion's belt wouldn't hold up a decent pair of corduroys, and as for scales, twins and pairs of fish- somebody needed a hobby.

After straying from the path several times as he stared up into the cosmos, Cuthbert reached the gate-posts. One of them was covered in moss, the other was rubbed clear. There was even a piece of tracing paper on the floor. Someone else had been here. Cuthbert quickly made a rubbing for himself and turned to go.

The light was there one minute and then it had gone. Cuthbert stood still and watched. The light flashed again. Someone was moving around out there. Cuthbert edged forward, watching the light darting about in between the headstones near the old church. He crept closer.

"Percy?" Cuthbert hadn't meant to shout, but his nerves had adjusted the volume. "What are you doing here?" Suspicion made his words thick with mistrust.

He wasn't really surprised when Percy retorted, "Gardening."

Cuthbert asked, "At night?"

Percy became defensive. "Deadly nightshade," he stated, "only comes out after dark. People waste hours looking for it in daylight, wear themselves out and then fall off cliffs."

Cuthbert stared. Percy was forced to explain. "That's why it's deadly."

Cuthbert looked Percy up and down. "Delicate little things, are they?" he asked.

"Oh yes," said Percy brightly. "Need special handling."

"With a shovel?" shrieked Cuthbert.

Percy looked at the tool in his hands as if it had just appeared and quickly said, "Moles."

"Moles?" asked Cuthbert warily, feeling his reality tip ever so slightly.

"That's right," insisted Percy, "can't let the moles eat the nightshade."

Cuthbert checked. "I thought nightshade was poisonous?"

Percy nodded. 'It is.'

Cuthbert pressed on. "Then the mole would be dead?"

Percy nodded again and replied, "Definitely, after I hit it with a shovel."

Cuthbert's volume climbed again. "So you hit it with your shovel to stop it poisoning itself?"

Percy nodded once more. "Them are country ways," he said, before adding, "Gotta go, Cuthbert. Gnomes and gardens wait for no man."

"Gnomes?" spluttered Cuthbert.

Percy sneered, "I suppose that a townie like you thinks they get themselves up in a morning?"

As Cuthbert wrestled with his own thought processes, Percy was off, darting through the gravestones like bacteria amongst rotting teeth. Cuthbert stood for a while. It paid to wait and readjust after spending time with Percy. It was like rearranging the contents of a drawer just because the thing you wanted had never been in there.

Checking around to try to decide what Percy had been up to, Cuthbert found little curled up pieces of tracing paper and it was obvious that Percy had scraped some lichen from an inscription. Cuthbert directed his lamp and gasped. The design looked like a UFO on a stick. He sat down heavily. This was an experience that the valley was keen to forget.

Chapter 27

Nick Bottomley was a newly-wed. He had brought his young bride to the valley and was shocked to discover that she didn't think that the place was normal at all.

She was becoming increasingly restless and disillusioned and Nick began to meet his old mates for a game of poker. In his head he had been preparing the other players and lulling them into a false sense of security.

His theory was that the more he drank, the more acute his senses became. Just when they thought he was incapable, he would pounce and clear the table. That would show his new bride what an asset he was. His fellow poker players also liked his strategy and continued to take his money. They already knew what an asset he was.

After one particularly blurred hand when the Queen of Diamonds insisted on winking at him, the others all folded and, scooping up Nick's money, they left. Now Nick was in a situation where he was ready to pounce but he had no-one to pounce on, and nothing to pounce with.

Now he really did feel an asset.

Wandering home with a stagger for company, Nick became lost and asked directions from a stone angel with a wreath in one hand and the other one pointing along the path. Thanking her profusely, Nick promptly fell into the grave Cuthbert had dug the day before. He tried to climb out, but it was hopeless. Cuthbert never cheated on depth, but Nick had been cheated on height so he fell asleep in the hole.

Early the next morning, the widow Bishop came to the graveside. She was early for the ceremony, but needed to make sure that the sides were steep enough to keep the old devil in. Peering over the edge, she gasped.

There, sleeping peacefully, was a young man. Now, widows are conditioned to realise that a chance missed is one less memory to keep you warm at night, so whooping with delight and throwing back her veil, she jumped in.

Nick, finding himself in an embrace, assumed that he had found his way home. After a lingering kiss, he opened his eyes and gazed at his new mother-in-law.

Now overlay that thought with the scene of several mourners peering over the rim at them, including a tearful new wife who had just announced that her husband had been out all night. Cuthbert shuddered at the memory, but had to smile as Nick had explained it all.

"Aliens," he had screamed. "Abducted us, bright lights, whirring noises, horrible, left us in a hole." This would never have worked at any other time or other place.

But so many people were embarrassed on so many levels that it was easier to accept it than it was to enquire into it.

Even the village gossip took an afternoon off after this one. It would have stayed a local matter too, but Avril had been there to report on the funeral and she passed the story on to the Nationals as a good stringer should. The world then discovered the valley.

The interest was immense. The roads were gridlocked. It was even worse than when both carts met at the crossroads as the ducks were being transferred to a new pond. Every hilltop grew a make-shift camp of people in foul-weather gear and woolly hats. The skies hadn't been studied this intently since the druids moved out.

Reporters knocked on every door. The lack of response didn't worry them. They reported whatever they wanted to anyway. It would have all died down in a day, but then things became complicated.

Cuthbert had remembered from somewhere that if he didn't maintain a working farm, he may well have to worry about money after all, and the corn in the top field was due to be cut. Cuthbert couldn't see the point of having a tractor taking up space all year round, so he simply bought a horse when he needed it and returned it when they had exhausted each other's patience.

He relied upon 'Smiling Jack' in the next village for this. Jack's smile always became bigger when he saw Cuthbert coming, but as Cuthbert's mum used to say, "If you can make someone smile, then at least you haven't hurt them."

Smiling Jack led Cuthbert over to the furthest paddock. It was as if he always kept a special one for Cuthbert. Cuthbert had no real affinity for horses and they watched each other suspiciously all the way home.

Passing the blacksmith in his new wooden forge, the man called out, "Morning, Sunshine."

"Morning," replied Cuthbert.

The blacksmith hesitated, "Oh, Morning, Cuthbert. I was talking to the horse."

Cuthbert stopped. "The horse is called Sunshine?"

The blacksmith replied, "Oh yes, right little ray of sunshine that one. Always makes the children laugh."

"Why?" spluttered Cuthbert not seeing anything remotely funny about three tons of horse flesh with teeth at one end and manure at the other.

"Well," the blacksmith replied, "have you noticed how he holds his head and one eye bulges more than the other?"

Cuthbert quickly checked and said, "I thought all horses looked like that."

The blacksmith was affronted. "Only when they've got two legs shorter than the other two," he said ,appalled at Cuthbert's insensitivity.

"What?" shrieked Cuthbert, "Which legs are shorter, the front or the back?"

"Neither," came the reply. "The two on the left are shorter than the two on the right; he can only walk in circles."

Cuthbert paused; there was a flaw in this argument somewhere. "I didn't have any trouble getting him along the road." he said suspiciously.

"Well, you wouldn't," agreed the blacksmith, "The road curves all the way from the next valley. Wait until you try to take him back."

"Can he work?" demanded Cuthbert huffily.

"Well, yes, but only in circles. See, he's making me laugh already."

Cuthbert stumped along the road noticing the curved hedgerows for the first time. *No wonder Jack was smiling,* he thought.

Cuthbert fastened Sunshine to the harvesting machine and tried all sorts of clicking noises and flips of the reins, but Sunshine wouldn't move. Eventually, the horse became bored and wandered off on its own wondering why the machine was following him.

Sure enough his track began to curve. Cuthbert tried to make him walk straight by using brute force, but the brute was stronger than him. Cuthbert gave up and stood in the field silently raging against life when the horse came full circle and nudged him in the back. Cuthbert realised that at least some of the corn was cut. By standing in front of the horse and annoying it, Cuthbert found that he could set it off in a different direction so even more corn was cut. At the end of the day as the horse and his apprentice went back to the barn, the field was dotted with tufts of uncut corn in all sorts of strange patterns. Cuthbert looked up at the nearby hilltop. *Thank goodness those reporters are all looking the other way*, he thought.

Chapter 28

The next day exploded into Cuthbert's life with the clatter of helicopter blades. Huge trucks with satellite dishes were everywhere, with serious looking men mumbling into microphones for gravitas and pretty young women doing the same for attention.

The local children ran up and down shouting, "The Martians are coming."

Cuthbert smiled. "Makes a change from the Russians," he muttered. The children were performing for the cameras, of course. Every child was a member of the valley Mafia and had probably already stolen a missile launcher from somewhere. Behind this irreverence, the truth was nibbling away at Cuthbert's resistance like a rat with a power line. When the answer came, the shock was very similar too.

Skulking through the crowded town where Mrs Biggle had sold out of Mars bars without seeing the irony, Cuthbert made his way up the hill. In a locust storm of whirring cameras and clicking shutters, Cuthbert's field was being immortalised. Cuthbert had to admit that it looked pretty impressive and the mathematicians on hand had concluded that the crop circle showed the best landing site for an imminent visitor. TV stations urged everyone to learn Martian and someone made a fortune selling books on Esperanto with the covers torn off.

Nick and his new wife moved quietly away. The widow Bishop married a reporter after guaranteeing his safety because 'she had met the head Martian and made a deal'. Cuthbert let the rest of the corn lie where it was and stayed inside. Sunshine? Smiling Jack picked him up in a truck and found him a job dipping his tail in a paint pot and marking out helicopter landing sites.

After returning to the farm, Cuthbert smoothed the piece of tracing paper out and compared it with the other designs he had seen. It was identical, except that it seemed to point downwards. He fetched his father's old magnifying glass and double checked.

The glass was a beautiful piece made from a deer's horn back in the days when people realised that animals could die of old age. It brought back childhood memories for Cuthbert. Not only had he cleared the village of ants, he had frightened away the local pest too.

The local drunk had made an art out of being annoying. Once he was drunk he systematically aggravated everyone in the village. They all bought him a drink to get rid of him and so the cycle continued.

Cuthbert's encounter came about when the drunk had completed his self-appointed tasks of serenading the local lamp post and demonstrating how a fountain would look if the village had one.

He also managed to water the hanging baskets outside the police station at the same time. He was on his way home for a nap to prepare for the night shift when he spotted 'that strange kid from the farm'.

Cuthbert sat astride a rotten log and seemed to only have one huge eye. Even the drunk knew that Cuthbert was a bit strange and he usually staggered across the road to avoid him, but this one-eyed vision interested him.

"Watcherdoin', Custard?" he slurred.

Cuthbert was engrossed and merely pointed to the cracks in the mossy trunk. The drunk tried to marshal his few remaining brain cells, but the conflicting signals made his brain ache. Snatching the magnifying glass, he peered through it, deep into the log. It was an epiphany.

He was faced by a world of tumbling writhing creatures fitted with mandibles and incisors designed to smash pre-stressed concrete.

The drunk moaned and throwing out his arms cried to the heavens. "Is this hell?" he asked, "Is this what you have in store for me?" he cried. "Show me a sign, Lord, show me a sign."

Just then the sun came out from behind a cloud and caught the lens of the magnifying glass. Cuthbert watched in fascination as a blister appeared on the drunk's forehead and the charred skin began to peel away.

"Aaaargh," screamed the drunk and, mistaking the glass for a mirror, tried to inspect the damage. Instead, he got a close-up of Cuthbert and another blister.

Dropping the glass, he fled, never to be seen again. Rumour had it that he was now selling body armour to sinners so that they could band together on the far banks of the River Styx and fight back against the demons. His latest line was a rather fetching Kevlar shroud.

Some members of the valley held Cuthbert in high regard after that, but the pub landlord hated him. He had just lost his best customer. Soon after that, he was told that he must allow for twenty-four hour drinking. It was the last straw. Why should he shut an hour early?

Oddly enough, the hanging baskets wilted away and were replaced by a blue lamp.

Cuthbert had now accepted that the symbol was identical in all cases, but this one was pointing down as if it was a marker. He suddenly realised that he was the only person who could dig up a grave without arousing suspicion.

Was that why everyone was helping with the play, so they could keep an eye on him? Cuthbert rubbed his chin. Having an imaginary friend suddenly announce that you did not exist could have a permanent effect on someone as sensitive as Cuthbert. Having an agoraphobic reflection didn't help either. Who was a friend and who wasn't?

Percy had obviously found the gate-posts and the headstone. Should they combine their knowledge? Henry was probably the best bet, but his brother Ronald seemed quite unstable and prone to random acts of violence. Cuthbert didn't understand violence.

After a difference of opinion two men would threaten to re-arrange each other with anatomically impossible threats and end up stood facing each other, gasping for breath, convinced that 'that would teach' the other one.

Surely the only reason to have an opinion was to find out if anyone else had the same one? In Cuthbert's experience, a situation would either resolve itself or one of the combatants would forget what the problem had been in the first place.

Chapter 29

Cuthbert headed for Percy's bijou residence. On the way, he noticed that someone had re-covered the scrape in the lichen, and then he heard a scream.

A scream in the valley was about as welcome as a grass snake at a picnic. Everyone had to do something, but no-one wanted to go near the thing.

Two gravestones further on, Cuthbert found Belinda with her hands held up to her face. She pointed silently at her father's gravestone. The moss had been scraped away and the name stood out clearly. "Edward Shakespeare Truffle". Cuthbert looked at Belinda. He had never seen her full length before; she was always behind the bar.

"His middle name was Shakespeare?" asked Cuthbert.

Belinda was still horrified at this vandalism, so Cuthbert explained the hobby of 'grave rubbing'. Belinda shrieked to the heavens, because she thought he said 'grave robbing'. Cuthbert waited for the decibel level to settle and calmed her down.

He asked her again about the unusual middle name. "It's not unusual," she sniffed. "My middle name is Ophelia." She then added dreamily, "Belinda Ophelia Truffle. My father said he could set it to music," she sighed.

"Good job it wasn't Belinda Bottom, then," quipped Cuthbert, ruining the mood instantly.

Belinda snorted, "All real valley folk are named after the bard," and she flounced off. Cuthbert sat. He hadn't heard that one for years. His parents had come here, so that his father could farm and his mother could follow her theatrical destiny, which, like most other actors' ambitions, promptly petered out. Oddly enough, his mother's middle name had been Tatiana, Shakespeare's Queen of the Fairies. Perhaps she had been 'real valley folk'.

Percy's shed looked even more derelict in the early morning light; it seemed to lean over to one side too. The door creaked open- it would have been really disappointing if it hadn't. Cuthbert liked everything to play its part properly. There were very few places to hide anything, but after accidentally kicking the plant pot holding the settee up, Cuthbert found one of them. Old newspaper cuttings told the UFO story in detail. Several of them showed a reporter doing his piece 'to camera'. It was Henry Chisolm.' So he had been here before.

"Found anything?" asked an oily voice.

Cuthbert turned slowly. *It certainly isn't Percy,* he thought.

Straightening up and completing his turn, Cuthbert came face to face with the butler.

Cuthbert breathed a sigh of relief, "It's you," he said. "No-one saw you after the fire."

The butler smiled. "Oh it wasn't hard to disappear after a conflagration like that. Congratulations, by the way. Whoever trained you knew what he was doing."

"Did he?" asked Cuthbert, bemused.

The butler motioned for Cuthbert to sit, so he sat. There was something menacing about the way the man was blocking the door. The butler continued, "The occupants of the Hall were convinced that you had special training. I wasn't convinced until I saw you infiltrate their defensive perimeter, neutralise the booby traps and use their improvised explosive devices against them, and all without leaving any messy bodies. "Excellent work, Custard."

Cuthbert automatically began to answer, "Thank y ... Custard?" He looked closer as the butler and swept a lock of hair from his forehead. The star-shaped scar still gleamed and if you imagined the eyes more blood shot and a good bit of stubble, you would recognise that the drunk was back. Cuthbert stared.

The man was working himself into a frenzy. He glared at Cuthbert, "You drove me from the village, Custard. Because of you, I have made millions. I cannot count my cars and properties, all because of you."

Cuthbert grinned inanely, "Don't mention it."

The man really lost it now. "… mention it. You dropped me into the shark pool of commerce. Meetings, back stabbing, mergers, acquisitions and taxes." He spat out the last word before quietly asking, "Do you know how hard it is to get Chinese children to sew Kevlar vests with radium tipped needles?" The man paused for breath before hissing, "Well, Custard, I'm back. I was going to send some men to kill you."

Cuthbert gulped.

The butler watched him carefully, "But I'm not sure that they would return. I then thought that *I* might kill you, but then I realised I could simply buy the Mandrake Arms and have my old life back." Cuthbert smiled. "Then kill you," the man added.

Cuthbert gulped again.

The butler asked smoothly, "Anyway, where is this wonderful thing that everyone is looking for?"

Cuthbert shrugged. "I have no idea," he said honestly.

The man snarled, "You don't know when you're beaten, do you?" He took a step forward, "As if the last member of your family wouldn't know the whereabouts of the lost ..."

Booooiing.

The sound reverberated around the shed and the man fell flat on his face. Percy stood in the doorway holding his multi-purpose spade. "Bit of luck that," he said. "We need an excuse to dig a hole." Checking his spade for damage, he said to Cuthbert, "Don't thank me, mate. He was only going to kill you."

Cuthbert spluttered, "He was about to tell me the secret," he snapped, before adding contritely, "then he was going to kill me."

Pushing an old wheelbarrow with the butler wrapped in a mangy carpet, the pair headed for Cuthbert's farm and discussed their findings on the way. Cuthbert described his puzzlement over the symbols.

Percy laughed, "I'll ask my cousin," he said. "He knows all about cymbals, he's a drummer."

Chapter 30

Cuthbert lay in bed that night and thought about people wanting to harm him. It was a strange feeling. Cuthbert had never knowingly harmed anything.

He had had several near misses himself, of course, like the time someone had a kite string caught around the weathervane and pulled the whole thing down just as he was passing under it.

Then there was the time a wagon load of hay ran down Gallows Hill as he turned the corner and led a funeral procession that way. Everyone else went the other way as if they knew something.

Hmmm, he thought, *what if there is something in this real valley folk business?*

He fell asleep dreaming about people in Shakespearean dress pointing at him and hissing, "Outsider."

*

Cuthbert pushed the old wooden wheelbarrow back up to the cemetery where he met Percy. The butler was still wrapped in his carpet and his arm swung limply over the edge as they bounced along.

The carpet parted just enough for the man's grey face to peek out. One of the valley Mafia look-outs sat on a wall and watched him pass.

Cuthbert heard him mutter, "Penny for the guy? This bloke needs a new calendar."

Meeting Percy at the grave, they studied the headstone. Percy's UFO on a stick now looked more like the feather in an ink-pot that Cuthbert had been finding.

"Right," said Cuthbert rolling up his sleeves. "Perfect excuse to solve a riddle and lose a body at the same time, eh, Percy?"

Percy was looking towards the gate. "What do we say if someone comes along?"

Cuthbert answered distractedly, "Oh, subsidence, loose headstone, that sort of thing."

Percy asked, "What about him. Do we need papers or anything in case someone checks?"

Cuthbert glanced over at the wheelbarrow. "No-one has checked here for years. We'll just chuck him in when we fill the hole."

Percy was still looking back down the path, "If someone did check, what would he look like?"

Cuthbert wanted to get on with it, so he snapped, "An officious little twerp with a briefcase. Looks like a stick with a hat on."

Percy stood to attention, "Morning, sir, Come to inspect have you?"

Cuthbert sighed, "Nice try, Percy, now get digging" as a shadow fell across him.

Horatio Penn was an inspector. He had been born to inspect. He inspected everything. His parents had barely dared to speak in case he reported them in his school diary. He had been drawn to the local authority like a moth to a flame after his report of bricks hidden in a bin for household waste had been taken very seriously indeed.

His parents had been heavily fined and they had never forgiven him for that. He had enjoyed a meteoric career, which began when he spotted a supervisor walking on the grass, and ended after he caught the Mayor watering his garden fifteen minutes after the hosepipe ban started.

The new Mayor was taking no chances. Horatio was now the official Graves Inspector for Towns, or as he was known in the local authority, 'The official G.I.T.'.

Cuthbert glared at the fawning and obsequious Percy and tried to appear calm before the inspector. This man could smell confusion.

Mr Penn had not changed at all. His face betrayed not one whit of warmth or humour. His life was simply a column of boxes waiting to be ticked. Horatio gazed at the scene before him, "And what is this morning's endeavour?" he enquired before asking, "Was I notified of major structural upheavals?"

Percy took this to be the first sign of closet sarcasm and laughed obediently.

The tundra coloured eyes crept across to Percy. "And you are?"

Percy panicked. Standing to attention, he touched his forelock and said, "Percy Plumm, m'lud, Gardener sir, man and boy. I came to help this stranger with the body, m'lud."

Horatio's eyes traversed towards Cuthbert like the turret of a panzer tank. "There's a body?" he asked bleakly. A viper tongue flicked out and licked a pencil. A cross was marked in a box.

Cuthbert's torment had begun. He glared at Percy and hissed, "Thank you very much."

Percy began to jabber, "But he's got a briefcase and a clipboard and a bowler hat and … everything."

Horatio began his inquisition. Where was the hearse? Cross the box. Where were the mourners? Cross the box. Is this grave already in use? Cross two boxes. He had a moment of panic when he came to the bottom of the page, but sighed with relief when another sheet of boxes appeared underneath.

Cuthbert was looking around for Percy and wondering how many bodies he could get into one hole.

Horatio paused. There was something not quite right about this scene. He looked around hurriedly. An empty wheelbarrow, an old carpet, so where was the scruffy little one with the spade and why did this one have a completely blank face? He mentally totted up the component parts of the puzzle. He had an undertaker, he had a grave and he had a chap with a spade.

All they needed was a body. Gulp. Suddenly months of hints and forebodings returned to haunt Horatio Penn- the way in which his parents had crossed their fingers when they served his meals; the way the outgoing Mayor had almost strangled the incoming one with the Mayoral chain whilst looking straight at him.

He shuddered; all his anonymous notes had been on headed paper so that he could claim the air-miles reward every month. This was pure Macbeth. He could smell the damp earth. Someone had put out a contract on him.

Cuthbert stopped looking for Percy and turned to face the music. There was no music. The only sound was the rapid 'bip-bop, bip-bop' of the upside down bowler hat rocking to a stand-still.

The discarded clip-board flapped disconsolately on the floor. The Government Issue pencil had been fastened to a lapel by a safety pin. Both now lay in the ornamental gravel. The man was all over the place.

Percy re-appeared buttoning his trousers, "Where is he?" he asked.

Cuthbert shrugged, "I don't know, his bits are here, but he's gone."

Percy frowned, "Not him, the other chap you made me hit with a spade."

Cuthbert was about to retort in his defence when he realised that part of what he had just heard was important. Words and apostrophes tumbled over themselves for prominence, but Cuthbert rejected them all and gaped. The body had gone. Eventually he managed, "Where is it?"

"He," corrected Percy distractedly.

"Who?" asked Cuthbert.

"Him" replied Percy.

"What?" shrieked Cuthbert.

Percy explained patiently. "He can't be an it. 'Its' don't walk."

Cuthbert spluttered, "Neither do dead men. You couldn't even do that right, could you? Some assassin you are."

Percy was affronted, "I'm a gardener."

"Oh yes," cried Cuthbert, "So, where then did you get the nerve to kill him?"

Percy looked abashed. "I pretended that he was a big mole," he said, shuffling his feet.

The pair of them sat and calmed down. They sat on the edge of the hole, dangling their feet like kids at a seaside pier. Then, lanterns aloft, they began to descend. Percy had brought his spade in case it was a huge mole hole.

*

The twins were rolling about amongst the gravestone with their socks stuffed into their mouths. "Wait until Cuthbert tries to use his fake body in the play," they giggled.

The butler leant against a headstone, not a word was spoken. With the childhood affliction of instant boredom, the twins wandered off towards the old church. Of course, they had watched Cuthbert and Percy start to descend and after a few minutes they pushed the wheelbarrow into the hole. They would need it to retrieve the body later ready for its introduction to the drunks at twilight.

*

Down their new hole Cuthbert and Percy moved slowly. The walls were dry and the stone seemed safe enough.

The 'thump' from somewhere behind them was worrying though. They had nothing to fear from Horatio.

Without a body, all he had was two men near a potential hole. Neither of them thought about the missing body very much at all.

Cuthbert had misplaced so many in his time that it hardly registered as an event.

The steps led to the inevitable tunnel. Cuthbert led the way as Percy gazed around, fascinated. To pass the time and muffle his own heartbeat, Cuthbert explained the history of the valley and its tunnels. He also included a mention of the book he had found at the old mill and his thoughts about all the newcomers, forgetting completely that the strange little chap behind him with a spade was also a newcomer.

Percy listened quietly before commenting. "These stones are much older than the aquifer tunnels and their tributaries."

Cuthbert stopped, turned and looked behind Percy to see who else had joined them. "Pardon?" he asked.

Percy scratched his chin knowingly. "The stones are a denser material and most of them show tool marks. There was even a mason's mark on a lintel back there." He never blinked as Cuthbert examined his face in the lantern light.

After a pause Cuthbert tried, "Gardening magazines?"

Percy nodded. "Got to know what's under a garden as well, you know. Drainage, root systems, mole hives."

Cuthbert studied the face again, "Mole hives?"

Percy sighed. "You townies," he said in exasperation. "You think everything lives on an estate."

Cuthbert turned and plodded on. No longer worried about anything he might find ahead, he had enough on with the thing behind him. It was hard to know when to relax with Percy. When the sane genetic chain was operating, he could be quite worrying. When the random gene kicked in, he was terrifying.

To fill the silence, Cuthbert asked, "So these root systems get everywhere then?"

"Oh yes," answered Percy brightly. "Tree roots can crack concrete and damage foundations. Houses have to be knocked down when a tree decides to move in." They both made their way slowly forward, imagining the silent tendrils groping through the cracks towards them, fully intent upon strangling them and reducing them to plant food.

"Er, are we there yet?" asked Percy nervously.

*

The tunnel suddenly opened up into a much wider room, Percy dashed in front, relieved to be out of the tunnel at last. He stopped suddenly as he realised that everyone seemed to be grinning at him.

"Is this a charnel house?" he asked weakly.

Cuthbert was back in his own territory. The long-dead may insist upon grinning at you, but at least they kept quiet. Cuthbert held up the light to reveal niches cut into the walls, some packed with leg bones and others with shorter ones. Some of the small ones had tumbled to the floor.

"It's like a doggy supermarket," said Percy irreverently.

Cuthbert stared at the rows of skulls, all locked in the ironic grimace of one who knows what really happens after death. "Probably plague victims," he muttered. Then, realising the implications, he moved towards the next room. Percy matched him, step for step.

The next room contained old rotting coffins. Some had been stacked on top of one another and had collapsed in unexpected marriages.

Percy suddenly said, "There's the inkwell."

Cuthbert went over to him. "What inkwell?" he asked suspiciously.

Percy was standing in front of a lead coffin. It stood upright in a corner and the weight had split the seam near the bottom. Dust had trickled out. Percy pointed excitedly at the device engraved into the lid.

Cuthbert moved closer. "That's the symbol I keep finding. Why is it an inkwell?"

Percy jiggled about with excitement. "It took hours to write a document by hand in those days," he said. "Inkwells had wide bases to stop them from being knocked over. This one always has a writing quill in it."

Cuthbert managed, "So someone did carve it upside down as a pointer?"

Percy looked around, "Yes, but what is it pointing at?"

They studied the lead coffin before them and the little pile of dust on the floor. Cuthbert looked around. "We must be in the crypt under the old church. Only wealthy people were buried in lead coffins. It kept them airtight ready for the resurrection. It's probably one of the owners of Mandrake Hall. What on earth are you doing, Percy?" he yelled.

Percy was on his knees where the coffin had been damaged and had widened the crack with his spade. Now he had his arm inside, right up to the shoulder.

Cuthbert was appalled- this was grave robbing, this was sacrilege, this was … fascinating.

Percy grinned up at him and removed his hand like a grim parody of Little Jack Horner.' "Look at this," he breathed.

Cuthbert took the gold ring from him. It was engraved with the inkwell and quill.

Percy plunged his arm back in and continued to rummage around. "Huh, pile of old bones," he complained.

Cuthbert replied distractedly, "The body will have rotted and the bones will have fallen to the bottom." He turned the ring to catch the light. It was beautiful.

Percy was wriggling furiously below him and struggling to free his arm. His thumb was stuck in one of the eye sockets and he was banging the skull against the sides to try and free it. Cuthbert opened his mouth to comment when all hell broke loose.

The noise was everywhere- wheezing, wailing sounds emanating from tortured souls. The walls shook and dust fell from the cracks in an attempt to hide the scene of desecration. Cuthbert dropped the ring and ran for the steps in blind panic. The cacophony chased him down the tunnel. He galloped up the steps, but the exit was blocked.

The awful sounds stopped. The air was full of dust motes tumbling downwards. There was no air to make them drift. Cuthbert made his way back to find Percy re-enacting Hamlet with the skull stuck on his thumb. They were trying to out-stare each other.

Percy looked up. "Have we just discovered the earliest alarm system known to man?" he asked. The skull came off with a 'plop' and rolled playfully into the corner. Percy stood and brushed the dust off himself. "Come on, then," he said. "Your turn to put the kettle on."

Cuthbert slumped, picked the ring up out of the dust and stared at it. Percy studied him. Cuthbert looked pale. This in itself was an achievement. Cuthbert started off pale, anything else was on its way to translucency. He looked like someone who had died and reincarnated just enough to come and say goodbye.

"What's wrong?" asked Percy.

Cuthbert didn't look up. "Someone dropped the wheelbarrow into the grave" he said tonelessly.

Percy brightened. "Oh, that's good," he said, "Someone knows we're here. Oh," he added as the thought sank faster than the dust.

Several yards above them, the twins ran laughing into the sunshine. They were on a high. They had been stealing sticky tape and band-aids for weeks to repair the old organ and today they had tried it out. "What a noise," shouted the first twin.

"Fantastic," shouted the second one. "We must have awoken the dead." Forgetting about both the body and the wheelbarrow, they skipped off happily.

Somewhere behind a headstone, the butler groaned.

*

Cuthbert and Percy sat side by side. After all the broken nights, Cuthbert actually caught up on some sleep.

Even Percy had to admit that it was at least as comfortable as his shed. Gradually Percy began to explain how he had come to the valley.

The UFO story had caught his attention and he had sneaked into the valley and moved into the potting shed. This put him in a prime position to watch the landing sites and be first in line to hitch a lift. Percy didn't necessarily believe in alien life-forms.

He just hoped that they were all little scruffy chaps with red hair and wellies. They could train him up and send him back with a vaporiser gun and a tee shirt saying, 'Carrot-top? - the top of a carrot is green, Einstein.'

He still dreamt of this moment of revenge for all those 'copper-top' moments. He actually had the tee shirt printed and it became his reason for living. Rock concerts, protests and potential overthrows of Government. He attended them all. Wherever there was a crowd, there was a crusader, and Percy was his name.

The rock concert wasn't a roaring success actually. He was packed in with thousands of others and couldn't jump high enough to be seen. After three hours of brain numbing percussion and breathing strange smoke, his hair didn't seem to be an issue anyway.

He was the only one at the Government overthrow because the football was on and the police thought he was the clown on his way to entertain at a children's party.

The only time he really got everyone's attention was when he arrived late at a mass rally in Trafalgar Square. He forced his way through thousands of women until he was under a banner saying 'Women-4-ever, Men-never.' Turning to face the crowd, he whipped open his coat and was promptly arrested. The two undercover officers, dressed as dominatrices with handcuffs, reckoned he had been extremely lucky.

UFO watching had given Percy the right amount of solitude with just the hint of an escape route.

He and Cuthbert certainly had something in common. Percy enjoyed his own company because nobody interrupted. Cuthbert preferred his own company because nobody corrected his grammar.

Chapter 31

Being a schoolteacher was like any other job- either a vocation or a life sentence, depending upon whether you survived the experience or not.

He had been considered a child prodigy in his youth, amazing everyone with his command of the German language. It was a local phenomenon that no-one could explain.

The truth was he had grown up in wartime and been an incredibly boring child. The others didn't even call for him so they could throw mud at him. During some intense air activity, a Messerschmitt crashed onto the roof of the house.

The pilot bailed out and the aeroplane had remained lodged in the rafters. No-one came anywhere near it because of the dripping fuel and the large bomb hanging underneath. Young Joshua now had solitude.

People pushed supplies through the letterbox and ran away. He didn't know that oranges were hard to get, he just assumed that they wouldn't fit through his letterbox.

The only reading materials not damaged by the leaking fuel were the Luftwaffe flight manuals. Thus young Joshua emerged after the hostilities were over, fluent in 'Flying techniques and maintenance' for most of Willi Messerschmitt's products. Naturally, he was selected for training at a foreign university to represent his country's emergence into peace-time prosperity. He settled right in.

Being ignored in a foreign country was very similar to life at home. It wasn't that the foreign students disliked him, they just couldn't figure out why, instead of "Good morning" he advised them to adhere to "Keep the rudder straight on landing."

The students of his own age found him to be eccentric. If they needed encouragement, he would offer "Always keep your nose up on take-off', but when he greeted older members of staff with "Always allow for windage before dropping the bomb", they thought he was taking the mickey.

After a life-time of living through other people's books and being stared at by generations of valley kids who could see straight through him, Joshua Tweedie had moved on.

He hung onto the uniform of jacket with leather elbow patches and his air of indefinable superiority. Apart from that, he left it all behind-the class who faced him every day as if posing for the zombies reunion photo, his nick-name of 'Posh-Josh' and the fellow staff members who mumbled encouragement to themselves all day long.

He was now an historian and was exploring the next valley where rumours of a Shakespeare connection abounded. Though his beloved books were bound, he was not. He was free. Joshua could roam the earth and meet experience head on. He breathed in deeply. The gravestones around him spoke of the vanity of man.

'Meeting my maker,' trumpeted one. 'Together in the afterlife,' said another, without a hint as to whether he was bragging or complaining.

Joshua noticed a gravestone that had been scraped clear of moss and lichen. *Must be important if someone has taken a rubbing,* he thought and moved closer. The grave had been opened.

"Good heavens," he exclaimed as he peered in, "A burial barrow." It wasn't quite what he had expected, but when knowledge comes from books, there are bound to be problems with recognition.

Joshua heard a groan behind him. After searching half-heartedly, he came across a man slumped against a headstone inscribed, 'Lean your conscience against the Lord.' The man groaned again. This was reality. This was Joshua Tweedie's Andy Warhol moment. His ten minutes of fame. It was also his Dickens moment as he found the churchyard scene with Pip and the convict spread out before him.

The man groaned even louder and slumped even further. Joshua racked his brains for literary inspiration, *What would Ulysses have done?* he thought. Then he pulled himself up. *Which one? The adventurer or the James Joyce version?*

He looked around wildly, 'Cometh the hour, cometh the man,' sprang to mind. If he was going to come, it would be handy if he came right now, thought Joshua desperately. *What would T.E. Lawrence do?* Something useful, suggested his sub-conscious. Quotes from Virgil, Pepys and Freud clamoured for attention.

"Hospital," murmured the man.

Ahh yes, thought Joshua, *beat me to it by a whisker.* Who said that? Felix the Cat probably, supplied his sub-conscious again.

Determination hurtled through unused neurological channels and sent his arms to grasp the handles of the wheelbarrow. *Am I disturbing an artefact?* he wondered briefly. Pulling and pushing and trying to summon supernatural strength by imagining the Spartans at Thermopylae, he ran to the gate to catch a 'son of the soil' on his way home, but was forced to return to the scene of his inadequacy. The wheelbarrow was standing by the grave. 'Eureka'. Inspiring words really do work- the injured man had given up and staggered off down the path under his own steam.

Chasing after him, Joshua managed to catch him behind the knees, depositing him in the barrow and they continued downhill at breakneck speed.

The twins sat and watched. They had given this chap a wide berth. They knew elbow patches when they saw them. When he went for help, they pulled the wheelbarrow out for him and hid again. They knew he would pick up speed and they were waiting until he hit the gravel path at the bottom of the hill. Then they would head off to organ practice.

The air in the crypt was getting thicker. The falling dust just hung like a smudge. The two men sat gasping for breath and wiping the sweat from their brows.

The noise began again with a whooshing sound and then burst into the room like an express train- terror and panic gate-crashed and combined to promote flight. The two fled.

Bursting out into the cool air, Cuthbert sat on a grassy mound and watched as a man pushing a wheelbarrow very fast collided with a dry-stone wall tipping a bundle of rags into a passing farm cart and pulling off a forward roll to join it.

Oxygen starvation, he thought. *The hallucinations will pass soon enough,* he thought again as he heard yelling and the crack of rocks hitting headstones.

Looking around, he spotted Percy chasing the twins through the cemetery, throwing bricks at them. He was like a mobile Gatling gun. Cuthbert didn't have the breath to warn him, so he just watched and waited for the inevitable.

Cuthbert winced as the twins executed their 'horns of the buffalo' manoeuvre and started to reappear behind Percy. They had only attended one class on the Zulu Wars and had perfected it in an afternoon. Shaka Zulu would have been proud of them.

Percy paused for breath briefly and wondered where they were just as they pounced. Up went his jumper, right over his head, and the frog went down his trousers. The twins hared off in a zigzag evasion technique (which has since been adopted by the SAS) and disappeared.

Percy was faced with several different and entirely new sensations. His top half was in the dark and immobile whilst his bottom half was far from immobile. Cuthbert wandered over to admire the performance of 'River dance' with a 'Can-can' flavour, performed by a Morris dancer, and all choreographed from inside a jumper. Cuthbert took pity on him and pulled his jumper down. The trousers he left to the owner to sort out.

After a search, which revealed that the body, the carpet and the wheelbarrow had disappeared, along with Percy's dignity, they went home.

Chapter 32

The next day's inquest was a painful affair. It was held in Percy's shed, which didn't add to the comfort level at all. The two of them were occupied by cracked mugs and embarrassing memories, so the silence lasted for a while.

Percy was in a world of his own, when he should have been in someone else's. He thought deeply about the missing man, the missing carpet and the missing wheelbarrow. There was only one conclusion; it was an alien abduction and he had missed his ride.

Cuthbert began to pace. This consisted of one step forward, kick, one step backwards, kick. Kicking the plant-pot, he was reminded to ask Percy about the newspaper cuttings he had found. Percy confirmed that Henry Chisolm had been the reporter, but he added that Henry had known Geraldine.

"They knew each other?" asked Cuthbert.

Percy nodded, "Oh yes. Thick as thieves, they were. I caught them trampling my Begonia trees looking for tunnels."

Cuthbert spluttered, "Did they find any?" he asked desperately.

Percy looked slightly uncomfortable, "Not that I know of," he said.

"How hard did they look?" pressed Cuthbert.

Percy was squirming now and Cuthbert was getting suspicious. He peered at Percy, "How-did-they-know-where-to-dig?" he asked very slowly.

Percy cracked, "Look. She fancied me, right? If I showed her where the tunnels were, we could have lived happily ever after."

Cuthbert tried a quick reality check. "Did you know any tunnels, Percy?" he asked.

Percy shook his head, "I thought if we dug often enough, we were bound to find something," he said miserably. "Look, I was already fighting off the woman in the play, so I had to be careful with Geraldine. That TV chap, Henry, was after her and he had a great big trailer. I hadn't finished doing this place up yet."

Cuthbert glanced around and wondered how far Percy had got with it since. Cuthbert sat and sighed, "How did you become the local expert?"

Percy became quite animated. He explained how he had drawn maps and spilt cold tea on them to simulate age. Cuthbert glanced down into his cup and pictured his ageing insides. Percy and Geraldine had spent hours in each other's company, digging and picnicking together. It had all ended when a summer shower washed all the lines off one of the maps. "After that, she didn't believe me."

"Well, that's not surprising," said Cuthbert.

"Why?" demanded Percy.

"Because you made it all up."

Percy sulked for a while and then muttered, "She didn't even look at the new map I found."

Cuthbert sat up. "New map?" he asked, "Which new map?"

Percy reached down into his welly "This one."

Cuthbert took the rolled paper. He laid it reverently on the floor, weighted the edges down and stared at it in awe. The dark stains of age, the spidery writing, the smell of tea. "You did this one as well, didn't you?" sighed Cuthbert.

Percy grinned, "All's fair in love and arrrrghhh …"

Percy's face began to blur and his hat fell off. Cuthbert shook Percy until all his pockets were rattling. Letting go, Cuthbert stood up to leave.

Percy gasped, "But I did copy it from the brass in the church.'"

*

The church had once been the thriving heart of the community, until a new vicar had been appointed. He was not 'real valley folk' and he tried to introduce too many changes.

The last straw was when he tried to stop the turnip fair. The Bishop was approached, but he had spent ages getting rid of this chap and he ignored them. Gradually the locals began to meet in each other's houses.

Then they partook of a nip of something to ward off the night's chill on the way home. Soon the houses weren't big enough and the Mandrake Arms already served drink anyway. So, the vicar was left without a congregation, not to mention a housekeeper.

Without invitations into his parishioners' homes, the vicar's appearance began to change. His hair and beard reached biblical proportions and he took to striding around the valley with a large wooden staff looking like an ancient patriarch looking for someone to smite.

After running out of cassocks, he wrapped the white altar cloth around himself and completed the image. Now his mission was to destroy this modern Sodom and Gomorrah and bring the flock back into the fold. Checking himself in the holy water, he noticed his resemblance to the renaissance paintings of God. He was at one with God. He looked like God. He was on God's mission. Ergo, he was God. It was time to show this rabble just who they were messing with. He would move across the face of the valley and improve on the original creation by removing the 'real valley folk'.

A new sect had sprung up in the village too. They actually believed that the vicar was responsible for death. They reasoned that by going to church and being named in prayers and entered into ledgers, you were drawing attention to yourself.

They seemed to think that heathens lived longer and definitely had more fun. Whereas, with the vicar, the only reward was death anyway.

That lot deserved more than boils on the bum, he thought. But first he had to remove some screws from the church door.

The screws didn't surrender easily and, even then, years of home-made varnish kept the hinge where it belonged. All the vicar could do was practice a few moves and rely on heavenly guidance on the day.

The churchyard was still in use and Cuthbert's father was due to bury a local. He had never really found the vicar to be necessary and besides, it would mean splitting the fee, so he never gave advance warning.

The vicar hid in the porch and waited until the locals were assembled. As he waited, he felt the stone slab beneath his feet rock slightly. This had caught his notice early on. The locals always skipped sideways as they entered the church when they reached this slab. This pagan dance would stop too, he promised himself. The crowd was assembled. He was ready.

As the coffin was being lowered and everyone was concentrating on what they were doing, the vicar leapt into view. Standing four-square in the porch and holding his staff aloft, the vicar roared, "No-one shall bar the path to the Lord." Turning, he smote the door a mighty thwack, knocking it open behind him.

Raising his staff again, he roared, "And be gone pagan dances of the devil." Smashing his staff down onto the slab, he split it asunder and teetered on the edge of a hole. The multi-layers of varnish held the door hinge and brought it flying back, knocking the vicar into the hole and finally falling off to cover him up. A dust cloud arose around the scene and then settled. The pall-bearers and the mourners didn't actually hear him over the wailing widow and only the deaf old quarryman saw the event.

Later on, in the pub, they played charades and all took turns to interpret what the deaf old fool had seen. By common agreement, they agreed upon the vicar shouting, "That's it, I'm bored. I'm off to a revel." and they never bothered to look for him. After all, they didn't want to get him into trouble with the Bishop and his stipend would come in handy.

If he had been a popular vicar who took an interest in the valley affairs, he would have been told about the agreement with the quarry workers. In return for prayers, the men had agreed to provide quality slabs for the church path.

A landslide missed the owner and merely killed his cat, and they only sent faulty or cracked ones after that. That was why the congregation always skipped to one side at that particular one.

It was said that sometimes on a dark, moonlit and lonely night at a certain time of year, a loud tapping could still be heard. People stayed indoors on that night even though it sounded just like Blind-Pugh trying to drink out of his frozen water bowl.

Cuthbert was treated to a view of Percy's rear end as he dug like a dog looking for a bone. Eventually, Percy produced a bent brass plaque with nail holes showing in the corners. "I hid this under the rubble before anyone unsuitable could find it," he gasped.

Cuthbert climbed up to join him and peered at the brass plaque. "You mean me, don't you?" he asked.

Percy ignored him and produced a bottle of brown sauce. "Brought a corned beef sandwich, have we?" asked Cuthbert sarcastically.

Percy ignored him again and began rubbing the sauce all over the brass before polishing it with his jacket sleeve. Cuthbert quietly watched as the brass began to gleam and the inscription showed clearly. Now Percy began to pontificate. "The skull and crossbones are quite typical," he announced. "They demonstrate the corruption of the body after death."

Cuthbert sighed, "I am an undertaker, you know."

They both peered at the other complicated design. Percy filled the silence again. "Now this probably represents the twisting paths of life. The ways that a soul can wander without purpose and lose sight of its goal ..."

Cuthbert interrupted, "It's not a map of the maze, then?"

Percy paused. "What maze?" he asked.

Cuthbert studied him. "The maze in the middle of your garden," he said. Cuthbert ignored the bewildered expert and began to climb.

As children, they had played in the old ruined church and one of the games had been to stand on top of the ruined tower directing their team from above.

The first team to the centre of the maze decided which games would be played for the next week. It was a boys' only event because girls' games were simply silly.

Cuthbert paused at the top to regain his breath and looked down. This was actually only the second time he had looked down on the maze because even his brain had 'two left feet' and he sent everyone in the wrong direction. After that, he was the one being blamed for 'not being fast enough'.

Percy joined him and they stared down at the outline of a maze with a hole in the middle.

"Have you been digging, Percy?" demanded Cuthbert.

Percy spluttered, "No. Have you?"

The pair slid down the pile of rubble and raced outside. Cuthbert stood over the hole and sighed. "Someone has dug something up," he noted.

Percy tutted and shook his head.

Cuthbert looked at Percy, then at the hole and back to Percy again. "Is that your spade?" he asked.

"Might be," said Percy shrugging.

"Is that your hat?" Cuthbert persisted.

"Similar," admitted Percy.

Cuthbert took a breath, "Percy, is that your hole?" he demanded.

Percy decided to wax lyrical, "Ahh," he began, "can any man claim the earth as his own? Does he own the stars?"

Cuthbert began to move slowly towards him. "There's some earth over that wall that can definitely be yours. I have a spade and I can even arrange for you to see the stars."

Percy backed away. Cuthbert kept on coming. Percy dropped into a crouch, elbows bent and fingers clawed as if trying to grasp reality.

"I'm versed in the marital arts," he yelled.

Cuthbert stopped, "I thought you were single?" he asked, bemused.

Percy straightened up, "I am," he replied equally bemused.

Cuthbert opened his mouth, but his brain supplied the anagram just in time and he simply said, "Oh." The moment had gone.

They sat on the edge of the hole together and sighed.

Cuthbert spoke first. "I thought we were a team. Do you really want to solve this alone?"

Percy swung one leg with its turned-down welly attached and replied vaguely, "Lonely are the brave."

Cuthbert spluttered, "The brave are only lonely because they are reckless and everyone else gets killed. Where do you get this stuff from?"

Percy swung the other leg in opposition without realising that it made him creep towards the edge of the hole. "It's an old Chinese warlord, Tsun-Beam," Percy said enthusiastically. "His teachings have lasted for a thousand years."

Cuthbert looked at him pityingly, "As an undertaker, mate, I can assure you that after a thousand years your 'Tsun-Beam' is very lonely indeed."

Percy opened his mouth to reply, but the edge of the hole gave way and he fell into the excavation. Sitting at the bottom, Percy tried to pretend that it was all quite normal. "You shouldn't mock the dead," he muttered.

Cuthbert agreed. "Quite right, mate," he said. "By the time I've finished mocking the living, most of the day's gone." Cuthbert borrowed a calm voice from somewhere and asked, "What was in the hole, Percy?"

Percy squirmed, but didn't reply.

Cuthbert persisted, "What was in the hole, Percy?" Percy squirmed again as he said, "You'll laugh."

Cuthbert sighed before stating flatly, "You are already in a hole, Percy. I am an undertaker and this is a shovel. Which of us will decide what comes next?"

Percy foolishly scratched his head and Cuthbert scooped up some earth. "All right, all right," exclaimed Percy, rummaging inside his welly.

Cuthbert waited as Percy climbed out and showed him a note scrawled on the back of an old used envelope.

The note was written in red marker pen. It read, 'We've got wot u want. Wotts itt worth?'

Turning the envelope over, Cuthbert wasn't at all surprised to see that it was addressed to Margery, the twins' mum. "So, they beat you to it?" asked Cuthbert.

Percy nodded mutely, before adding, "I dug part-way down and when I came back, I found that."

Cuthbert considered the facts. The influence of the twins ran through the valley like a thread in the fabric of confusion. "Come on, Percy," said Cuthbert as he marched away clutching the letter. "We need to pay a visit."

Chapter 33

Marjorie's cottage wasn't as old as Cuthbert's, but it blended into the valley nicely. The 'minefield' warnings and scrawled childishly-written signs warning everyone to keep to the path were slightly unusual, though.

Marjorie was already apologising as she opened the door. Apologising for the twins was a well-practised routine for her, and it took some convincing before she accepted that Cuthbert wanted to discuss a treasure hunt with the boys and there wasn't a nasty court action looming.

Margery led the two men into her sanctuary. Everything was chintz and overtly feminine. She locked the door behind her and offered them tea. Tucking a stray strand of hair back behind her ear, she smiled at Percy and he was promptly smitten.

"They can get in, of course," said Marjorie, nodding towards the door. "Those two can make a key in seconds using ear-wax and a melted down toy soldier." She poured the tea as Cuthbert looked nervously over his shoulder. "Oh, they won't disturb us," she laughed. "We have an agreement." Cuthbert suspected that it went along the lines of, 'Stay out of my room and I will make tea for the neighbours whilst you wreak havoc in the valley all you like.'

Cuthbert wove a tale of a valley treasure hunt in which the twins could be involved as organisers, and felt a pang of guilt as Marjorie beamed at him. "The responsibility will do them good," she said and patted his knee.

Percy sat simpering and cradling his cup as though it was a religious relic. He would have liked a pat on the knee, but he was tongue-tied and his finger was stuck in the cup handle. Cuthbert caught Marjorie watching him very carefully, but the look disappeared and she offered more tea.

Cuthbert accepted and found himself wondering how this delicate feminine being managed to evade both the local constabulary and the truancy squad on a regular basis. He put the thoughts aside and sipped his tea.

Margery sat back and smiled at the door. It seemed to be a signal. The door crashed back against the wall to flatten anyone hiding behind it and there stood the twins. One of them held a hair grip where the lock would have been. The twins surveyed the room, eyes flicking across the visitors like snakes' tongues.

Cuthbert smiled and squirmed. The squirm was noted and the smile analysed. Cuthbert withered under the concentrated gaze. This is why he preferred to deal with the dead- anything with a pulse had the capacity to terrify him. Marjorie addressed the twins as if they were normal human beings and they both focused on Cuthbert. A bead of sweat ran down Cuthbert's spine carrying an Arctic chill with it.

The twins exchanged a glance and announced, "Park swings in one hour." The door closed and they were gone. Cuthbert tried to regulate his breathing and Marjorie began trying to tease her valuable cup from Percy's finger. Cuthbert wasn't convinced that stroking the back of Percy's hand was really necessary.

*

Henry sat alone in the bar of the Mandrake Arms. He idly watched as the urchin began to cross the road outside.

The words "Park swing one hour," were barked out at Henry's shoulder and he jumped as the same youth appeared beside him. Henry checked- the youth was still outside and Henry was alone. How did he do that, he wondered before calling for Ronald.

Cuthbert and Percy left the dubious safety of Margery's home. Suddenly Cuthbert was inclined to take the warning signs seriously.

Percy was in love. "Isn't she wonderful?" he asked. Cuthbert was remembering 'the look' and he wasn't so sure.

Percy sighed. "That laugh, like a breeze through the bluebells." He stooped to pluck a dandelion, still wet from a passing fox, and inhaled its scent. Eyes streaming from ammonia fumes, Percy tried to forget his latest conquest and see whatever it was that Cuthbert was going on about.

Cuthbert had spotted Henry, Ronald and the Captain also heading for the park. "Crafty little blighters," he said, "They've set up an auction." Then, seeing Percy frantically wiping his eyes, he snapped, "Nothing to cry about Percy, it's only business, you know."

The five grown men converged on the park gates at the same time. They managed to subtly ignore each other as only grown men can before filtering into the play area.

The desolate patch of bald grass designated for allowing the local children to let off steam was decidedly under-used. By the time school had finished, meals were eaten and stray cows were rounded up, the local children dutifully yawned and went to bed.

Then the play area came into its own. As the children made their escape by various ladders, tunnels and rope slides, the swings became the centre of an empire. The twins ran the valley Mafia from this spot.

Sentries could lurk unobtrusively around the perimeter, tinkering with a bicycle or tying a pesky shoelace for the umpteenth time. The threadbare grassland made a natural 'killing ground' around them. No-one took the Mafia by surprise.

The adults looked around at the desolate expanse and subconsciously moved closer together.

A swing creaked ominously, hinting at recent occupation. The see-saw thumped down unexpectedly and everyone jumped. They jumped again as a tinny voice boomed out, "You are being watched. Do not move." The voice emanated from a litter bin with a swing lid.

Cuthbert noticed a wire leading to some distant bushes. The men decided independently to regain control and a rebellious muttering ensued. Twilight was falling and a bush rustled. Shapes flitted between distant trees. An empty drinks can rolled noisily across a concrete path. The fact that it was a soft drinks can somehow seemed to make it even more menacing.

"Be quiet," snapped the voice and the adults found themselves back-to-back as if the Sioux nation was about to attack. The voice continued, "We have what you are looking for. You are merely pawns in plans for the future of the world." Sounds of an amplified scuffle came from the litter bin and a new voice took over. "What are you prepared to pay for the treasure?" it asked.

Henry used his broadcasting experience to project his voice. "What is the treasure? None of us have seen it."

A muffled discussion took place before the voice barked, "What is he doing, the one who walks like a cartoon penguin?" All eyes slid to Ronald, who had begun to crawl into the deeper shadows. He stood and sheepishly brushed himself down.

The voice continued, "We have the thing you strangers are looking for. Leave a note at the old church before lunch time tomorrow. It should give your best offer, otherwise we go public. Weigh it down with that posh bloke's watch. We'll have that for a start."

Henry was about to protest when his mobile phone rang. As usual it had changed the ring tone on a whim and the sound of gun-fire echoed around them in the gloom. Bushes disintegrated and shadows fled like roosting bats. The men were alone.

Walking together, without acknowledging each other, Henry was the first to speak. "We are going to have to work together on this, chaps. Why don't we have a drink and discuss things?" The rest agreed reluctantly and they gathered around a table in the Mandrake Arms. Henry took charge. "What are we going to offer these twerps for whatever they have found?"

The others shrugged.

Ronald offered, "I don't even know what I'm looking for, so I won't know even if they have found it." Shrugs, nods and vague expressions all round pretty much confirmed that this was a general state of affairs.

Henry sighed. "It doesn't matter what we offer them. They have to show us the item at some time and, if it's not what we expect, then we don't pay." He sat back, happy to be in control.

"What do we expect?" asked Cuthbert.

Henry looked around, "What do you expect, Percy?" he asked.

Percy answered immediately, "Bags of gold." he said.

Ronald guffawed, "Gold. Why would there be gold in this dump?" he asked.

Percy was affronted. He needed to put this newcomer in his place. "Saint Grizelda's foot," he announced. "People came from miles away to study it."

Ronald looked suspicious, "Why, did it smell?" he sneered.

Percy replied, "It would do now, it was hundreds of years ago."

Eyes slid reluctantly sideways as each person hoped that someone would know of a way to stop Percy.

Percy squirmed in his chair to get comfortable and began. "Long ago there was a nunnery around here and the Vikings heard of a great treasure stored inside. Plus, it was full of women so there was a consolation prize if it turned out to be a rumour." The men bent forward to listen.

Percy continued and inclined his head politely as his glass was filled. "The raiding party was spotted coming ashore and the alarm was raised, but in a community without men, most of the women were outside the gates gathering wood and herding livestock. As the Vikings got closer and the women crowded into the outer gate, it became obvious that someone would have to be sacrificed to slow them down as they reached the huge inner gate.

"Now, Grizelda was a big girl and not a particular beauty by any standards, so they tripped her up so that she would be the last in line. They considered that no-one could do her much harm and it might just slow their attackers.

"Grizelda looked back at these huge Norsemen with their fearsome weapons and realized that when she had taken her vows, she hadn't really been paying attention. It seemed such a shame to close the gates and miss out on an opportunity to put some sin on her C.V., so when the other nuns slammed the gates shut, Grizelda stuck her foot in the gap and gave the Vikings a welcoming smile.

"The first poor Viking dropped his axe in shock and severed her foot, allowing the gates to close after all. The nuns thought that Grizelda had lost her foot fighting for their virtue and the Vikings threw her foot down in disgust and cleared off. The foot was made part of a shrine and venerated. Pilgrims came from everywhere and left offerings to the foot."

"What happened to Grizelda?" asked Ronald in awe.

"She hopped it," said Percy, looking him in the eye.

"Who are you?" asked Henry.

"I'm the gardener," said Percy.

The adults separated and made their way home. They were none too pleased that the valley Mafia had the upper-hand, especially as that particular upper-hand didn't even shave.

Ronald sat by the fire thinking about the set-up in the valley. He admired these kids. In his day, the Coppers wore tall, funny hats and you could see them coming. Now, they had dogs, helicopters and sirens, which seemed to come from everywhere at once. Ronald had seen a demonstration of a tazer gun and even he thought of going straight, although the fantasy of putting fifty thousand volts through Cuthbert cheered him up, and he nodded off in the chair with a smile on his face.

*

The next morning everyone awoke with a note pinned to their clothing. It read, 'We think yoor speshul. What doo yoo offer?' It was written in red marker pen.

Ronald awoke with a start as the cold morning grabbed his attention, felt the piece of paper, blew his nose on it, and flung it into the embers where it flared like a lost opportunity and died just as dramatically.

Henry was the possessor of Olympian snoring techniques and his note didn't stand a chance. It cavorted around the room like a whirling dervish and settled under the settee where it was recycled into mouse droppings by mid-day.

Cuthbert slept as a man should- alone- in his opinion. The note was pinned to his lapel and as his reflection didn't bother to show up, he didn't see it. Minutes later, a flash from an over-active frying pan ensured that there was nothing left to see.

The Captain tore off his regimental night shirt and, as he changed into a track-suit, the note fluttered to the ground. Slamming the door behind him, he went for a run. The note was found by his wife, Elspeth who almost swooned. At last, a secret admirer.

She read and re-read the note before ironing it lovingly. She remembered the secret panel that had sprung open when she was dusting and she placed it carefully inside with all those dusty old scrolls.

The only representative of the reluctant alliance to actually see his note was Percy. On cold nights like these, he wrapped himself up thoroughly in his shed. In fact, there was only his nose showing, so that's where they pinned it.

Recognition at last They had obviously identified him as a leader. He was the cream, smooth as custard, knees like jelly. Not a man to be trifled with.

The deadline was lunchtime today at the old church, so Percy needed to contact the valley Mafia before then. He would be the only one bidding on whatever it was that they had and he didn't. He headed for the park.

The park was deserted. The same swing creaked forlornly. Percy approached the swing-top bin. "It's me," he whispered. A crisp packet skittered across the park. "Percy reporting …" The bin sat there with its mouth open. Percy tried a gentle nudge whilst chanting, "Testing, one-two-three." The wind moaned. Percy tried "Cuthbert had a little lamb, its fleece was white as snow. When Cuthbert found some mint sauce, the lamb it had to go."

Nothing, not a sound,

116

Percy rocked the litter bin. The lid clanged shut. Percy began kicking the thing because his fingers were in the opening. His nose was throbbing because the pin had stayed in when he tore the note off. Pulling the pin out with his other hand resulted in splashes of blood on the lid. Wrestling with the thing smeared more blood on the sides.

Constable Beeching had been watching all this. He had been ignoring reports of clandestine meetings and 'strange goings on at night'. He had waited until daylight so that everyone would have cleared off. Now he only had to handle a funny little chap in a hat.

A large shadow fell across Percy, who now sat under a bin that leant at a forty five degree angle and refused to go any further.

"Is this something I should know about?" asked the constable.

"Er, maintenance," said Percy quickly.

"Maintenance?" echoed the officer.

"Yup," said Percy standing up. "Got to see if it comes up to standard."

"And does it?" asked Beeching.

"Oh, yes," said Percy. "Right as nine pence." He walked away saying, "Must dash, forms to fill in."

The Constable recognised that as official jargon and prepared to shamble off satisfied, when some spark left over from his training lit a fire behind his eyes and he asked, "Is that blood?"

Percy came back, "Where?" he asked, rubbing the offending spot with his sleeve.

"You can't do that," wailed the constable. "That's DNA, that is."

"What's DNA?" asked Percy innocently.

Constable Beeching spluttered. "Damned Necessary Accessory," he raged dragging out his notebook, "We have to test that."

"What for?" asked Percy.

"To see if it's blood."

Percy scratched his head. "You've already said that it's blood."

The Constable floundered, "Oh, yes well, er … that's for the lab to decide." He remembered the phrase just in time. Glancing up from his writing, the Constable asked, "Are you a friend of that Cuthbert?"

Percy hesitated. "Might be. Who is he?" he said carefully. He was watching the notebook.

Cuthbert was fascinated by the spiral on some notebooks. Percy was afraid of all notebooks. They had no memory, so how come they never forgot anything? He had a memory and he forgot things all the time-explain that. Many a time he had been on the brink of talking his way clear … until the dreaded notebook appeared. He saw them as spiteful devices of revenge, invented by someone harmed by his ancestors.

The Constable wasn't used to being ignored. "I asked your name," he barked, "What is it?"

Percy looked around and spotted a passing rodent. "Squirrel," he said. "Sammy Squirrel."

The offended rodent glanced across and wondered if he should phone his agent.

"Occupation?" barked the officer, firmly in control now.

"Bee-keeper," said Percy, really enjoying himself now.

"Sammy Squirrel, beekeeper," repeated the constable, sticking his tongue out to help him concentrate. For some reason the game of Cluedo came into his mind, but he dismissed it as his radio squawked. The Constable stood to attention and muttered, "Yes, Sarge," several times before looking at Percy again. Tapping his breast pocket, Beeching warned, "You're in here now, Sammy Squirrel my lad."

Percy hadn't the heart to point out that the book was still in his hand.

The officer set off towards his next task, arms pumping and getting very little progress from it.

"Hive a nice day," called Percy the beekeeper cheerily.

*

Time was now of the essence. It was nearly lunchtime. Percy glanced up at the sun before checking the length of the shadows and doing a quick calculation. Next, he leant to the left and looked at the park clock. He began to run.

The others were leaving the old church ruin when he arrived. It was obvious they thought that he should have been there. Henry confirmed that they had left a written offer weighted down by his watch, and he invited Percy to the pub. Percy hesitated and said that he would hang around here in case he could learn something.

Ronald snarled, "First time for everything," and they parted company.

Percy knew he was being watched. He made his way past the old gravestones and he could sense movement always just out of his sight.

118

A bush seemed to be swivelling to keep him in sight, so Percy approached it.

Standing in front of the bush, Percy announced, "I'm here because I'm special."

"Course you are," said a voice behind him, "I bet your mother loves you."

Percy turned to face the twins. "I went to the park and spoke to the bin, but there was no-one there."

One of the twins laughed. "Do you really think we leave a kid in the bin all night just in case Coco the clown comes back?" Turning to the rest of the Mafia, the twin added, "They've picked a real leader here, lads."

Percy was appalled. "I'm not one of them," he gasped.

"Whatever you say, sweetie," came the reply.

Percy was almost speechless. He wasn't used to this. Kids were bad things that happened to good people as far as he was concerned. "But I got your note," Percy said lamely.

The twin gaped at him. "Out of five adults, only one got the note?" he asked incredulously, "It's like dealing with children."

It was Percy's turn to gape. "You sent one to everybody?"

The twin was biting his nails, "Yeah, fat lot of good it did us. No wonder the economy is in a mess with you lot running the shop."

A silky voice behind Percy asked, "Why don't we take a hostage?"

The nail biting stopped. "What a good idea. We will need someone special."

Percy backed away and bumped into a gravestone. "Take Henry," he said, "He's got money, or Cuthbert, yes Cuthbert would make a great hostage," he babbled.

The silky voice was close when it said, "Not Cuthbert. We may need help to get rid of a body."

Percy fainted.

*

The meeting in the pub was a very informal affair. They had nothing to discuss. There were no demands to make and no suggestions were forthcoming.

In fact it was just four chaps having a drink. As they sat watching condensation steal their drinks, there was a thud outside.

"What's that?" asked Henry.

"No idea," said Cuthbert.

"Probably kids playing football," suggested Ronald.

Another thud.

"Not very good at it, are they?" said Henry.

The Captain barked, "Rugby, man's game, that's what they need."

"I know what they need," muttered Ronald, conjuring up his experience with explosives.

From outside came the sound of an argument and another thud. A young voice whined, "Oh all right, go on then," and something was lobbed around the door heading straight for their table. The men showed a speed and dexterity known only to middle aged drinkers under threat. The glasses were whisked into the air whilst the threat was assessed. The 'threat' landed with a thump and rolled to a standstill in the middle of the table.

"What the devil is that?" asked the Captain.

"It's a turnip with a hat on," supplied Cuthbert.

"Well, thank the Lord it's not Grizelda's foot," said Ronald.

The glasses were returned to their places exactly equidistant from each other and Henry read the note attached to the turnip.

"Weeve got him - wots e worth?" read Henry. It was written in red marker pen.

Cuthbert asked, "Is that Percy's hat?"

The Captain focused and replied, "Good Lord, yes. Where was I? Oh yes, rugby ...."

*

Percy sat on a hard chair with his hands tied behind his back. The bag on his head smelled of a burger and fries, and he was trying to live off the fumes.

The place he was in was a mystery. The Mafia had turned him around several times, when he recovered consciousness, to disorientate him. It smelled fusty and was obviously not fit for human habitation.

Could be a stable, thought Percy. It seemed an age before the door crashed back against the wall and someone entered. The bag was whipped away and the twins looked at him ruefully. They began to untie him without a word.

Percy babbled in relief, "So they paid up then, lads? Well done. How much did you get?"

No-one answered.

He persisted. "Go on, how much? We can always do it again and go halves." he suggested, rubbing his freed hands.

The silky voice sounded by his ear, "Nothing," it spat, "not even the price of the turnip," and they left.

He dashed outside and shouted to them, "What did they say when they saw it?"

"Nothing," came the reply.

He persisted. "What did they do?"

One of the twins turned, "They auctioned your hat," he said flatly.

"Auctioned … my … hat …" spluttered Percy. He stumbled about in shock and then noticed the building he had just left. They had imprisoned him in his own shed.

Percy was fuming. He would show them. He would confront them, solve the mystery, find the treasure and run off with the woman.

His humiliation was complete when he charged into the pub and found the turnip sat in the window, wearing his hat and smoking a cigarette.

Chapter 34

Geraldine sat in the corner. This was her part of the asylum. She liked this corner and it was her corner. She could see all the angles and no-one could sneak up on her.

She didn't have any friends in here even though some had made an effort. It wasn't that there was anything wrong with the people in here. Good Lord, if the white coat brigade ever visited the valley, they would need to hire convoys of buses to ship everybody back here.

This was actually why Geraldine was still here. Every time she referred to the valley, conversation stopped and the pill trolley appeared.

They were convinced that the valley was a mythical place where she escaped from reality whenever she needed to. In fact the opposite was true. The valley was where reality went when it needed to escape from itself. That one had earned her two pills yesterday.

Her only crime as far as she was concerned was in not finding what she was looking for. As a professional Researcher and Historian, she shouldn't have to tip-toe around people's privacy and sensibilities. She should be able to rip up gardens wholesale and dig trenches across motorways - this was heritage, for goodness sake.

We could not hope to see into the future and yet the past lay smirking at us under our feet. Who wouldn't want to dig it up?

Her old professor had tried to rein her in with the comment, "Don't try to discover it all, my dear. Leave some for future generations."

"What are the present generations doing?" she had replied. "Concreting over Roman villas and destroying Saxon tombs to extend airports. Will the future be any better?"

The professor had peered at her as if she had just appeared from a stratified layer on a fascinating dig. "Good Lord," he said, "a militant archaeologist." His eyes glazed over.

He recalled his student past. "You remind me of a young me," he said wistfully, "only without the 'Ahem', of course, and I actually had a beard. We started a movement, you know. We had a rallying cry and used to shout 'DIGGERS OF THE WORLD UNITED'. We marched on London, but unfortunately it was during the Miners' Strike and we were baton charged. The police were exhausted when the real miners came through and they escaped scot-free. We never met again after that. Several went a bit funny and tunnelled under Parliament looking for their rights." Memory clouded his vision for a moment and then he brightened and said, "You go for it, young Geraldine. Don't stop until you've found your share of secrets."

Geraldine had heeded his advice. She decided that the fly-infested plains of Mesopotamia or the Valley of the Kings where donkeys fell into holes and someone groaned, "Oh, not another one, we'll never get this mall finished," were not for her.

For her, it was the fields of England where history had whipped itself into a frenzy and overlaid the evidence into one big Koala Bear shaped layer cake. The valley had been almost hypnotic for Geraldine. She had been sent there as a punishment for digging up everyone else's pottery shards after they had gone home.

Good grief, what difference did it make? They could already see what they were- another day wouldn't have made them any more exciting. It was ordinary stuff, the Roman equivalent to Tupperware.

She didn't know that Prince Charles was coming the next morning when she hid a bra and a packet of condoms under the dust waiting for the final brush-off. The ensuing embarrassment ensured that Geraldine was on her way into exile forthwith.

The rural museum in the valley had welcomed her with an open arm. The caretaker had lost the other one, the way he seemed to lose everything else. He liked to joke that "Someone came in with a real treasure once and I made the mistake of saying, I'd give my right arm for that." It had been funny the first several times and then Geraldine started to spend a lot of time in the basement.

The valley had seen everything in its time. They had a monastery that took part in a game of monopoly with Henry VIII, and lost. There were hints and rumours of a Roman baggage train buried under an avalanche with its treasure still intact. Of course, the urban legend had grown to where the mules were still loaded down under panniers of gold and jewels, and the soldiers were still fully armed.

Where were the Roman soldiers going with all that gold? thought Geraldine. There was nothing to spend it on, that was for sure, and if the Romans wanted something they tended to send a load of skilled negotiators with sharp swords and big shields to get it.

It was something else that caught Geraldine's eye. Scanning the parish records, she noticed that every birth and death involved a middle name taken from Shakespeare. She found it odd that anyone in this valley could even read Shakespeare, let alone dedicate anything to his memory.

She didn't discover the valley's obsession with the theatre until the caretaker showed her a pamphlet either done in authentic 16th century style or written by a chicken, which announced a performance of *The Tempest*.

Anything to cause Geraldine to suspend belief for two hours was riveting indeed, and then the performance had started. This of course was when she had met Cuthbert and shortly after that she had met Percy. The mention of Cuthbert and his foibles had seen Geraldine promoted to the black pills, which caused even the trolley dolly to be impressed. She hadn't dared mention Percy after that.

On top of everything else had been the rush to buy property in the village. Mandrake Hall and the old mill had changed hands and Percy seemed to be a newcomer for all his pseudo knowledge. Cuthbert didn't even know him.

Geraldine had begun to question the butler after she caught him looking at some books left out in the library, but he seemed to be just trying to improve himself.

She was sure that Cuthbert was the key. He lived in one of the oldest buildings. It seemed to have its original furniture and it was linked to the tunnels.

The tunnels had excited her at first, until she read about the reservoir and that seemed to clear things up. Yet the thought of tunnels kept coming back to her.

She had also just discovered a book with the inkpot and quill engraved on the spine. Having already spotted the gate posts, it was her next investigative step, but the catastrophe at the Hall had interrupted all that.

Had she really meant to murder Cuthbert? She could certainly have merrily strangled Percy, but Cuthbert seemed harmless, until he was challenged, that is.

Just then, a commotion in the corridor attracted Geraldine's attention. That braying noise sounded familiar somehow.

Peering around the door, Geraldine was astonished to see three burly 'Restraint Managers' being flung around like rag dolls and the trolley-dolly hurtling past astride her chrome plated steed shedding pills like chicken feed. At the centre of all this excitement was a large tweed covered gal with a pony-tail and a syringe in her bum.

"Good Lord," said Geraldine quietly, "that's the daughter from Mandrake Hall."

A plan began to form.

Chapter 35

Over the next few days, Geraldine sought out the company of the other woman at every opportunity.

No-one knew her name, and because of the teeth and pony tail she was referred to as 'Arkle', usually in muttered tones and with the rubbing of whichever limb had been bitten this time.

She had been found in the next valley snorting at fences and thundering towards them at full speed before crashing straight through them and releasing all the sheep. The sheep, being genetically stupid did not exactly run amok, as they hadn't realised that they were captives in the first place.

When a local farmer had investigated the damage, 'Arkle' had rolled his Massey Ferguson over, prompting a local policeman to put out an alert for an ex-tractor fan. The culprit had been rounded up with the aid of cattle prods and a team from the wildlife park who owned a special vehicle.

But now, thanks to Geraldine's need for an accomplice, things were settling down. 'Arkle' was responding to a friendly face. Geraldine had something to occupy her time, the staff were slowly healing and the therapists, as usual, took all the credit and prescribed each other one of the black pills as a celebration.

Last thing at night, when the night shift had settled in and the riot squad had begun a poker marathon in a locked staff room, was the time for action.

One man, alone with his book and his fears, was on duty. He sat in a pool of lamplight at a desk in the centre of the ward and glanced around nervously.

Why, he thought, was it considered ideal to sit the guard under a light? All the nutters could see him, but he couldn't see them. The shadows moved in sympathy with his plight and probably out of spite as well.

Unfortunately, his book was a fantasy involving a Gollum, and his imagination was just supplying the image when Arkle entered the pool of light. Her huge shoulders shuddered as she flicked her pony-tail teasingly. Sashaying towards the guard, she slipped her jacket open provocatively, and then she smiled.

However, from the guard's perspective, this huge thing slithered into view whipping its hair about like Medusa, ripping open its clothes to reveal a blouse full of brawling puppies, and then showing him those teeth.

Before he could reach for the panic button, Geraldine came up behind him and slammed both his hands into separate desk drawers, giving Arkle the chance to tape him stuck to the desk with duct tape.

As his vocal chords fought with the instincts of panic and survival, Geraldine slapped a huge sticking plaster across his mouth.

Standing back to admire their handiwork, Geraldine and Arkle celebrated with a 'High-five', but unfortunately Arkle missed. When Geraldine came to, the place was in an uproar. The riot squad was tramping down the corridors with shields linked like a malevolent tortoise, sirens were blaring and Geraldine had a hand-shaped bruise on her forehead.

"What's happening?" she managed as an orderly pulled her out of the way of the advancing phalanx of storm troopers who were now beating truncheons against their shields to bolster themselves and terrify others.

"Arkle has tried to escape," he gasped. "She has destroyed one squad of the riot team and barricaded herself into the medicine closet."

"She must be mad," said another orderly.

"Errrr ..." said Geraldine.

*

The crashing of shields and truncheons ceased but the lull was soon filled with a cry of "Charge" from the senior riot plod.

The men tightened their grips and entered that higher plane where a samurai prepares for death before dishonour. They charged.

The men swarmed forward and the charge became a high-octane ballet as they slipped and skidded on thousands of pills released by Arkle from the closet. Men and helmets collided, shields buckled, truncheons flew as the charge degenerated into 'Tom and Jerry on ice'.

As the men tangled into utter confusion on the floor, Arkle burst out of the closet holding a plastic funnel to her mouth. By filling the cone with pills she was able to keep up a constant barrage of suppressing fire before retreating to reload her improvised pea-shooter.

127

Geraldine shook her head to clear several thousand scattered images and looked around. Panic and chaos were the order of the day, all set to the back-beat of sirens. Geraldine did the only thing she could do; she took advantage of the situation and joined the other inmates streaming out of the front door.

"I think that went rather well," she congratulated herself.

Chapter 36

The evening meetings in the pub weren't going very well at all. Everyone seemed to know something they didn't; even 'Cuthbert the clown' seemed to be ahead of them.

The daughter of the house was missing, Geraldine was no longer sending postcards and Ronald hadn't attacked anyone for ages.

Henry Chisolm had received a strange visit from a scruffy youth who always seemed to be in two places at once. Henry had politely turned him away at the door only to find him staring in at the back window. When he glanced back down the street, there he was again - strange and mildly disconcerting.

Without Geraldine, Henry had no access to the museum, and without the library at Mandrake Hall he was completely cut off from his sources of research. It was a frustrating time and he was not a man to sit around.

He had tried following Cuthbert and Percy, but they obviously knew he was there because of the ridiculous lengths they went to just to evade him. All this disappearing down holes and hiding in graves for hours on end? Did they really think that such childish tricks would fool him?

He had wandered around in the tunnels and even found his way into Cuthbert's cellar, but he did not enter. After Ronald had been peppered with almost every missile known to man, Henry had adopted the careful approach.

He thought of his old contacts at the television station, but serious subjects never were their forte. At this rate, he would never find the secret of the valley. He didn't stand a ghost of a chance.

"Wait," he said aloud. Ronald and an old sheepdog glanced across at him, but soon lost interest when he kept the thought to himself. Now ghosts were the bread and butter of a television station like theirs. Had anyone ever done a programme about ghosts in the valley?

Henry took out his phone. He also took a deep breath and prepared himself. As the main presenter to camera at the station, he was required to own certain props for dramatic moments. His watch was one. He could barely lift his wrist to look at the thing, but it displayed beautifully as he lifted the microphone.

His phone was another. At certain times his producer would stage a dramatic phone call to interrupt a mundane announcement. Henry would pull out his state of the art phone and give the impression of the imminence of World War III, all for the benefit of the viewers.

He took it out now and stared at its single malevolent blinking eye. Henry was convinced that this phone was a reject picked up on the cheap during station cutbacks. It changed ring tones every time it felt like it, and whenever a phone rang near him he had to check it in case it had changed again.

His worst moments had been trying to master 'predictive text', the product of some warped Japanese mind. The idea was that you typed in a text and the machine would try to guess the word before you finished it. It is like a portable parlour game played against the devil.

Apparently it could save the user lots of time. In reality, it was confusing, argumentative and took eight times as long as his old steam-powered one had. It had also cost him the love of his life. His relationship with Liza had been perfect. She was suitably impressed with his job and put up with his absences when filming away.

All she asked in return was that he would always respect her and never talk down to her. That was simple, because he really did respect her. But along came 'predictive texting'. Every time Henry entered 'Liza' the machine guessed at 'Lizard'. What on earth happened in Japan to make a designer assume that all phone calls would involve a lizard?

It took so much time trying to correct messages that in the end he sent this one as it was, "Loves my Lizard - home soon."

He would clear up the matter when he got home and they would laugh about it. Not so, with a surname like Green, Liza was not forced to share this particular joke and she, her clothes and his car were long gone when he returned.

Henry pondered this flip-down monstrosity as he scrolled through the maze of contact details. That was another thing- he was sure he didn't know anyone in Tokyo, but there he was in between Kawasaki and Yamamoto.

He found his editor's number and pressed the button. He could only hope that the senior staff had begun to forget his mishap over the Queen's visit. The cavalcade had approached, the limousine door had opened and out had stepped her Majesty. Henry had stepped forward with his microphone and the man beside him had fainted.

He was the cameraman and he had forgotten to put in a new film. Henry leapt into the breach, whipped out his new phone, activated the camera by flipping it open towards her Majesty and pressed the button. Instead of the picture everyone else got of her Majesty's security men all diving on top of her, Henry transmitted a colour photo of the inside of his nostrils.

It was a long and tortuous phone call during which Henry whined, wheedled and gave up his bonus to get what he needed. The results would be with him tomorrow.

He closed the phone with a snap and it retaliated by turning up the volume and loading the sound of gunshots as his new ring-tone.

Chapter 37

Cuthbert knew it was time to stage the annual play and for rehearsals to begin. All his new found friends had offered to take part.

He was convinced that they simply wanted to keep an eye on him. Cuthbert sighed. Sometimes the theatre tradition was a real chore. The fall-out went on for months.

Last year the postman covered his face with burnt cork to play Caliban. When it wouldn't come off, his bosses at the Post Office had threatened to give him the sack. Cuthbert always giggled at that one.

Mister Croft, the joiner, had refused to make any more scenery after he made a ship for the Tempest. The twins started rocking the poop deck and ended up wrecking it. Prospero's daughter had been played by Belinda the barmaid and her cleavage alone could have capsized the ship. Cuthbert sighed again; it gave his brain time to cool down between thoughts.

He loved the association between the valley and Shakespeare, but he didn't really understand it. This insistence by the newcomers on staging a play involving pirates had been a ruse to cover the excavations noises.

He knew that now, but it would offend the locals. Perhaps he should have a meeting. An old memory from his childhood leapt to his mind unbidden.

His parents once had a problem staging the 'Two Gentlemen of Verona'. Seeing that the leads were played by the local pig farmer and the night soil man, it wasn't surprising. They were hardly type-cast for the role. The un-gentlemanly fisticuffs had doomed that idea.

Cuthbert remembered sitting on the bend in the stairs and hearing his father say, "Perhaps it's time to show something new."

His father had gone out into the night and Cuthbert had followed him all the way to the old mill. Watching through a back window, the son had watched the father open a secret panel with the owner of the house and remove some old scrolls.

Cuthbert only just made it back into bed before his father returned and his parents had sat up all night in heated debate. In the end, they had staged Hamlet, which even Cuthbert knew wasn't exactly hot off the press.

The police had been in the valley for weeks after that production. All the valley grievances appeared when some fool handed the swords out. It took ages to get the stage clean. Hamlet had been known as 'The cursed play' ever since.

Cuthbert had forgotten about the panel and the scrolls. Somehow, if his father knew about them it didn't seem much of a secret. Surely they couldn't be what everyone was looking for? He looked outside with a view to visiting the old mill but the rain had begun. This was real rain, valley rain, lashed by spite and intent on vengeance.

'Capture me in your reservoirs and ponds, would you', it seemed to say. 'Trap me in your horse troughs and puny gutters, force me into your inadequate down pipes,' it gurgled. 'Keep me hostage in rain butts and puddles, would you', it hissed.

The farmyard seemed to dissolve and simply run away. Roads were streams and streams were torrents. Cuthbert's house hunched its shoulders and allowed the rain to pressure-wash its thatch, clearing out ticks, fleas and sometimes small mammals as the water cascaded from its beetle brows. Cuthbert opened the door and the volume of water increased. All that wonderful farmyard patination destroyed, all those glorious smells gone, to be replaced by enough fresh air to give anyone a headache.

Cuthbert put the kettle on and prepared to wait. Then he remembered the tunnels. He need never really get wet again. He went down into the cellar, lit a lamp and stepped through the hole in the wall.

The tunnels stretched before him, cool and dry. Cuthbert did a little dance. The rain had beaten him all his life. Some clothing may be guaranteed 'rainproof', but they forgot about its accomplice, the wind.

Any loose flap or ventilation point was soon flipped up to allow the icy fingers of rain inside, but not anymore. Chatting happily to his shadow, Cuthbert walked merrily along the tunnel. If he hadn't pretended that his shadow was answering him, he might have heard the wall of water bearing down on him.

As it was, he was lifted off his feet and his lamp went out as he was spun around by the maelstrom. Suddenly lonely, now that his shadow had deserted him, Cuthbert flashed past the entrance to the old mill as the water chuckled around him.

'Whose laughing now, mortal?' it seemed to say as it spat him into the icy lake. Cuthbert spluttered to the surface by climbing up a discarded supermarket trolley. There wasn't a supermarket in the valley due to health and safety- no-one had the health to push a loaded trolley uphill and it certainly wasn't safe when it hurtled back down- and yet there was always a trolley. Cuthbert sometimes worried that they were boundary markers for a subtle invasion.

He slid along the path like an otter until he bumped against the mill wall. He was covered in mud from head to foot. The sun promptly came out to encourage people to come out and spot the mud monster. Thunder rolled like a fat man laughing.

The old door nearby opened and Henry, Ronald, the Captain and even Elspeth emerged and headed for the village. Cuthbert suddenly felt very alone. The newcomers had each other and the valley folk were united in their mutual distrust.

Catching sight of himself in the window covered in mud, Cuthbert remembered his mother saying, "Cuthbert, don't stand there like a chocolate bobby. Give me a hand."

Then, his father usually overlaid it with, "Cuthbert, get out of that hole and stop snivelling."

Cuthbert opened the door and entered the mill as the mud dried on him and began to crack.

Percy watched him go. He had strapped a grass divot on his head as a disguise and Cuthbert hadn't spotted him. He smiled to himself.

Behind Percy, one of the valley Mafia sniggered at the attempt at a disguise and adjusted the decoy duck on his own head. He settled down to wait.

Whilst Cuthbert was inside, Percy had time to consider his grievances- not all of them, nobody lived that long. Rubbing the patchy stubble on his chin caused by shaving with a sharpened trowel and broken mirror, he thought back to his days at agricultural college. Percy had been a keen student.

He had soaked up knowledge like a sponge and attended every lecture. If they had allowed him inside the building, he would have been a master of his trade. As it was, he crouched outside the windows of the classrooms with a notebook.

Unfortunately, most of the lecturers had a habit of pacing so Percy only heard the middle bit of each sentence. Then there was the odd freak who insisted upon shutting the window. He thought back now to the things he had half-learned. He would show them. Gardeners knew things, they had ways. An odd sound behind him made him turn. A duck had just banged its head against a gate-post. One sounded as solid as the other.

The Mafia sentry adjusted his decoy duck after the impact and hoped that this would be worth the wait. If not, he would show them.

The Mafia had ways, they knew things.

Percy's mind drifted back to college. One of his favourite lecturers had been 'One-thumb thingy', so named because he was easily distracted when using secateurs and, anyway, Percy couldn't read his name on the blackboard from where he was.

Another favourite was Miss Vaughan-Williams. She was known as Miss 'Vine-Weevil' because if you asked her a difficult question she would play dead and then bolt for the corridor at the first opportunity.

Percy felt the chill night air and sub-consciously flicked his scarf back around his neck. The association made him smile. He had worn an extra-long college scarf, which wound around his neck several times. It had been his trade-mark.

Everyone admired it until it became caught in the automatic doors of a bus. Percy had leapt onto the platform just as the doors closed at the top of the hill. He had hung on until his wellies began to smoulder and then he let go of the hand rail.

Spinning furiously, he had careered down the hill until he was almost screwed into a storm drain cover at the bottom. This had become a tradition whereby someone was elected to 'Do a Percy' at the start of the term and the whole college would gather to see the attempt. Percy's name would have been on the cup if he had ever enrolled. He still held the record.

Percy still had fond memories of those times. He had shared many a laugh with his classmates but, being outside he was always a heartbeat behind them and they would glance around nervously when they heard him.

The pride of the engineering department was a radio controlled tractor. Visitors came from all over to watch it go round in circles.

With all these students around, the principal had insisted that the steering be locked. He might have been an academic, but he was no fool.

With the carnival coming up, Percy decided that it made more sense for the tractor to pull the college carnival float, so he set to work re-coupling the steering linkage for forward running. He had absolutely no idea that the other students had entered it into a tractor race and fitted a bigger engine. He had been at the wrong window at the time.

On the day of the parade, 'Miss Bountiful' sat high up on the float surrounded by the college's display of organically grown fruits and vegetables.

Gracefully inclining her head to the principal and waving to the crowd, the button was pressed and the parade began. So did an awful prolonged screeching and the smell of burning rubber.

Percy had disguised the tractor by draping an advertising banner for laxatives over it. This proclaimed, 'Feeling sluggish, having trouble getting going? Not anymore'.

He had also bagged himself a lifetime's supply of the product and now it would be heading for the valley's water supply.

The tractor reared up like a speedboat until all surplus tread had been burnt off the huge back tyres and it had left the starting blocks. It also left 'Miss Bountiful' and her miniature harvest festival looking like an emergency appeal poster after hurricane Wilma. Witnesses could later only recall a series of freeze-frame images. Looking around in horror, all eyes alighted upon the only man holding a spanner. This is why Percy had been running for the bus in his long scarf in the first place.

Cuthbert ran his fingers over the panelling. Someone had bricked up the window he had looked through all those years ago and he could not pinpoint the right place. The mud was drying on him and dropping off in little chunks as he moved around.

With an audible 'click', a panel moved and he felt a draught on his face as if the secret cupboard led to the outside somewhere. Cuthbert groped around in the dark until his hands closed over a pile of scrolls. He scooped them up and tucked them into his pockets.

He didn't notice a single sheet of paper amongst them and it went with the rest. Whistling merrily, Cuthbert entered the tunnels, which were drying out nicely, and made his way home.

Now Percy concentrated upon his up-to-date grievances. He had justification, he had targets and he had a lifetime's supply of laxatives.

Percy remembered Margery. She was the only person who had ever offered him another cup of tea. It must be love. She was really smitten.

Somehow he must warn her and at the same time make sure that the twins got a double dose. He had seen her drink tea and she definitely cleaned her teeth, so this was going to be tricky. If the twins had been his, he would have fed them outside from the horse trough, but his beloved would not be so cruel. What could he do?

Percy made a decision. The poor woman must be suffering. He would grant her heart's desire and propose to her. That way, just before they left on their honeymoon, he would put 'Mister Shifter' in the reservoir. Abandoning his post, and leaving a wooden duck gently snoring behind him, Percy headed for home. His stubble needed sorting out and margarine usually flattened his hair. It also attracted wasps.

And he needed flowers.

*

Elspeth sat in the bar of the Mandrake arms. She closed out the burble of male conversation and stared at her drink.

It had an umbrella in it. 'Why?' she asked herself. Her husband had always handed her a drink whenever they went out together. Even during the rigours of foreign postings there was always an umbrella. She had no idea what the drink actually was. It was just something she stared at until they went home.

Glancing around the table, she took in her husband beaming at Henry and Ronald as they swapped war stories. Henry had been a big shot war correspondent and Ronald was a mysterious mercenary type who never sat with his back to the door and always knew where everyone was in the room.

Elspeth sighed. Her life had brightened marginally when she found the note. She had never been called 'speshul' before and longed to know who her secret admirer was.

As soon as she got home she would take out the letter and read it again. Somehow, it always said the same thing, but meant so much more every time she read it.

She tapped her fingers under the table in an attempt to encourage time to increase its tempo.

Percy approached Margery's house. Stopping at the gate, he bent to re-tie his shoe-lace and spotted the trip-wire. Further on there was another one. *So that's how they know when we're coming,* he thought. Stepping over the wires, Percy clutched the flowers to his chest and added a few more from the borders as he went. Hearing sounds of raised voices from inside, Percy risked glancing through the window.

The twins stood in the middle of the room looking at the floor. They had their hands clasped behind them and seemed quite normal. Someone was giving them a right tongue-lashing, but Percy couldn't see who it was. Had the husband returned? Percy panicked and stepped back into one of the wires, bells sounded inside the house and the door flew open.

"Are those for me?" asked one twin.

"Or for me?" asked the other one.

Percy spluttered until Margery appeared and the twins fled upstairs. Margery ushered him into the sitting room and Percy was relieved not to find an adult version of the twins in the room. "You look nervous, Percy," said Margery kindly. "What is it, dear?"

Percy hesitated and then blurted out, "I thought your husband had come home."

Margery paused with the teapot in her hand and flashed a glance at the window. "What did you ...?" she began, but settled down and said, "Oh, Percy, there is no husband. That's just something I say to keep people quiet." She resumed pouring.

Percy was nervous and his mouth would simply not obey his brain. It was out of practice.

"But I heard ..." he began.

"What?" snapped Margery, before calming herself and adding, "am I thinking of, Percy? I haven't thanked you for the flowers, dear."

Percy was sweating, He knew that passion could incite mixed emotions, but he had never imagined this. His college half-courses hadn't covered any of this at all.

He suddenly wished that he was somewhere else. Margery was staring at him as if he was her next meal and alarm bells began to ring.

The twins answered the door saying "Are those for me?" and "Or me?" and in came Henry.

Percy noted the perfect clothing and the cellophane around the flowers, and gave in gracefully. He ran. Kicking over the milk bottles on the doorstep, he destroyed trip wires, flower beds and gate hinges in his rush to escape.

Safely back in his shed, Percy sat and recovered from his ordeal. Then he noticed the paper lodged in his welly. It must have been in the top of a milk bottle.

He unfolded the paper and gasped. It read, "Moor milk pleeze and speshul creem for party. Thanx, Margery.' It was written in red felt tip.

138

Margery was the head of the valley Mafia. Percy quaked. Suddenly his little shed didn't seem very solid around him.

*

Cuthbert stared into the twilight. If that was the crow that sat on his wall, it had eaten something huge. Then he spotted the hat. "Is that you, Percy?" he called.

The shape came closer and Percy sat at the large table. Cuthbert poured him a cup of tea and waited for Percy to speak. When the words came, they tumbled out in much the same way that 'Miss Bountiful' had tumbled off the float before being saved by her melons.

So Henry was courting Margery. Cuthbert wondered if it was a ruse to get close to the twins. He shuddered; he would sooner get close to two angry alligators joined at the hip.

Percy was muttering like a drunk with an audience, so Cuthbert made an effort to hear him. "I know she loves me, but can I give up my friends and career?" he asked. Cuthbert's stunned silence only encouraged him to continue. "I could have been the making of those boys, you know. I would have moulded them in my own image."

Cuthbert pretended to fill the kettle, putting his head in the oven to muffle any sounds.

Percy eventually convinced himself that he must give up Margery, for the sake of his friends and career, of course. Besides, he admitted, he felt as though he had just survived an interview with a black widow spider.

Cuthbert watched as his friend relaxed and asked, "Would you really have put all those laxatives in the reservoir, Percy?"

"Good Lord, no," said Percy indignantly. "Only about half. I've got tons of the stuff."

*

Elspeth was on her way home. The Captain was being particularly irritating tonight. Every time someone said 'Goodnight' he thought of something else to say and delayed things.

She could hear the rustle of the paper as the note opened and revealed the dramatic urgency of the red letters. She smiled at the thought of the coded spelling to disguise his identity. She really needed to get home.

Cuthbert had shown Percy the scrolls and they had found the note written in red. This in turn led to Percy's revelation about Margery, and the two of them were trying to absorb volumes of information, which neither of them was equipped for.

"So, what are they?" asked Percy.

Cuthbert shrugged. "Old copies of plays, as far as I know," he replied. "My father kept them at the old mill in case he needed a new play sometime." Undoing a ribbon, Cuthbert smoothed out one of the scrolls and they peered at the dark, crackling parchment covered in spidery scrawl.

Cuthbert sat back. "Well," he said, "I won't find a new play here. I can't read them."

"No, but I can," said a voice from the shadows. Geraldine stepped forward. The glint in her eyes matching the glint from the wicked tip of the crossbow bolt. "I have been exploring, Cuthbert," she said. "Why didn't you tell me about the carvings of quills and inkpots in your house?"

The voice was calm, but the crossbow moved to cover Cuthbert as he stammered, "Er, er, hello, Geraldine."

Percy said, "We thought it was a UFO," and gulped as the crossbow swung towards him. "Or Cuthbert did," he added quickly, watching the weapon move away again.

Cuthbert suddenly caught up with events and blurted, "I thought you were in ..."

"A rest facility?" asked Geraldine in a dangerously calm voice.

"Yes, that's it exactly," agreed both men in stereo.

Chapter 38

Noting the tension in the room, Geraldine quipped, "I haven't got an axe, you know." Then, seeing both men stare at the crossbow, she said, "Oh, this old thing?" She shook her head dramatically, "It wouldn't hurt a fly."

The large bluebottle just above the cooking range was pleased to hear that just before the bolt embedded it several inches into the wall. "See?" shrilled Geraldine. "It didn't feel a thing." Her maniacal laughter drove both men under the table, but when they peeped out, Geraldine calmly sat reading a scroll. They resumed their seats cautiously.

She glanced across at them and dismissively pushed a sheet of parchment over to Cuthbert. "You left this on the bed, Cuthbert. I presume you found it hidden somewhere?"

Cuthbert nodded. It was the one he had found in the roll top desk. Geraldine sat back and took a deep breath the way the therapist had taught her. "The other scrolls were moved to the old mill because a museum curator was getting close. Your father thought they would be safer there, Cuthbert. Did you read the letter you found?"

Both men nodded mutely. Geraldine nodded at some private thought and continued. "The letter was written by Queen Elizabeth the First, gentlemen." She paused for effect. "It was sent to the then owner of Mandrake Hall. Apparently William Shakespeare took a teaching job for that family early in his career. It seems that he wrote his first play there and it did not show the Queen in a good light. The owner was tasked with finding the play and sending it to the Queen so that she could destroy it. Of course in those days poor old William the playwright wouldn't have just had his licence revoked. Oh no. His insides would have become his outsides and his head would have had a wonderful view over London."

Geraldine paused again. "William Shakespeare had made many friends in the valley whilst he was here and they all conspired to keep him safe. The play never came to light and Shakespeare was content to view London from ground level. The people of the valley have always celebrated the association by staging one of his plays on an annual basis. This is the secret that brought all those strangers to your valley,

Cuthbert." She tapped a long fingernail against the parchment. "And this is the missing play," she added dramatically.

Everyone relaxed as they absorbed this revelation, until Geraldine whispered, "What tales would the walls of Mandrake Hall tell us now?" she asked before screaming, "if some fool hadn't burnt it down …"

*

Elspeth dashed into the house, threw her coat onto the table and went to open the panel. She lifted a lamp from the wall and turned the corner. The panel was open, the cupboard was bare.

Elspeth looked around in panic stricken horror, shock sent for rage and fury gate-crashed. Elspeth discovered her inner-woman and it was terrible to see. She noted the brown shards of dried mud on the floor leading away to the tunnels. The thief had gone that way. She plunged into the tunnels, only to recoil at the sight of all those cobwebs. Grabbing a duster, she set off in pursuit.

Henry and Ronald had said goodbye to Elspeth and the Captain. One of Henry's old newsroom colleagues had been in contact and warned him that Geraldine had been involved in a mass breakout from the asylum. Henry thought it was only fair to warn Cuthbert. Ronald would have rather hidden outside Cuthbert's farm and watched the fun. They made their unsteady way along the lane. Neither of them commented upon a wooden duck dashing about as if it had lost something.

Geraldine had taken a black pill and settled down again. Cuthbert and Percy watched as her lips moved when she read the document before her. When the shrill scream shattered the peace, both men were watching Geraldine- and it wasn't her. The lamp was blown over and scrolls crackled as they were scooped up to the cry of "Mine, they're mine."

Poor Geraldine simply could not take the shock. Her mind shattered like glass with shards of memory flying in all directions. Cuthbert scrabbled around under the table until he had enough bits of lamp to be able to light something. He couldn't find the wick, so he lit Percy's coat.

When light and order were restored, Cuthbert was breathless and Geraldine was in shock. Percy was smoking, and the scrolls were gone.

Someone had come through the cellar, taken the play and escaped the same way. Only the note in red pen was left.

Back at the old mill, Elspeth laid the scrolls back in the cupboard and wept. Her note was missing. Her only link to her admirer was gone. It crossed her mind that the burglar had been after these old things. She was tempted to destroy them so that someone else suffered a loss.

The Captain appeared behind her. "There you are, you silly old thing," he said, very unwisely. "What have you got there- more cleaning tips, eh?"

Elspeth turned and the Captain gulped. It was like confronting a hound from hell.

He backed away, "Er, I'll make my own supper then, shall I?" His training had included how to deal with a mountain gorilla and he used the advice wisely, wishing that he had some male company to hide amongst.

*

Henry and Ronald entered Cuthbert's kitchen unannounced and were miffed to see that the dangerous lunatic sat peacefully staring into space.

Cuthbert explained what had happened and the history of the scrolls, and Henry sobered up immediately. "We must get them back," he announced.

Everyone grabbed a lamp and they headed into the tunnels. Ronald led the way trying to be stealthy as the rest of them cannoned into each other and squabbled behind him. Percy had brought two bottles of elderflower wine from Cuthbert's cellar in case they were gone for a while, and he was nervously shaking them as they entered the tunnels.

Cuthbert grabbed one of the bottles just as Ronald turned to tell them all to be quiet. Snatching the bottle provided one agitation too much and the wine exploded.

The cork shot out and hit Ronald right between the eyes. "I'm hit," he cried as the cork ricocheted around the tunnel walls. Then he saw Cuthbert holding the bottle. "He's done it again," he roared and launched himself at Cuthbert.

Elspeth heard the commotion in the tunnel and kicked the back of the secret cupboard in frustration. The back swung open revealing another tunnel leading upwards. Elspeth grabbed the scrolls and fled.

As the limbs were untangled and order restored, the procession continued to the old mill. The Captain appeared at the top of the stairs as Henry and his gang appeared at the bottom.

"Have you got the scrolls?" demanded Henry.

The Captain gaped. "No," he began. "Oh, is that what Elspeth was playing with in the cupboard?"

Henry snapped, "Yes, you nincompoop, where is she?"

The Captain bristled. Damn man was only a civilian after all, but he saw Ronald glaring and nodded to the newly revealed tunnel. They all surged in, with the Captain tagging on behind.

When soil and heather appeared on the floor of the tunnel, someone asked, "Where are we?"

Henry answered, "Must be the moors. Not much heather in the valley."

Leaving the tunnel, they spotted Elspeth posed dramatically amongst the heather. A warm breeze caressed the moor and Elspeth's hair and dress billowed out around her.

Henry spoke, "There she is. Captain, get the silly mare back here before she loses the scrolls!"

The Captain bristled again. *There he goes again, damn civilian, twenty years ago I would have ...*

"Today!" snapped Ronald.

The Captain swallowed and barked, "Elspeth, here, now woman. Front and centre."

Henry gaped at him. "Oh, that will do the trick," he said sarcastically.

Elspeth's nostrils flared as she spotted them. She was poised like a springbok, ready to flee.

Henry sighed, "Not like that, you fool. Entice her. Cajole her."

"Eh?" said the Captain.

"Elspeth, my love," said the Captain. Or at least his voice did. They were all watching him and his lips weren't moving. The voice continued, "Come to me, darling. The moon shall light our way and our passion will surpass the sun. For you are special."

Percy's impression was faultless and Elspeth gasped, "At last, at last," she cried and ran towards them with her arms stretched before her. This was her Heathcliffe moment, her time had come.

"Go on, you fool, run to meet her," urged Henry. With a shove from Ronald, the Captain stumbled forward, arms outstretched the way hers were. At the point where they should have met, the Captain fell down a badger's set and Elspeth ran straight over the top of him. The witnesses to this event covered their eyes as Elspeth looked around, panicked and ran off in the opposite direction. They all gave chase, ignoring a cry when someone trod on the Captain.

Elspeth was distraught. Her moment had gone, her lover had gone, and she would end it all. The pursuers cannoned into each other as Elspeth appeared on top of a large rock, arms held up to the scudding clouds like a Valkyrie summoning the host.

Henry gasped, "We need to talk her down."

Percy tried desperately to compose something, Henry started to climb, and Ronald wondered if he could get her with a well-aimed rock.

Cuthbert just stood there.

Elspeth screamed into the wind, "Take me. Take me now, I have nothing left." She began to throw the scrolls into the air where they were whipped away by the wind and hurled across the moor. Then she turned towards her pursuers like a stag at bay and cried "Farewell", before casting herself backwards and out of sight.

The Captain gasped. Percy stopped composing. Henry stopped climbing. And Cuthbert still just stood there.

Ronald looked at him admiringly, "You are a cool one," he said.

Cuthbert shrugged. "Spent hours up here. There's no drop behind that rock. It's flat."

An undignified scramble began as they raced to the summit. Elspeth lay spread-eagled like a discarded snow angel and the scrolls were rolling faster and faster downhill. It was going to be a long night.

Chapter 39

Morning found them dejectedly around Cuthbert's table. Elspeth was making tea and managing to be even quieter than when she didn't speak at all.

There were three scrolls before them. No-one knew how many they had started with, but it was definitely more than this.

Cuthbert yawned. "Does anyone think the twins are bluffing?" he asked the room in general.

Henry snapped, "I hope not. They've got my watch."

Percy saw his chance and asked slyly, "Perhaps Margery will get it back for you?"

Henry blushed. "Sorry about that, Percy, but I really think we have something between us."

"Yeah, the twins," snarled Ronald.

Percy airily waved a hand and announced, "I withdraw from the contest. My career and my friends come first."

As the exhausted minds tried to grapple with this, Elspeth came alert. She recognised that voice from the moor. With a long look and an arched eyebrow, she poured Percy a second cup of tea. Percy gulped.

Ronald asked, "Where did you learn such flowery phrases then, Percy- talking to the plants?"

Percy shuffled, "Didn't I tell you about my ancestor, the poet?" The room cleared and Percy was alone.

*

Geraldine had taken to wandering around Cuthbert's house. The low-beamed ceilings and the inherited furniture made her relax. She was comfortable in the past. The past was when the bad things hadn't happened to her yet.

She ran a finger along the inkwell carving and traced the outline of the feather. Clues surrounded her all along. It had been the strange habit of giving everyone in the valley Shakespearean middle names that caught her interest at first and then she saw the letter found in Cuthbert's desk.

146

This was her way back into the hierarchy of her profession. Who would remember a little stress breakdown when all the witnesses had been eliminated?

She began to giggle, but promptly slapped her own hand over her mouth and stifled it. *Not yet, girl,* she thought. The scrolls were out there somewhere. *Stay sane for a little while yet.* The jump from lunatic to eccentric was much easier with a doctorate to hide behind.

*

Percy sat at the farmhouse table. He swung his little legs so that his wellies scuffed each other as they passed.

It seemed to stimulate his thinking processes. "Do you realise," he asked, "half the valley seems to be looking for a secret and the other half already knows it?"

Cuthbert had been nimbly avoiding the tongue of flame that lurked inside the cooking range and shot out just as you were distracted. He was also perfecting a technique for filtering out most of Percy's twitterings. This was rendered impossible because the irritating little twerp sometimes said something useful- like now. Cuthbert paused and the flame caught him behind the knees.

Limping around the table, Cuthbert sat opposite to Percy and said, "You're right. If we could bring them all together, it would save a lot of trouble."

Silence reigned for a while with only the rhythmic swish of Percy's wellies as he powered his thoughts.

Percy spoke. "You would think that they would all be interested in helping with the play, if they are so keen on Shakespeare, wouldn't you?"

Cuthbert tried to snap his fingers. He could never fully enjoy a 'eureka' moment. "That's it." he said instead. "I'll invite everyone to take part and they will work together, act together and all become friends." He stared admiringly at Percy; perhaps he had underestimated him. "You are a genius, Percy. Any more thoughts?"

Percy swung his legs and said dreamily, "I was wondering if I was the only one to grow bananas in the valley."

Cuthbert gaped; his friend was back.

*

147

Geraldine had been very busy. She found the carved inkwell on the coffer. She found the crypt under the 'theatre' and was building up the evidence she needed for her dissertation.

To log everyone's movements, ready for the reckoning, she really needed somewhere to stay, close to everyone.

Cuthbert gazed at the ceiling and remembered something Percy had said. "What was that about your ancestor being a poet?"

Percy shuffled and answered brightly, "Oh, we have a history of poets in the family, all the way back to that Lord Bryon."

"Do you mean Lord Byron?" asked Cuthbert incredulously.

Percy smiled, "A common mispronunciation," he said before sitting upright and reciting,

A barren soul,
His father dead
Childe Harolde
Wept instead.

Cuthbert wasn't at all sure about that one, but perhaps somewhere there was a valley stuffed with long lost poems and he could send Percy off to look for them.

As evening fell, Cuthbert took himself off to bed. Sinking into the feather mattress, he thought of Percy sleeping downstairs. He had reluctantly agreed to put his garden and his renovations on hold to assist with the play, and he would stay with Cuthbert. Cuthbert suspected that it would be like having a flea in your ear- a constant droning and pretty hard to get rid of.

*

Geraldine snuggled down in her new dwelling place. It was warm, it was dry and it was a haystack.

She daren't be found wandering the countryside whilst the asylum vans were patrolling. The vans had actually been grounded.

The crews had been a little too enthusiastic and they now had more inmates than they had started with.

*

Ronald lay in his bed at the Mandrake arms. He could hear his brother, Henry, begin to snore in the next room, so he dressed in black and set off for the moors.

During his career as a mercenary, Ronald had become used to night manoeuvres and general creeping about. He figured that there would be a fence somewhere and things got caught up on fences.

Ronald was right. He found three scrolls along one stretch and slipped them into his special pockets. The others wanted to offer a bounty to the valley Mafia, but Ronald thought it was a waste of chocolate.

Humming to himself on the way back, Ronald was taken by surprise and hit from behind. The first assailant came in low and knocked him off his feet.

Then the rest waded in to give him a good kicking. Only Ronald's specialist skills allowed him to fight his way free and escape.

In the morning he felt as though he had been trampled by a flock of sheep. Oddly enough, he saw a lamb with a black eye.

*

Constable Beeching was worried. He was fending off more emergency calls than usual lately. All these strangers, and even stranger goings on.

The valley was like a powder keg and it was ready to blow. The officer didn't hesitate - pulling out his pen he began to fill in his holiday application form.

Margery was worried; she was used to having the valley covered. Belinda the barmaid passed on information from the Mandrake Arms. The village gossip filled in the gaps and the Mafia foot soldiers did the leg work. However, the newcomers had begun meeting with the 'not-real-valley-folk' and the twins' ransom demand was being ignored. It was time to turn the screw.

One of the twins sidled along behind Cuthbert's farm wall. The decoy duck on his head seemed to be waddling along the top of the stone. The crow watched carefully.

Cuthbert opened the back door, then the front door to achieve a through-draught.

A twin fastened a note to an arrow. It read, 'Last chans- tressure worth millions-pay up.' Of course it was written in red felt tip. The twin heaved back on the bow as Cuthbert was framed in the doorway.

149

Even Cuthbert will find this note pinned to his coat this time, he thought as he fired.

Cuthbert turned to wake Percy and something whistled past him and straight out of the back to land in the manure heap with a warm 'plop'.

The twin gaped, found another note and fitted another arrow. The crow moved closer.

Cuthbert roused Percy and suggested that he carry the old tin bath up to the theatre while he made breakfast. The buckets just weren't keeping pace with the leaks.

Percy grumbled as he put the bath on his back and bent forward to clear the doorway.

Clonking against each side of the frame he left the house. The arrow hit the sloping side of the bath and zipped up into the thatch to disappear forever. Percy peered curiously out from under the bath before continuing on his way like a geriatric armadillo.

The twin shook his head. He had brought enough notes and arrows for each of the doors- Cuthbert's, Percy's shed, the mill and the pub.

He had wasted two already. The door had closed gently in the breeze and the twin took aim at the static target. He leant against the wall for stability and dislodged a stone.

This revealed the pair of boots left by Cuthbert poking out from under the wall. The twin knew about Cuthbert's reputation as an undertaker, but this was sloppy even by his standards.

Trying to keep one nervous eye on the boots and the other one on the door, he pulled back on the bow. The crow noticed that this arrow did not have a note attached and he chose this moment to tap the twin on the shoulder to warn him.

The twin yelped, the bow fired and the crow flew. The arrow arced gracefully and dropped cleanly down Cuthbert's chimney. The shower of sparks was testament to a nice hot fire burning below.

Outraged, the twin leapt onto the wall and took aim at the crow. The crow saw it coming and executed an 'Immelman turn' to neatly evade it.

A clang in the distance drew the eye of the twin. Percy's tin bath had spun around with him still under it and was still on its way to the theatre.

The twin wrestled with the bow and managed to twist it into a wooden Jews harp when its natural urges took over and it sprung back into shape, throwing him off the wall.

Cuthbert stopped what he was doing to answer a tapping at his door. When he opened it, he was greeted by a twin. The twin silently handed him a note and walked dejectedly away, dragging the wreckage of a bow behind him. Once out of sight, the twin sat down and, for the first time in years, he had a good cry.

Cuthbert met Percy in the theatre and showed him the note. Cuthbert asked, "Do you think we should set up a meeting?"

Percy could still smell the old fries from the bag on his head and panicked. "I'm not meeting the twins alone again."

Cuthbert pointed out that they had all been there, but his voice tapered off when Percy wouldn't meet his eye. He leaned in and plucked a hair from Percy's nostrils. Percy confessed quickly and wiping his eyes told Cuthbert about the kidnap and the turnip head.

"So that's why you were sulking," said Cuthbert.

Percy was indignant. "It was a strategic emotional retreat."

Cuthbert had a thought. "I wonder if Margery knows what they've found?"

Percy became fidgety. "Er, I wouldn't go there, Cuthbert," he said, and confessed a little more.

Cuthbert exploded. "Dealing with you is like a one man band covering up his instruments so that the others don't know what they are."

Percy thought about this analogy for a moment before asking, "Wouldn't they still hear each other?"

Cuthbert gaped and stormed off the stage and out of the theatre.

Percy smiled. "Another strategic emotional retreat, I reckon."

*

Cuthbert stormed up to Margery's front door leaving a tangle of wires in his wake, kicking over the milk bottles just as Percy had done.

A note lay beside them, 'Two pints please, Margery'. It was written in red felt tip. Cuthbert paled. Percy was right. Innocent, harassed Margery was the head of the valley Mafia.

He turned to leave as Margery appeared and slammed the gate behind her. The impact of the gate sent a ripple all the way around the picket fence until it came back again. "Come to see me, Cuthbert?" she snarled.

Cuthbert spluttered until his brain saved him from a 'Custer' moment. "I've come to offer you the lead in the new play," he said quickly.

Margery's eye's narrowed. "Really?" she purred.

"Oh, yes," Cuthbert pressed on. "Leading lady, beautiful woman, big frocks, everything."

Margery melted; she could hear the applause already. Cuthbert vaulted the fence and fled.

Cuthbert burst into the theatre, ran onto the stage and grabbed Percy by the lapels. Neither of them spoke, but for entirely different reasons. Cuthbert shook Percy sideways and then forwards and then sideways again because he was fascinated by the fact that his hat wouldn't fall off.

"Why didn't you tell me about Margery?" cried Cuthbert.

Percy tried to answer but he sounded like a faulty spin-drier and waited until Cuthbert let go.

"I did," he insisted.

"But why didn't you tell me when I was listening?" screamed Cuthbert.

*

Margery stood before the full length mirror. She had wrapped a shawl around her head and extra skirts around her waist to simulate long, historic clothing.

The twins burst in and stood gawping at her.

"Ahh, yon scoundrels have returned," she said. "These vagabonds of yore to warm me in my winters of discontent."

Then, to thoroughly frighten them, she ruffled their hair.

152

Chapter 40

Cuthbert and Percy sat on the edge of the stage. Each of them had a letter written in red felt tip pen.

Percy broke the silence. "You know," he began, "I was once called in to solve a murder by analysing handwriting."

Cuthbert stared. The thing about Percy was that you never knew what he was going to say next, but whatever it was, it had a way of evading all checks and filters installed as standard at birth.

Percy took the stunned silence as encouragement and continued. "Do you remember the case where a milkman was murdered and the killer left a note saying 'Three pints tomorrow or I'll kill you'?"

Cuthbert nodded cautiously, so Percy elaborated. "It was down to me to prove that the man was innocent and get him a full pardon," said Percy, puffing out his chest.

Cuthbert watched him cautiously. He had already learned that Percy was a man of many parts, but he tended to assume that none of them actually worked.

"How did you do that?" he asked with reluctance and regret elbowing each other for attention.

Percy shuffled to get comfortable and Cuthbert recognised the sign.

He sighed, and waited.

"Well," began Percy, "the facts were that the milkman didn't return to his depot one night and his milk-float was missing. A search began the next day involving depot workers and the police. They retraced his route and when they reached Lakeside Cottage ...."

Cuthbert was suddenly alert. "Lakeside Cottage? I remember that. The Lady in the Lake murders?" He was all ears now.

Percy stumbled a bit. "Well, yes, that one, except that there wasn't a woman. It just made a good headline." He glared at Cuthbert and snapped, "Can I continue?"

Cuthbert nodded mutely.

Watching carefully for more outbursts, Percy went on with his tale. "When they reached Lakeside Cottage, they found a note, which said ...."

"Three pints tomorrow or I'll kill you," interrupted Cuthbert before slapping his own hand over his mouth and mumbling, "Sorry."

Percy glared at him and started slowly before picking up speed.

Cuthbert pressed his lips together like a Muppet and even sat on his hands in his eagerness to hear the story.

Percy watched him closely and went on with his narrative. "Three pints tomorrow or I'll kill you," he said very deliberately and watched for any subversive movements from his listener.

"When the police interviewed the owner of the cottage, he admitted writing the note, but claimed that he hadn't seen the milkman at all. He had been having trouble with this new milkman and hadn't received any milk for days. The police arrested him anyway, assuming that the milkman had got it wrong again and the cottage owner had murdered him."

Cuthbert listened patiently.

Percy paused for dramatic effect and announced, "Then they found the milk float in the lake. All they needed was the corpse delectable."

Cuthbert asked, "Was it stolen from the float?" He didn't know any Latin and assumed that it was a yoghurt.

Percy flapped his hands, "No, it's Latin for a body. Anyway, I made a dramatic entrance into the courtroom a few days later to prove that the cottage owner couldn't have written the note because he only had one leg."

Cuthbert stared. Percy sighed and added, "His writing would have leaned to one side if he had written it."

"Would it?" asked Cuthbert hesitantly.

"Course it would, stands to reason," snapped Percy dismissively. "Anyway, everyone stood and applauded, and the man was set free and I was the hero," concluded Percy proudly.

Cuthbert applied the brakes to his spinning thoughts and asked, "Well, where was the milkman?"

Percy explained. "Apparently the road leading to the cottage ended in a lake and the regular man would wait for the ferry. But whilst he was away on holiday his replacement looked at the lake and assumed that a milk-float had a logical reason for being called that and he drove straight in. Both the water and the vehicle were taken by surprise and this allowed it to drift to shore further down before it sank completely. The new chap realised that all the stock would be taken out of his wages, so he spent the whole day diving in and rescuing everything. This was exhausting, of course, and he fell asleep, missing all the excitement."

Cuthbert gaped. "So the milkman was alive?"

"Yep," said Percy.

"There was no murder?" asked Cuthbert.

"Nope," said Percy.

"No body in the lake?"

"Nope," said Percy again.

Cuthbert went for the fine details. "So, there was no milky or lady in the lake at all?"

"Correct," confirmed Percy.

Cuthbert looked at him carefully as he asked, "Who was the regular milkman, Percy?"

"Oh, that was my cousin," admitted Percy brightly.

Cuthbert persisted, "Were you filling in for him, Percy?"

Percy grinned, "Of course. That's what families are for."

Chapter 41

Margery stood before the full length mirror. She threw a cashmere wrap around her shoulders and laughed gaily at her reflection. This was her secret dream.

She didn't know anything about the play, not even which period it was set in. This was her chance to shine in public.

Margery could already act. She had been fooling everyone with her down-trodden single mum performance over the years. The twins would get parts too. They could be a right pair of thespians when they wanted to be.

A thought occurred to her. Cuthbert had been sweet on that Geraldine woman. She had been seen back in the valley; she might persuade him to give the part to her.

Margery would increase surveillance on Cuthbert's farm. They didn't call her 'the Godmother' for nothing. Opening a window to shout for the twins, she remembered that one of them had not been the same since he delivered a letter to Cuthbert. She had no idea which one it was, but one of them seemed odd.

*

The newcomers sat around Cuthbert's table. The atmosphere was splintered. Margery was the head of the valley Mafia. Henry was stunned.

Elspeth was intrigued- women with secrets were nothing new, but women with secrets and ambitions, that was worth watching.

Ronald wasn't surprised- he never bothered to get to know who was who anyway, then when things got confusing he was ahead of the pack.

The Captain changed the subject. "Have these blasted twins got a secret or not?" he barked.

Everybody shrugged.

Henry said, "We expected another note, but I haven't seen one yet."

Cuthbert coughed apologetically and produced the crumpled note from his pocket. Everyone craned forward to read it.

"So the treasure is worth millions, is it? Why won't they tell us what it is?"

Henry suggested, "Perhaps they only think it's treasure. They're not the brightest bunnies, are they?"

Ronald muttered, "They keep giving us a whipping."

The word treasure stirred something in Cuthbert and he quietly slipped away and checked the cellar. Returning to the kitchen, he announced, "They've got treasure all right, but not from that hole."

Over the years, people in the valley had donated any scraps of broken jewellery or glittering costume jewels to Cuthbert for the plays. Eventually, it filled a medium sized trunk and was used as the prop in Cuthbert's productions. The Mafia had come in through the hole in the cellar wall and taken it. Everyone around the table was in stitches. The relief was obvious when they all accepted a cup of Cuthbert's tea without a thought for the health risks. Then Henry remembered his watch.

*

The twins were fuming. No reply to their note and Mum seemed to be in another world.

There would be no instructions from her for a while. Perhaps this was when the chicks flew the nest and took matters into their own hands. Ignore a Mafia ransom demand, would they? For a moment, they were tempted to go global and tell the kids in the next valley, but it would make them look weak.

It was time to move into the wide world of commerce.

The antique dealer, Martin Hepplewhite, was in the back of his shop coating a statue from the garden centre in yoghurt.

When it went mouldy and moss appeared, he would casually lean it against an outside wall to be discovered by a tourist on the way to the ruins of the old abbey. He sighed; the glory days were gone.

When the Americans had been keen, dark furniture had fled the country like lemmings following signs to the cliff top. Now all he got were the television prompted 'experts' with no money.

His father had defined the word 'expert' as "An ex is a has-been and a spurt is a drip under pressure." It still made him smile when someone came in hurriedly hiding the new antiques guide behind them and trying to appear casual.

The shop bell jangled and Martin wiped his hands and adopted a fatherly expression as he entered his shop from the back. All was as it should be except that the bell over his door still quivered, but the shop seemed empty.

Feeling rather silly he called, "Anyone there?"

"We've got something," said a voice.

Martin peered over the counter and recoiled. Two scruffy urchins had dragged an old box right across his polished floor.

"We've got something," repeated the other twin.

"Hope it's not catching," tried Martin gamely.

The twins stared. The lights seemed to dim. "Long way over here," said one twin.

"Not designed for bikes, these roads," said the other.

Martin asked where they were from and then paled as they named the valley. Not only was he still raw from his encounter with Cuthbert, he had heard about these two. *Better make this quick,* he thought. "What have you got then, lads?" he asked jovially.

The twins hefted the box onto the counter with a shuddering crash. One side fell off and trinkets cascaded across the wood. One of the twins offered Martin his eye glass.

"Er, no thanks," he muttered. He could recognise the sound of dross hitting mahogany a mile away. "This is all rubbish," he exclaimed, "This is the sort of junk a theatre company would use."

The twins exchanged a look. "King's ransom there, mate," said one twin.

"King's ransom," agreed the other twin.

Martin didn't have time for this. Horse brasses don't bury themselves in the garden, and he lost his patience. "Look, kids, this is rubbish. It wouldn't ransom King Lear."

The twins began scooping the 'treasure' into various pockets and left him the broken box. Martin gazed at the drag marks on his lovely floor and was distracted as the twins neared a huge Chinese vase near to the door.

"This valuable, then?" asked a twin.

"Yes, very ..." said Martin absently, staring at his floor.

"... valuable," said the first twin.

"Oops," said the other one.

*

The group around Cuthbert's table were getting down to business.

158

Henry announced, "Gentlemen, it's time to play poker. Everyone show his hand and lays his cards on the table. We must work together."

Percy rummaged in his welly and produced a scroll. Ronald sneered and raised the ante with his three scrolls. Cuthbert saw them with two scrolls and a 'speshul' note. Elspeth felt her heart leap at the sight of it. She deflated visibly as Percy produced another 'speshul' note and topped everyone with a ring inscribed with an inkwell and quill.

Geraldine pounced on the ring and went into a trance whispering, "The Bard, the Bard."

Henry added some research books he had salvaged from the Hall. Cuthbert added the rubbings taken from the coffer, the gate-posts and his house. He then nudged Geraldine, who added the letter from Queen Elizabeth the First.

"Quite a haul," breathed Henry.

Geraldine spoke. "You don't know the half of it," she said reverently, before adding, "What is the most valuable artefact we could have found?"

"Saint Grizelda's foot?" suggested Ronald impishly.

Geraldine's glare impaled him and he re-arranged everything on the table trying to look useful. Geraldine turned her attention to Cuthbert. who related the story of the crypt and the upright lead coffin.

Neither he nor Percy mentioned Percy's thumb being stuck in the eye socket. It didn't seem wise somehow.

Geraldine turned the ring this way and that to catch the light across the design. "What," she whispered, "if this was the Bard himself?"

Everyone sat up. Henry and Ronald saw its worth immediately. Cuthbert saw a little room with bars on the windows. Percy wondered if any of the magic had rubbed off onto his thumb. He began to practice a few sonnets just in case.

Reality seemed to wander into the room by accident and they all settled down again.

Henry became practical. "Shakespeare is buried in Stratford and I think we all agree that his death is much better documented than his early life."

Geraldine was twirling the ring and humming to herself. "Okay then," she began, "what if we are correct about the missing play? What if these rings were owned by the conspirators as a way to recognise each other? Perhaps they were loath to destroy the first play written by

Shakespeare, but if it was discovered they would all share the same fate."

Henry added, "His plays were performed for Elizabeth and later for James the First. Perhaps they were due to announce the new play now that Elizabeth was dead."

Geraldine took up the thought. "The ring in the crypt would have belonged to the owner of Mandrake Hall. Perhaps all the conspirators were dead and the secret died with Shakespeare himself."

Henry sat back. "Only local memories and tradition kept the idea alive, but the location was forgotten."

Geraldine finished the sequence with, "The engravings on the gate posts would have announced a safe house and perhaps the scrolls were first kept in the coffer with the same carving."

A feeling of satisfaction suffused the room and they celebrated with a glass of Cuthbert's elderflower wine. All past animosities were forgotten. Some of them even forgot their own names.

Percy saw that Henry was alone and sidled up to him. He confided that he had actually touched the bones and went on to describe how it felt having a thumb stuck up someone else's eye-hole.

"What if it really was the Bard?" mused Percy.

"Hope not, old chap," slurred Henry blearily.

"Why not?" asked Percy.

"Because, if I remember rightly, his tomb says 'Curst be he who moves these bones'."

Percy snorted derisively and wandered off. A few minutes later he returned for clarification. "Did you say 'first' or 'curst'?" he asked worriedly.

Henry adopted a drunken pose and boomed, "Curst old boy, as in curst, curst and thrice curst."

Percy wandered off again muttering, "Okay. Okay, I get the picture."

Percy felt rather foolish as he read the experimental sonnets he had scrawled on some old blank parchment he found under a cupboard. With a resigned sigh he pushed them back there. A stuffed owl watched him from the window and the twin strapped under it noted where the scrolls had gone. Mother would be pleased.

It was arranged that Geraldine would stay in a spare room and begin to translate the scrolls. The party gradually broke up and contented people followed strange pathways in an attempt to get home.

160

"She did what?" screamed Margery.

"Stayed the night," confirmed the twin. "Just her, Cuthbert and turnip head."

"She is making her move," cackled Margery, practising her Lady Macbeth.

This is better, thought the twins. *Mum's back.*

The twins stayed silent about the scrolls. They were determined to begin their own empire now and bribes would be needed. Ninja Turtle figures didn't come cheap.

*

Martin Hepplewhite was behind his counter. He didn't like being surprised, so he had fitted a stable door to the shop. The top was open and there was nobody in sight. He looked up as he heard a scratching sound. The bottom half of the door swung wide and a twin stood there with a hairgrip in his hand. Martin quivered. The twins advanced side-by-side until they disappeared in front of the counter. A grubby hand appeared over the wooden top and a scroll rolled towards Martin.

"Got something," said one twin.

"Worth a King's ransom," said the other one.

Martin hadn't realised that his eyes were shut until he opened one and looked down. Gingerly he opened the scroll. It crackled as he unrolled it and it insisted upon rolling back up again. He noted the 'chicken scratch' writing and the uneven edges. He noted the word 'curst' and several uses of 'ye'. It was a poem, he could tell that by the spacing. These two had actually come up with something.

Rolling up the scroll, he asked nonchalantly, "Just this one?"

"No mate" said one twin, "there's more.

"Worth a King's ransom they are," said the other twin.

"Well, specialist job, not much demand. Foreign buyers have all dried up you know …" The terms tripped out of him as he tried to think.

A grubby hand appeared and grabbed the scroll causing an unseemly tug of war.

"I can give you pocket money for them, lads. I can't say better than that, can I?"

The scroll disappeared over the counter and Martin heard a scratching noise. Then the twins walked out of the shop with the scroll.

Martin dashed to the door to lock it top and bottom. Breathing a sigh of relief, he walked back and spotted the reason for the scratching noise. They had carved 'Weel B bak' into his beautiful mahogany counter.

Chapter 42

Cuthbert's farm was a hive of activity. Geraldine was translating the scrolls. It was a play, but the introduction was missing.

That must have been the first scroll. A search of the moor revealed nothing, so they would see what Geraldine produced and improvise.

The men were preparing the theatre. Henry seemed adapt at turning up and making a huge show of rolling up his sleeves, but never actually touched anything.

Ronald was in several places at once without drawing attention to himself. Cuthbert caught him trying on hats. The Captain was expert at barking out orders just as the task was completed, and Elspeth poured the tea. Cuthbert noticed that Percy had twice as many cups as anyone else.

He had been meaning to have a word with Percy. Geraldine had found a pewter inkwell like the one in the carvings and had asked Percy to find her a quill to go with it. The farmyard was a blood-bath. Even the crow was missing a few feathers and the ducks looked like vultures.

Percy had offered no explanation, but he was the centre of attention now. He was demonstrating the correct way to angle the tip of the quill so that the ink would flow correctly. The secret, he said, was to allow the ink into the stem and restrict the flow back out.

It was Ronald who broke the cardinal rule and asked, "How do you know all this, Percy?"

Percy sat on the edge of the table and shuffled. Cuthbert groaned.

"It was passed down through the male line of our family all the way back from Geoffrey Quiller himself."

Henry asked reasonably, "So your name's Quiller, then?"

"No" said Percy and continued. "Geoffrey had the contract to supply the Royal Court and the Inns of Court with quills. This contract was 'the big one' and he would have been made for life. He may even have supplied Shakespeare himself," he added, impressing everyone. "The one problem he had was that he didn't actually own any ducks or geese. So, he carried a sack and plucked one from any bird he passed on the way into London."

"He nicked them from anything with feathers, then?" asked Ronald.

Percy nodded.

Ronald snorted. "Nobody is that dumb," he said. "Who would buy a black quill?"

Percy tapped his nose. "That was the clever part. He even colour-coded them. The white ones were extra fine and expensive and the others were priced on a sliding scale so that everyone could afford them. He convinced undertakers that a black crow quill was far more appropriate than a merry white one, especially during the plague. He even sold sparrow feathers to school kids."

Ronald was impressed in spite of himself. "What happened next? He must have made a fortune."

Percy sagged. "It all went wrong just as he was getting established. Some chap followed him all the way into London, exposed him as a cheat and stole the whole bag of feathers. No-one trusted him after that."

Ronald sympathised and asked, "Did the chap who stole the feathers take his trade, then?"

Percy sagged even further and replied, "No, he sold the whole bag full and got the credit for inventing the pillow."

*

A weary band of men trudged back to Cuthbert's farmhouse that evening. They settled around the huge table and Elspeth fussed around them pouring tea.

When all the shuffling, creaking and coughing stopped, Henry asked the big question. "Do we know what the play is about, Geraldine?"

Geraldine pursed her lips and looked around the room. "Yes," she sneered, "apparently all the men are heroes and all the women are fainting ninnies."

"So?" asked Ronald, genuinely puzzled.

Geraldine registered the uncomprehending male faces around the table and sighed. "Elizabeth the First was not a fainting ninny," she shrieked, making the cups bounce as she thumped the table for emphasis. The men suddenly remembered where Geraldine had just escaped from and paid attention. Margery and Elspeth exchanged a look. Elspeth slid a black pill out of her apron pocket just to be on the safe side.

164

Geraldine paced up and down the room watching the faces of the men for any sign of rebellion or, in Cuthbert's case, any sign at all.

"You lot are really convinced that you are superior, aren't you?" She grasped the scroll as if it contained a lightning bolt. "Whoever wrote this tripe had Elizabeth standing on Drake's flagship with a heaving bosom and fluttering eyelashes, telling all those big strong men that she would have gone with them, but loud noises made her jump and confrontations made her cry."

"So?" asked Ronald again, quieter this time.

Cuthbert asked, "Wasn't she a redhead? I have an Aunt Liza who's a redhead." He shuddered.

Geraldine began to rant. "Elizabeth the First was the strongest woman in the land and the strongest ruler after her father Henry. She ran the country, fought off offers of marriage, resisted the church and all of this whilst surrounded by men. That's what I call multi-tasking."

"That's what I call propaganda," muttered Ronald.

Geraldine was incandescent. "Propaganda, propaganda. She didn't need propaganda. What use was propaganda? It's rubbish."

Percy straightened. "Just a minute, young woman," he said. They were in his territory now. "Where would my plants be without propaganda?"

Henry whispered, "That's propagating, Percy. Propaganda is where someone exaggerates or lies to make something look better."

"It certainly makes my plants look better," agreed Percy.

Cuthbert leaned forward. "Is that those little heated boxes?" he asked. "I had one for a gerbil once."

"Did it grow?" asked Percy. "Cos you need a special bulb, you know."

The Captain chimed in, "Not for propaganda, you don't. We used leaflets in my day."

Geraldine gawped as Cuthbert assured them that it could definitely make animals grow because when his gerbil died it was replaced by a rabbit.

Geraldine sauntered over to the women as the men leaned forward and the conversation became really confusing. Geraldine addressed the women. "This is how wars start- a bunch of men avoiding the truth. Why can't they be like us?"

Elspeth patted her on the arm and asked, "Nice cup of tea, dear?"

Geraldine turned to Margery and demanded, "Will you back me up. What are you thinking?"

Margery roused herself and said, "I was wondering whether the milkman will be a good kisser."

Geraldine used the shriek that always brought the pill trolley running and ran upstairs to seek the sanity that all the others pretended they had already got.

Cuthbert left the discussion and tapped on Geraldine's door. She was calm now. Finding a black pill in her bra had helped tremendously.

"Sorry about that," said Cuthbert. "They don't seem to like it when things get serious."

Geraldine sighed. "I only know serious, Cuthbert. I have always taken everything very earnestly. Anyway," she brightened, "I have a surprise for you."

Cuthbert tensed. He had often been promised a surprise, but as someone with no imagination, everything was a surprise anyway, so he was always disappointed.

Geraldine said, "Remember how you don't have a Shakespearean middle name like the real valley folk?"

Cuthbert nodded.

"And you don't like your name?"

Cuthbert nodded again.

Geraldine paused to build up the tension, but realised who she was dealing with and just came out with it. "The hero of the missing play is named Cuthbert. Instead of a middle name, your parents thought so much of you that they gave you the first name of the hero. It was all part of the family secret."

Wandering downstairs in a daze, Cuthbert met Percy sneaking back into the front door after he had forgotten where he lived. They said 'goodnight' and went off to dream separate dreams of heroism and desire, but now Cuthbert's dreams had a name.

The twins waited until the sounds abated in Cuthbert's farmhouse. It took a while because one set of noises was simply replaced by another. They passed the time firing wine bottle corks at each other in the tunnels. Then they sampled the plum brandy and really warmed up.

Climbing the cellar steps, one twin asked, "Which way did you say we had to go?"

"Right," said the other.

"Which way is that?" asked the first.

166

The other twin sighed. "Can't you remember that teacher banging on about 'Write with your right'?"

His brother replied, "Yes, but then she found out we were left-handed and said that we 'write with our wrong'."

The reply in the dark was, "Oh. We'd better split up then."

One twin headed for the warmth. The heating, cooking and hot water all came from the huge cast-iron range in the kitchen. It sat malevolently in its place and Cuthbert almost had to ask permission to approach it. The twin had no such reservations. He began opening doors and leaving them open. Smoke began to dribble from one of the doors and ash dripped menacingly to join the mysterious liquid oozing from underneath. Rumbling noises built up inside the labyrinth of chambers and the pressure gauge began to climb.

One door was known as the sausage crematorium because all it ever did was burn sausages. The next door was one Cuthbert never went near, but the twin did. As his brother grovelled under a cupboard amongst Percy's scrolls, a flame shot out and scorched his backside with pinpoint accuracy. Both twins yelped and ran for the cellar to escape.

Cuthbert awoke with a start. The house was vibrating. He dashed downstairs to find the cooking range dancing off its moorings. Smoke, flames, dust and ash flew in all directions. Silhouetted against this vision of hell was Percy, still in his nightgown and still wearing his hat, arms flying about as he closed doors and opened valves in an attempt to quiet this demonic Wurlitzer organ. Gradually, the smoke began to leave by the chimney and the doors were staying closed. The range was resuming its rhythmic chugging noise and Percy was wiping the sweat from his brow.

He turned to Cuthbert and grinned. "Did I tell you my granddad was head boiler man on the Titanic?"

Outside, one twin stood guard whilst the other one sat in the horse trough steaming.

Upstairs Geraldine dreamt on. When she came down in the morning and saw Cuthbert and Percy on their hands and knees cleaning, she shook her head and simply assumed that she was still dreaming.

Chapter 43

The shop bell rang. The twins entered and Martin took a tablet. The twins seemed subdued and Martin asked if they had the other scrolls.

"Difficult," said one twin.

"Painful," said the other one.

"Alarm system," said the first twin.

"Damned effective," said the second one rubbing his behind.

Martin panicked. "Don't say that," he said, looking around wildly.

"Why not?" asked the first twin.

"Mum lets us swear," said the other one.

"Not the swearing," insisted Martin, "the alarm."

The twins looked blank.

Martin explained, "Look lads, all antiques have changed hands that many times that no-one rightly knows what belongs to whom or where it really came from. So don't mention alarms, okay?"

The twins still looked blank.

Martin sighed. "Right," he began, "if you bring something from someone's garden, knock the soil off, all right?"

The twins nodded. One of them was still rubbing his backside and muttering about Cuthbert.

Martin interrupted him, "Cuthbert, from your valley?"

The twins nodded cautiously.

"Gormless chap, undertaker, buries people in the wall when he runs out of space?"

One of the twins was confused, but the other one nodded.

Martin lowered his voice and began to describe a carved coffer he would like to buy.

*

The cast began to assemble. The milk man turned up with his horse and cart. Elspeth seemed to spend an awfully long time buying milk from him, but there was a lot of tea to make.

Margery paced rehearsing her lines. She almost fainted when the milkman appeared and caught her in the full beam of his teeth.

Snatching a prop sword, he practised his swashbuckling on an innocent stage curtain, which promptly covered him in dust, and he retired to the wings coughing. Margery had seen his muscles ripple, though, and she thought, *I'm going to enjoy this.*

It was up to Cuthbert to announce the new play. It was also the opportunity to reveal the secret of the valley and ask everyone to co-operate. He walked to centre stage and wondered why everyone was looking at him. Then he remembered and dropped all his papers.

As Cuthbert scrabbled around on the floor, Geraldine strode forward and took over. In a stentorian voice, she began. "Ladies, and other valley bottom dwellers, we believe that we have discovered an unknown play by William Shakespeare."

Pausing for effect, she trod on Cuthbert's fingers before continuing. "There is evidence that he worked as a teacher at Mandrake Hall, long before someone burnt it down." She emphasised this by screwing her foot into Cuthbert's other hand. "We believe that he wrote this play and hid it in the valley due to the political climate and the fact that he was a man."

There was complete silence in the theatre; even the pigeons had moved up for each other and nodded silently. Cuthbert's finger bones re-arranged themselves around her spiked heel as she turned from one side to the other.

He managed to free himself and crawled painfully to where Percy sat in the wings. "Something going on between you and that Geraldine?" he asked Cuthbert.

Geraldine continued, "We will perform this play for the first time ever. There is no introduction as the first scroll seems to be missing. We will welcome anyone from the valley to either assist or add anything to our knowledge." She then turned and walked away.

"Exactly what I was going to say," said Cuthbert, sucking his fingers.

Percy looked at the blank sheets of paper scattered across the stage and said, "Yes, I can see that."

The theatre was humming with conversation. They could make sense of some of the pages, but no-one seemed to know the overall picture.

Ronald ended everyone's torment by asking, "What's it about?"

Silence returned and so did Geraldine. She had been dreading this. She began, "The author of this play, some man, expects us to believe

169

that the most famous and most powerful woman in English history …"
She caught the men shrugging and shaking their heads at each other.
"… Elizabeth the First," she shrieked.

The men muttered things like "Oh, her" and "right, carry on", but
the prize went to the Captain when he asked Henry, "Did she really
play for England?"

Geraldine turned away and fumbled in her bra, hoping to find
another stray pill, but she was out of luck. She turned back and, taking
a deep breath, said, "He expects us to believe that Elizabeth was so
upset by the threats of the nasty Spanish and French that she panicked
and rode all the way to Plymouth harbour so that her fleet could save
her from all the brutes who were shouting at her. When she arrived,
Captain Frobisher had left for a sailing holiday and Captain Drake was
off playing bowls somewhere. The only person left was a chap called
Cuthbert." Muttering under her breath she added, "They probably took
the keys out of the ignition when they left him in charge."

Her audience was riveted and the real valley folk were nodding
approvingly towards Cuthbert.

Geraldine ploughed on. "This Cuthbert was dispatched to all the
inns and ale houses to recruit enough seamen to man the fleet and repel
the invaders. He then set sail with the dregs of England, survived a
mighty storm, thrashed the Armada and refused the Queen's hand in
marriage for the good of the country."

The crowd gave a collective "Ooooh" and applauded Cuthbert, who
blushed for the sake of the country.

Geraldine exploded with rage. "This is rubbish," she screamed, "this
is an adolescent fantasy written by an imbecile. If Shakespeare wrote
this, there's no wonder they locked it away." Geraldine stood, shaking
from exertion and pill deprivation.

The crowd gasped and looked around for Elspeth. They had worked
up quite a thirst.

Geraldine had stopped speaking and was regaining her breath. She
was surprised when the crowd let out another "Oooohh" followed by
an "Aaaaghh" and then realised that they were looking behind her.

"He's behind you," shouted one of the twins.

"No, he's not," she snapped automatically.

"Oh, yes he is," shouted the other twin.

Geraldine turned. A 'Restraining Technician' from the asylum crept
towards her with a very unfashionable buckled jacket in his hands.

170

Behind him was his back-up with a dart gun. Geraldine jumped for the stage curtain and pulled it down in a cloud of dust over her attackers. Then she leapt from the stage, wrenched the tractor seat aside, caught the badger safely and disappeared into the tunnels. The tractor seat thumped back down and she was gone.

The stage curtains rippled like a pantomime camel, not sure whether to have one lump or two, as the men strove to escape. Having people standing all the way around the edges didn't help either.

Ronald suddenly asked loudly, "So, it's Cuthbert and the Spanish Armada, then?" He was pleased to be the first with a suggestion.

"Cuthbert rides again," shouted one twin.

"Cuthbert goes to town," shouted the other twin.

"Cuthbert all at sea," suggested the Captain ungraciously.

"Crafty Cuthbert dashes Spanish hopes on rocks of despair," suggested Henry, allowing his inner journalist to escape for a moment.

It was Margery who surprised them all when she stated, "No, gentlemen, there is only one title for this play. Think of Shakespeare's Hamlet, Shakespeare's Romeo and Juliet ... what is wrong with, 'Shakespeare's Cuthbert'?"

Spontaneous applause broke out around the theatre and everyone gathered around Cuthbert to clink teacups. This allowed the men from the asylum to escape because no one was standing on the edges now. They slunk away leaving a cute buckled jacket somewhere under the curtain. The cast also toasted Geraldine's escape. She may be a nut, but she was their nut. Anyway, by valley standards, she wasn't that bad at all.

Percy waited for everything to quiet before he asked the theatre at large, "If Queen Elizabeth was such a ninny, did she invent femmy-ninny-ism?"

The cast groaned and all began to clear things away. Tomorrow was a very big day. The costumes would appear. Everyone was here. Until yesterday, no-one had even known which period the play would be set in. Of course, being Shakespeare narrowed it down a bit.

Cuthbert had never had such co-operation. It was as if the valley had been holding its breath for generations trying to keep the secret.

Actually, thought Cuthbert, it would explain some of the strange facial colourings around here. The local joiner had relented and he was making a life-size galleon with a figure-head and masts with real sails.

The blacksmith was fitting the Captain's cannon and making some fakes to fit along the deck. Everyone had relaxed now that the twins had fired the only cannon ball and used up all the black powder.

They wouldn't have been so smug if they had spotted them emptying a load of fireworks into a bag, and they still had the stone ball from the gate-post at the old Hall.

The race was on for the best gear, but over the years Cuthbert had amassed quite a collection, and trunks full of stuff were dragged onto the stage. Ronald grabbed the biggest cod-piece and let the twins push the rest up their jumpers as fake boobs.

Percy discovered a wonderful doublet, but put it back when he thought that the sleeves were ripped. Henry grabbed it and held onto it in awe. It fitted him perfectly.

Percy sneered until Henry explained the fashion for 'slashed sleeves' that showed the silk lining underneath. A peeved Percy stuck a feather in his own cap and declared himself ready.

Margery was in her element. She swished around in her full length frocks and sampled every wig she could get hold of. Both she and Belinda showed off the low neck-lines to perfection. Margery even found herself distracted away from the milkman. That Henry certainly looked fetching and he seemed rather taken with her.

The doublet and hose bit seemed to be causing some problems as the men struggled into their tights. Backstage was full of hopping, swearing males standing bow-legged as the crotch stubbornly stayed at knee level.

Margery walked past causing a rash of defensive hand movements and blushes, and said sweetly, "Welcome to my world, boys."

The twins had returned the treasure hoard after the posh bloke suggested that they could be the Gunners. They nudged each other happily. Cuthbert was delighted. He looked around at all the activity and enthusiasm and beamed. This was no longer a local project, this was theatre.

The cast trudged home weary but happy. Couples walked arm in arm, positioned so that the man's sword-hand was free, and recited lines to each other in the dark. Most of the women wore their costumes home on the flimsy excuse that 'things needed taking up'.

Cuthbert smiled when he entered the farmhouse and the kettle was warm. The desk was open and the scrolls were still being translated. He left some more paper out for Geraldine and reminded Percy not to block the hole in the cellar.

The lights went out at last and the twins moved into position. They each had a stuffed duck strapped to their heads so that they could pop up over the wall and alert each other with the appropriate duck call. The ducks appeared to glide along the wall towards the barn.

The crow was asleep in the guttering. The contours fitted his barrel-shape perfectly and he dozed. Now, the wrong type of bird-call at the wrong time of night wouldn't mean much at all to most people, but to a bird it meant an awful lot. The crow snapped awake and watched the two ducks slide along the top of the wall.

He had heard about these birds that stayed up all night and liked to be out on the tiles. He always missed out because his nights were spent on the thatch. Hopping along the gutter, he followed the ducks to the theatre.

Maybe they were stage-struck? He'd heard about those birds too. He stopped and watched in amazement as the two ducks both rose vertically and levitated across the yard whilst uttering the cry of the sea-eagle. "Squawk," cried the crow, "unidentified flying objects."

Then, he fainted.

Percy opened the window for some fresh air just as the crow's claws caught on the guttering and he received a beak straight between the eyes. Percy stared at the upside down bird and then focused on the two ducks running across the farmyard with a box between them.

"Body snatchers," screamed Percy. The crow opened its eyes, saw Percy at close range and let go of the guttering to stick beak first into a sawn tree trunk below where he quivered gently to and fro.

Cuthbert awoke immediately. He rolled off the bed and came up with the Blunderbuss in his hands. Dashing down the stairs, he was in time to see Percy charging ahead, nightshirt flapping, hat on his head and a large pitchfork in his hands. Cuthbert felt the draught blow up his own nightshirt and galloped after Percy.

Cuthbert shouted, "Where did they go?"

Percy gasped, "Towards the road." He was having trouble with the long handle on the pitchfork and had to hold it horizontally as they leapt over moonlit ground and dark shadows.

Suddenly, Percy reached the farm gate. The handles hit both stone posts at the same time, bringing him to a shuddering halt. Cuthbert cannoned into the back of him and the Blunderbuss lit the night.

There was a yelp, followed by a thud. "I think you got them," yelled Percy triumphantly. They moved forward slowly. They seemed to be following a trail of potatoes.

"Who do you think they were?" asked Cuthbert.

"Two ducks," said Percy, peering ahead as he walked.

Cuthbert stopped. "I beg your pardon?"

Percy replied irritably, "As I said, two ducks."

Cuthbert took a moment before asking, "So two members of the French aristocracy came into my farmyard in the middle of the night, dug up a coffin and simply ran away with it?" He stopped and gave Percy a very puzzled look.

Percy halted, matched him puzzled look for puzzled look, and replied, "Pardon?"

Cuthbert tried again. "Two French nobles, let's say for arguments sake, the Duc de Orleans and the Duc de Rouen, came into my farmyard in the middle of the night, dug up a coffin and simply ran away with it?"

"Don't be silly," said Percy.

Cuthbert tried to recover some logic from the rock-spoil of Percy's conversation. "So, in actual fact, two ducks came into my farmyard in the middle of the night, dug up a coffin and simply ran away with it?"

"Yes," said Percy.

Cuthbert slapped his own forehead dramatically and said, "Of course, silly me. One of them must have been a Drake auditioning for the part of the Captain."

"Now you're being silly again," said Percy sulkily.

Cuthbert felt as though he were spitting feathers as he berated Percy all the way down the farm track and then they stopped.

The trail of potatoes had come to an end. There on the ground was the old carved box from the barn and at one end of it was a scattered pile of feathers.

"Who feels silly now?" asked Percy.

Smugness radiated from Percy. He carried his end of the coffer back to the barn and helped to lower it gently back into place without saying a word. He even went back and helped to pick up the potatoes without uttering a sound. Cuthbert had never known him to be so irritating.

*

174

A low hum had filled the valley all night. Old treadle sewing machines had been dragged out and thrashed into action. Every home helped to alter and prepare the costumes ready for the performance.

Even old Mrs Figgis, who was a slave to her arthritis, had a go. She could push the treadle down with one foot, but couldn't fetch it back up again ready for the next stroke.

By pushing her fat sleeping cat underneath, she found that the treadle bounced back nicely and between them they hummed and snored away merrily for the rest of the night.

The cat didn't mind because it saved it breathing under its own steam.

Chapter 44

The valley was gradually coming under the spell of the play.

Cuthbert went off to the Post Office for more paper and spotted Henry, in costume, bowing to Margery, also in costume. He produced a wonderful flourish and Margery coloured demurely.

The twins had become 'Young knaves' and the Mandrake Arms apparently accepted doubloons. The valley Mafia were bowling barrel hoops down the street with a stick and Ronald held his cape across his face like a sherry advert.

Just in case the diet changed as well, the geese were splashing mud onto each other as a disguise, and the swans took it on the wing into the next valley. The place was like a film set.

The contagion had spread everywhere. When they all gathered at the farm later, Geraldine decided to drill them in the finer points of archery. She refused to have 'stout English yeomen' on the stage that couldn't pull a bow without shooting the audience. As she was in hiding, all the instructions had to be shouted through an upstairs window.

Now, as any drill instructor knows, it is impossible to form people into a straight line if you can't see them. Added to that, some people will not know right from left, some will be deaf and in denial, and there is always one whose reactions are a heart-beat behind the others. But in their theatre costumes, at least they looked the part.

All the ingredients were there to make a complete pudding of the whole exercise. So, when Geraldine shouted, "Form a straight line, face left and aim high and fire," Geraldine had no idea where this rabble was actually aiming.

The result was that when the bus company sent the bus on its annual run to keep the route open, it came back looking like the Deadwood Stage out of Apache Springs. The fact that the driver's name was John Wayne from the next valley, meant that this was only discussed in the depot in secret.

In fact it replaced the annual discussion about which of the villages celebrated some ancient rite by smothering the front of the bus in sheepskin rugs.

Cuthbert returned to the farm in time to witness the aftermath of this first volley. People were hopping on one foot because the one in front had stepped back to watch the arrows flight and trodden on the chap behind.

Most were rubbing an arm vigorously because the bow-string had removed a veneer of skin from their forearm, and Percy was acting very strangely, even for him.

Cuthbert panicked when Geraldine shouted down and asked if anyone had 'Hit the bull?' but then he remembered that he didn't own one since his had left with a bucket on its foot.

He beckoned Percy over, but found that he was reluctant to leave the thatch overhang. When Cuthbert insisted, Percy jinked across the open ground with one eye on the sky. When he arrived at Cuthbert's side, he was holding a dustbin lid over his head. ,

"What on earth are you doing?" asked Cuthbert.

Percy spluttered, "That bow was so big that I could only fire it straight up. I haven't seen the arrow since."

Cuthbert looked up. Only Percy could make a beautiful blue sky into something dangerous. A whistling sound seemed to get louder and a small black dot was getting bigger.

"Run for cover," yelled Cuthbert. Everyone panicked and set off in a different direction to everyone else.

Ronald was proud of his natural survival instincts. They had kept him safe in deserts and jungles. He had also survived Cuthbert.

He headed for the barn as the whistling increased, but he was suddenly gripped by the throat, dragged backwards rapidly and jerked off his feet. *This is it*, he thought. *Cuthbert must have sneaked up behind me and got me in the Peruvian choke-hold. I am doomed.*

Suddenly assailed by a terrible smell, he passed out.

Cuthbert and Percy had a grandstand view of the event. As Ronald ran for the barn, his cloak had billowed out behind him. The arrow pinned it to the milkman's cart and the horse bolted dragging Ronald through the manure heap because the horse didn't like loud whistles.

"Phew," said Percy in relief, "no humans were hurt in the making of this scene." He and Cuthbert grinned at each other.

In the background, Geraldine could be heard shouting, "Do we have the arrows back, people?"

The Captain snorted, "Nobody mentioned bringing the blasted things back." The cast began to drift away from the sound of

Geraldine's voice as she called, ever more plaintively, "Arrows, people?" and finally, "People?"

Of course, Percy knew exactly where his arrow was and moved over to where the milk-cart had come to rest.

Just as he stood on Ronald and tugged at the shaft, Cuthbert called. "That's smart, Percy."

Percy agreed. "Yep. I'm the only one to bring his arrow back."

Cuthbert shrugged and added, "It will certainly save Ronald some enquiries, mate."

Percy wiped his feet on Ronald's cloak and walked away whistling.

Chapter 45

This was a new one on Cuthbert. He had a stage full of actors and they weren't making a sound. They were queuing up to stare at themselves in the only full length mirror left intact. Cuthbert had broken all the others over the years, but his luck had never changed. It was assumed that he had some special dispensation.

Henry was stunned by the way Margery looked in her regal gown, but that damned milkman kept getting her to practise swooning into his arms and Henry could not get near her.

The Captain was puzzled by his tights. The knees were at the back giving the impression that he was running away from himself.

Elspeth had been given a maid's mob-cap, but it kept slipping down and she looked like a toadstool. The valley seamstresses had done them proud and everyone strutted about in character.

Percy's costume still consisted of a feather in his cap, so he didn't join the queue at the mirror. He leant against the wonderful ship's figurehead and watched the others. The carpenter had done a magnificent job.

He had carved a hollow busty woman draped in a Roman toga and holding a trident before her with golden curls trailing behind. She looked quite capable of ploughing through the high seas and raiding the Spanish Main. Percy was staring intently at it, not because he appreciated the carving particularly, but because it had spoken to him.

He sidled up to the figure as if admiring it and whispered, "Can you hear me?"

"Of course I can hear you," snapped the figurehead. "Be casual. Don't draw attention to me."

Percy took off his cap and twisted it nervously.

"Is anyone about?" asked the wooden goddess.

"Well, it's mostly me. The rest are over there," he said, nodding towards the mirror.

"I can't see them, you fool," snapped the figure again. "I have to sense things."

Percy gaped. He understood now, having heard of this. It was called the Oracle. All he had to do was ask the right questions and the riches of the world would be his. Then he remembered the Oracle always

179

spoke in riddles and only a wise man could interpret them. *She has come to the right man this time,* thought Percy.

The Oracle spoke. "Are there strangers about?"

Percy replied in kind. "Strangers in the night or stranger than fiction?"

After a short silence, the figure asked, "A stranger in the barn?"

"… is worth two in the bush," replied Percy promptly.

Silence reigned for a moment. Percy always carried a small notebook for moments like this and he was making notes. He had been writing in it for years and when he finished a page he would turn it around and write in the opposite direction, and then again when that page was done. If he ever coloured in the gaps he would have a marvellous mosaic of Jupiter killing a bull.

The figurehead spoke again. "Are you being cautious?"

"As a snake in the grass," said Percy.

"Is there anything to fear?" asked the Oracle.

"Only fear itself," said Percy quickly.

"Are you taking the mick?" asked the figurehead.

"Only if the mick is prepared to be taken," said Percy, still scribbling.

"IS THAT YOU, PERCY?" screamed the figurehead.

"Geraldine?" asked Percy as he stopped writing.

After much banging and thumping and scuffling, Geraldine backed out of the hollow figurehead and peered over the ship's rail. "You blithering idiot," she snapped, "I am hiding in here to make sure that Cuthbert doesn't take any liberties with Elizabeth the First."

Percy was indignant, Percy was insulted, but most of all Percy was baffled. He couldn't imagine Cuthbert taking liberties with a sheep, let alone a virgin Queen.

Geraldine stormed off to find another hiding place. Percy hung around to ask about the three-thirty at Chepstow, just in case, but eventually he wandered off as well.

180

Chapter 46

The stage looked amazing. The colourful cast milled about like a medieval market scene and Cuthbert spotted some of the 'real valley folk' lurking in the shadows at the back. *It is working,* he thought. *Everyone is coming together on behalf of the Bard.*

A strange, manure-like smell wafted around Cuthbert and he sniffed curiously. He hadn't smelled that since they used real goats for the nativity scene last year.

Behind him, Ronald stood glaring at him. His fists were clenching and unclenching as he ran through various attack strategies, but in the end his injuries were hurting and he stank, so he went for a bath.

A sudden scream shocked everyone and both Henry and the milkman struck heroic poses near to a stricken Margery. She was pointing wordlessly to the pile of jewellery in the treasure chest. It was moving.

Geraldine stood up cursing amidst an eruption of glitter and fake pearls, and stomped off to find another hiding place.

Margery swooned, but Henry and the milkman were busy squabbling and they both missed her. The Captain had been put in charge of the mechanical side- it was his job to open the curtains, direct the lights and operate the wind machine. He even had to move the ship ready for the interior scenes.

The Captain had proven to be a wizard with pulleys and ropes. His wife, Elspeth, recognised some of the knots and giggled. When the Captain was finished, he could operate everything from one central point just by pulling a different rope.

The play was bringing out the best in everybody, except for Ronald. He sat in the bath trying to lie on something that didn't bear an injury and seethed quietly.

No-one else had as many injuries as him. No-one else seemed bothered about getting even with Cuthbert, except him. In fact, everyone else had a better part than him too. Crow's nest indeed. If he was stuck up there, he would have some sharp objects with him. He smirked at the thought.

Margery had recovered very prettily, everyone thought- just two slight staggers, enough to give each of her suitors a chance to catch her properly. It was all beyond the twins- this was the woman who kept piles of old copper pennies by her chair and could hit anywhere on the ground floor with pinpoint accuracy and the speed of a hummingbird's wing. Yet here she was going all girly and getting the vapours. They hadn't been back to the antique shop yet- failure had a strange taste and they were avoiding it.

Margery was having a ball. The only fly in the ointment was *that* Geraldine- she could lurk better than any woman had a right to. Cuthbert still hadn't announced who had the leading role publicly and the haystack hadn't been slept in for a while. There were two cats after this cream.

Elspeth was angling for the refreshments concession. Her tea was tried and trusted. Some awkward newcomers asked for coffee, but a cup of tea with a dash of brown sauce seemed to do the trick. She wasn't bothered about this acting lark. She was a people-person. It was a vocation. People had no idea what they wanted until someone told them.

Did a car salesman ask a customer what he wanted? Good heavens no. He looked the customer up and down and told them which car would suit them perfectly. By sheer coincidence, this was the same car that had a gear box full of saw-dust, and the engine sounded like a skeleton scratching. Elspeth was the catering equivalent.

The customer was always right, but if the choice was limited, it narrowed it all down rather nicely. She dusted her counter and sighed. So many of the old arts were being lost. Take dusting for instance; it wasn't enough to wipe a surface with a rag. Goodness me, no, the trick was in the wrist.

Dust motes would take advantage of up-draughts and thermal currents. As her husband had taught her, 'know your enemy'. The little blighters had to be panicked into the air like grouse, and then wrapped by a curving sweep of the duster.

On the downward stroke, the motes would be dropped into a bucket filled with precisely one inch of soapy water. Empty the bucket over next door's fence and the job was done. *Simple when you knew how,* she thought, casually wiping the figurehead's nose as she passed by.

Henry was surprising himself. He was really drawn to Margery. Even the twins seemed to be calming down a bit. He had spent years travelling the globe reporting on other people's problems.

Somehow, they were always solved by people shooting each other or even themselves. After a while, one conflict looked very much like another and the faces of the leaders blurred into a collage of all the others. He could write his memoirs.

That war where those very angry chaps in the desert were fighting those other angry chaps had been an interesting one ... come to think of it, the way he had covered most of the conflicts, perhaps a Hotel guide would be quicker. He had no idea how to be a father, but how hard could it be?

Wave them off to boarding school and send them skiing in the holidays. That seemed to pretty much cover it. He sneaked another admiring glance at Margery and spotted the milkman doing the same.

Henry sighed. There was his brother Ronald to consider. Henry had been saddled with him his whole life. On his first week at school he had chained all the teachers' bikes together. The second week had found the bomb squad making the school gates safe again.

The third week had seen them both thrown out. Ronald had entered all the teachers' names as volunteers in the Assassins' Monthly and no-one could concentrate owing to all these little men dressed in black jumping out of cupboards.

Ronald joined the army to kill people, but left because they were holding him back. Then he had entered the world of the holiday 'rep'- never in the same place twice and most of the deaths were blamed on the food.

Ronald had become some sort of mercenary and disappeared for long periods, but he always popped up again when he needed to lie low. It had to be admitted, though, that Henry owed him some of his best scoops, especially assassinations when Ronald always had inside information and usually a smoking gun. Perhaps it was time to cut more than the umbilical cord this time.

Geraldine peered out from amongst the spare clothing like a crocodile in a pond full of algae.

Cuthbert could not be trusted with representing Elizabeth of England. The great woman must be protected.

Cuthbert might be in trouble, though. Geraldine had a mission.

The cast were keen, but factions were forming. Margery hated Geraldine and Geraldine hated Cuthbert. Henry loved Margery and hated Ronald. Ronald hated Cuthbert and Cuthbert hated spinach.

Tensions were building. Eyes were becoming furtive.

Chapter 47

Percy slipped out of the back door and went to check on his garden. He had once left the gas on and now he always checked for leeks. Then he popped back in to see if the Oracle did requests.

It was the day of the full dress rehearsal. Lamps had burned late in the valley and shadows could be seen at most windows as the occupants paced inside, reciting lines.

Everyone had a script and almost anyone could step in and replace anyone else. This put the leading players under pressure in case they were substituted because they "Simply don't look the part, my dear." The women were quite catty too.

Owing to the missing scroll, Cuthbert had been tasked to write the opening scene. He envisaged the curtains swishing open and a cannon being fired to warn England of the approach of the Spanish Armada. Messengers would be sent to the Queen.

The curtains duly opened and, with thoughts for everyone's health and safety, the twins were only allowed to shout 'Booom'.

The gaily dressed crowd appeared flustered and pointed out to sea dramatically- a perfect representation of 'panic in pantaloons'.

The nearest the scene painter had been to the sea was a trip to the Isle of Bute, so the crowd were actually pointing to an island off Portsmouth with a stag on it.

Henry stood in the wings clapping coconut shells together as Percy leapt onto a vaulting horse carried by two men hidden by cardboard hedgerows as he was despatched to London to warn the Queen.

The curtains closed. The cast scuffled into new positions and the curtains whisked open. The throne room was lined by panelling taken from the Old Hall, and in pride of place on the throne sat Elizabeth the First surrounded by her courtiers.

Margery was resplendent in silks and frills and personified power and authority. She would run England the way she ran the valley Mafia. Her make-up began to run under the hot lights and a hand-maiden stepped forward to powder the royal brow. The maid was slightly heavy handed and the Queen disappeared in a cloud of talcum.

Percy giggled, but a pile of clothing behind him growled and he stopped it at once.

The scene changed again and they were back at the port. The Queen simpered as the galleon slid across the stage with the milkman posed heroically on the bow with his foot on the hand rail. "My hero has come to save us," lisped Margery, wringing her hands.

Geraldine exploded from under the pile of clothing, "No, no- a thousand times, no," she shrieked.

"Anything wrong?" asked Cuthbert innocently.

"No, Cuthbert, not *anything*. Everything," she spluttered to herself as everyone backed away. "A ship cannot just glide into port with a shop window dummy on the front."

"'Ere," said the joiner, "that's some of my finest work."

"Not the figurehead, you numbskull, the other dummy- the one with the teeth," she snapped before asking, "And where did the lisp come from?"

The 'other dummy' meanwhile was sailing merrily on his way across the stage until he disappeared stage left with a thump.

Geraldine was still ranting at Cuthbert. "There would be men swarming up the rigging, furling the sails. It's all to do with the wind."

"Don't mention wind to me ..." began Percy before Geraldine spitted him with a laser stare.

"The Queen wouldn't be simpering 'My hero', either," she spat. "She hasn't even met him yet. She doesn't know who he is." Behind her, the half-ship was being winched back into place with the milkman still posing because no one had told him to stop.

Cuthbert formed a scrum with the nearest male members of the cast and they muttered to themselves. Certain phrases escaped the huddle, like, "Afraid of her" and "Not me, mate."

The group broke up and Cuthbert walked over to Geraldine. As he came closer, he glanced over her shoulder and allowed his eyes to widen. "Love all the buckles, mate."

Geraldine's nostrils flared. She jumped up, grabbed a rope and swarmed up it to disappear amongst the pulleys, sandbags and gantries.

"Thank the Lord for that," said someone.

"I heard that, Percy," yelled Geraldine from above. Percy gulped.

The rest of the rehearsal wasn't perfect, but a lack of knowledge definitely made things easier.

Chapter 48

During a break when Elspeth took over his flock, Cuthbert could hear a rhythmic thudding from under the stage.

Climbing down a ladder, he saw Ronald alone in the gloom. He was throwing knives into a tall wooden board. That was the noise Cuthbert had heard. Cuthbert approached and watched as Ronald threw a knife into the board and then walked up to retrieve it.

"What are you doing?" asked Cuthbert.

"Practising," [thud] replied Ronald.

"Practising what?" asked Cuthbert [thud].

"Killing with a knife," [thud] said Ronald.

Cuthbert leafed through the script and said, "I don't remember your character throwing a knife." [thud]

"Who said I was in character?" [thud] asked Ronald.

*

It was generally agreed to keep the language simple and relatively modern. 'Forsooths' only made Belinda giggle.

After the rehearsal, Cuthbert had a surprise for the cast. He had contacted a theatrical costumier and a long wooden box had been delivered.

As everyone gathered around, Cuthbert held out an extended wooden rod at a certain height. "All those who can walk under this rod will stand over there, please," he announced.

Percy, the twins and Ronald all passed beneath it and Cuthbert didn't bother with anyone else. "Right," he said and lifted the lid. As the others surged forward to choose a sword, Cuthbert held the 'small' group back with the stick and the words, "Sorry, chaps. It's the law." He had cleverly separated anyone who might be a danger to anyone else and he was rather proud of himself.

"He made that up," snarled Ronald, fingering the knife in the top of his boot.

"Did he?" asked Percy.

"Course he did," said one of the twins. "Section seven of the act relating to knives and ceremonial swords states that 'Wheresoever the

186

previously mentioned borrower of the aforementioned cutlery shall be a person of reduced height, he shall not be refused ownership as it will affect his well-being'."

Percy was fired up. He stormed over to Cuthbert and snapped, "According to the sectional fencing act regarding long pointy things, I am entitled to own one because it affects my wellies. So there," and he grabbed a sword.

Cuthbert tried to intervene, but Percy stepped back and, jamming the sword point down into the stage, leaned upon it nonchalantly.

The sword and Percy slowly folded as the rubber collapsed and Percy fell flat on his face.

"Nice one, kids," said Ronald, exchanging a high-five with the smirking twins.

The evening ended with a sherry party. The Captain rigged up a pulley system and a glass wobbled its way up to Geraldine.

Everyone was in a good mood and the table of grievances had changed slightly. Ronald hated Cuthbert. Margery was wary of Geraldine. Percy hated Ronald, the twins, and Cuthbert. Cuthbert still hated spinach.

Perhaps if Cuthbert ate his spinach, equilibrium could be restored to the valley instead of it being a conspiracy known as 'the vegetable plot'.

When everyone else went home and Geraldine had skulked through the tunnels and gone to bed, Cuthbert found himself in the kitchen with Percy.

Cuthbert asked, "Are you still sulking?"

Percy snapped, "No, I'm ..."

Cuthbert broke in with, "I know you're temporarily emotionally detached, or something else entirely."

Percy glared- he was far beyond that stage and well into 'Entrenched bunker mentality' now.

Cuthbert held up his hands and said, "I didn't plan it at all, but I'm sorry if it became a cheap laugh."

Percy smiled slightly. "I suppose it was a bit funny," he allowed.

Cuthbert replied, "Oh yes, it really, really was."

"But not from where I was standing," snarled Percy.

Cuthbert sighed and started all over again.

Percy's friendship really was hard work.

During negotiations about Percy's sanity, Cuthbert had a thought. He remembered Percy's expertise with the cooking range and tried, "You know, Percy, I have a little secret I wouldn't show to anyone else. You might be the only man who would appreciate it."

Percy took the bait, muttering, "Well I wouldn't see anyone struggle, you know."

He followed Cuthbert out to one of the outbuildings. After fighting with a huge door and an antique latch, Cuthbert held the lantern up in the air.

Percy gasped. "What is it?" he asked in amazement.

Cuthbert said, "It's a tractor."

Percy circled the beast. "No, it isn't," he breathed. "This is what it would be before the bits were added to make it a tractor. This is the original prototype." He turned to Cuthbert, eyes flashing in the lamplight. "Does it work?"

Cuthbert stammered, "Of course it ... well, it should ... I've no idea."

Percy snatched the lamp, and grabbed an old piston-operated oil can from a shelf and produced an oily rag from somewhere about his person. Wiping a smear of grease across his forehead, he anointed himself 'Engineer' and dived into the middle of the machine. Cuthbert smiled and left him to it.

Chapter 49

The next morning Cuthbert took a cup of tea out to Percy. A greasy hand appeared and took the cup, and a disembodied voice asked, "Have you ever driven this?"

Cuthbert admitted that he had, but it was very unpredictable. He was okay whilst the wheels were trapped in the farm track ruts, but as soon as he had to steer, he was hopeless. "That's why I use a horse for ploughing," he admitted.

Percy's voice was muffled, "Which, the one that only goes in circles?"

Cuthbert was appalled. "Nobody knows about that," he yelled.

"I do," said Percy triumphantly.

Cuthbert stamped off to emotionally detach himself.

*

Later in the afternoon Cuthbert opened the front door to take another cup of tea to Percy. It was foggy. 'Thick as a bag', as the valley folk would say. Cuthbert was 'country' born and bred, but he hadn't seen any of the natural signs recognised by farmers everywhere.

His neighbour always said, "If you can't see the awning, it's foggy this morning." It was infallible too.

Cuthbert went to check the back door to stop large hairy animals wandering in to escape the fog. The sun was shining at the back. Cuthbert raced through the house to see if the whole weather system was trying to trick him.

Fog-sun-fog-sun. Soon even Cuthbert was sick of this juvenile game and he stopped. Then he noticed that the house was vibrating. Leaving the house by the back door, he discovered that the fog was in fact smoke and the outbuilding was vibrating even more than the house. Clouds of smoke had billowed out and congregated on the valley floor. There was no sign of the village.

Cuthbert stood outside the gaping doors and shouted, "Percy!"

Percy's reply was lost as he let out the clutch. The tractor made a break for the daylight and punched a hole in the smoke. Cuthbert flattened himself against the door as it went past.

Percy bobbed from side to side as the tractor went against the grain of ruts and pot-holes. His hat bounced jauntily and he wore a beatific smile.

Percy stopped the tractor outside the farmhouse and switched it off. The sudden silence caused more panic amongst the animals than the noise had. The machine produced a series of ticking sounds as the engine cooled down and Percy slid a pair of aviator's goggles up onto his head, leaving white rings around his eyes.

He had an affinity for machines that he didn't have for people. People simply didn't respond to a squirt of oil and a bit of tweaking.

Cuthbert eyed the machine warily. Percy had fitted a curved metal grill onto the back either as an extra seat or a luggage carrier. He sat grinning on the high seat.

Cuthbert asked, "Is that my cattle feeder welded onto the back?"

Percy nodded.

Cuthbert sighed. "Elspeth needs supplies for the performance. Do you fancy a trip to the hypermarket in the next valley?"

"What's a hypermarket?" asked Percy, intrigued.

Cuthbert shrugged. "It's like the Post Office, except they have two different types of crisps and they don't sell stamps."

"Okay," said Percy. "Hop on."

Cuthbert had no choice because at that moment Percy switched the tractor back on and the world became a place where sight was vital because hearing was rendered useless.

They went off down the track, bobbing about like something from Noddy's Big Adventure. Anyone seeing them from behind could have set it to music. In fact, many people could see them from behind because no one could get past and the traffic tailed back for miles.

When Percy pulled off into the hypermarket car park, all the drivers were waving their fists at them. Percy waved back happily and switched the tractor off. "Ahh, the camaraderie of the open road," he said.

Cuthbert said nothing. He had been trying to resist the vibration forcing him through the metal grill like a potato chipper and his arms ached. The tractor engine gave a last shudder like a wet dog, and Percy waved back at the tail end of their reluctant convoy. "Always a welcome in the valley," he said brightly.

For someone who had just wrestled four tons of machinery across rough terrain, Percy was hopeless at steering a wire trolley.

At first Cuthbert stayed with him, muttering a stream of apologies, but eventually he moved ahead and tutted and rolled his eyes along with the rest of the shoppers.

Percy couldn't grasp the fact that if he was staring at the shelves, then he had nothing left to look in front with. It was everybody else's responsibility to avoid him.

Cuthbert noticed that whenever he put something in his trolley, Percy moved up and put two of them in his. When they met up at the check-out, Percy said smugly, "I've got more than you."

Cuthbert nodded and replied, "You probably brought more money than me." Percy went quiet. When Cuthbert looked around, Percy's trolley had gone and he was eating an apple.

"All junk food in here," he said.

Cuthbert paid for his purchases and the girl turned to Percy. "That's ten pence, please, sir."

"Fott for?" asked Percy through hamster cheeks.

"The apple, sir," explained the girl patiently.

Percy pretended to tie his shoe lace and came up with normal cheeks.

The girl sighed and pulled a microphone towards her. "Cleaner to check-out four, please. Cleaner to check-out four."

Cuthbert took his place behind Percy and the delicate dance began, "Key, pedal, clutch, curse," until the engine started and they roared away bringing most of the traffic system to a complete standstill.

When they arrived home, Cuthbert was part way to solving the riddle of supermarket trolleys in lakes. Percy had tied the whole thing onto the back with baling twine and the store name was emblazoned all over it.

The joiner had made a market stall for Elspeth. It had a red and white striped awning and had shiny tea-urns standing at each end. Bottles of brown sauce stood suspiciously close to the urns.

There was even a machine for cooking sausages. The sight of all those glistening Frankfurters rolling and steaming made many a man cross his legs and hurry away.

Once again Cuthbert noted the similarity to a medieval market- it was springing up around the theatre in time for the performance. This was authenticity.

The squeal of children drew Cuthbert around the next corner and the astonishment stopped him in his tracks. Percy and the joiner had made a magnificent roundabout powered by a huge leather strap on the tractor's back wheel. The two men stood together surveying their handiwork as the children flashed past changing colour rapidly.

"Too fast, do you think?" asked the joiner.

Percy nodded absently. He was quite happy with the speed as long as the twins were on it.

The performance was today. The costumes were done. The rehearsals were complete. The people were coming. They were ready for the world even if the world wasn't ready for them.

The cast backstage were deep inside their own thoughts; some of them weren't happy with the things they found there either.

The joiner had accidentally caused a problem. He had taken it upon himself to add more seating and had constructed tiers around the walls so that wherever the actors looked, they saw the audience. This had caused a panic because the main refuge for amateur dramatics was to concentrate on a spot on the wall and pretend you were at home. What happened when there were no walls left to put spots on?

The smell of sausages crept in and upset everyone because no-one had dared to eat before the performance. Someone seemed to be practising scales, which was odd because there were no singing parts. Actually, the joiner had nailed Ronald's feet to the stage and they were pulling him free with a rope and pulley.

The ladies' dressing room was filled with the sibilant swish of silk, wafts of competing perfumes and high pitched insincere compliments that define women's dressing rooms everywhere.

The men's dressing room smelled like any man's dressing room anywhere in the world after a rugby final. It may even come in aerosol form. Half of the male cast were trying to apply make-up when the others weren't looking, and the rest were Morris dancing into their tights. The language was an intriguing blend of modern, Elizabethan and pure Anglo-Saxon.

The swords were displayed authentically in a rack, except for the one with a knot in the blade. Cuthbert had meant to have a word with Percy about that.

Cuthbert had climbed up onto the gantry high above the stage. He opened the skylight to help to ventilate the theatre and gasped at the amount of cars and television crews arriving. *It's a good job Elspeth has bought plenty of stock,* he thought. *But how did she know?* He would have a word with her later too.

Cuthbert enjoyed a moment's peace. Even the pigeons were at the far end grabbing all the best perches. He glanced down into the crow's nest where Ronald would spend most of the play. He seemed to have a supply of knives in there. *Still,* thought Cuthbert, *it will stop him getting bored.*

People were filing in and scraps of conversation floated up to him. "Good job we came early, these school productions are pretty popular." "I saw the last one. Didn't realise that Macbeth was a comedy until then …" "Good job I made you hurry, Sidney. See, there's only one front seat taken …" "Is that a badger?"

Cuthbert sensed someone beside him on the gantry. Geraldine was holding some of the script. Cuthbert smiled. Geraldine didn't. Cuthbert waited, Geraldine couldn't.

"Cuthbert," she began, "I have just been rehearsing with Margery and it's the first time I've seen the introduction you wrote."

Cuthbert gulped.

Geraldine watched him closely. "The spelling mistakes in your introduction are exactly the same as the ones in the lost play. How do you explain that?"

Cuthbert said, with a sickly grin, "I copied the style for authenticity."

Geraldine purred, "You didn't translate the scrolls, Cuthbert. I did. You only saw the papers I wrote with the mistakes corrected."

Cuthbert slumped and it all spilled out. "School project … used some old blank scrolls …. lost my pen … used pointy stick …. spilled the ink … used cold tea ... teachers laughed …. hid them in the secret place so my dad wouldn't see them."

"Good grief, Cuthbert. I wonder if you ever left the valley, would it all revert to normal, or would it fade away completely?"

She patted him on his dejected shoulders and said, "Come on, Cuthbert, these people expect a play."

Cuthbert took a moment before he followed Geraldine down the ladder. He thought of putting his feet on each side and sliding down dramatically, but when he last tried it he hit his chin on every rung.

Cuthbert forced his way to the main doors where the joiner was arguing with a television crew. "They are demanding the whole front row for filming, and she wants to talk all the way through it," spluttered the joiner.

'She' slinked her way over to Cuthbert and smiled seductively. Cuthbert looked over her shoulder and asked "Are those sausages burning?"

The television crew were pushed back outside and told to film from there because all the tickets were sold. The commentator began to broadcast through gritted teeth.

Elspeth stood behind her stall taking orders and waving her arms like a race-track bookie. Percy handed over the tractor controls to one of the valley Mafia, adjusted the feather in his hat and prepared to act.

Geraldine had donned a costume as a disguise and she walked to centre stage. Raising both hands, she appealed for silence. The murmur continued. "Now, people," she snapped.

'So much for the disguise,' thought Cuthbert. The audience froze.

Geraldine explained the circumstances of the discovery of the play and its apparent importance. She left in all the mystery and left out Cuthbert's role in it. She stepped back.

The front row murmured nervously again. "Not a school do, then …" "Hope it's funnier than her …" "It is a badger, you know."

Chapter 50

Geraldine bowed to the audience and the curtains opened.

The cannon boomed and the stone ball howled across the theatre, punching a hole in the far wall.

"Thank you," shouted the T.V. cameraman as he pushed his lens through.

Cuthbert shook his head to clear the ringing noise and peered through the smoke at the twins. He vowed to 'have a word' with those two as well.

On stage, the crowd milled about, pointing out to sea.

The front row muttered, "Is that a stag?" "No, it's definitely a badger ..." "Looks like a stag to me."

Percy leapt onto his trusty steed to ride to London and warn the Queen, but he bounced off into the crowd on the dock because the crotch of his tights was still at knee height.

At the front door, a commotion distracted Cuthbert. He turned to look just as a knife thudded into the wall beside him. Above, Ronald cursed.

'Arkle' was bounding down the aisle halfway out of a strait-jacket. Buckles flew in all directions as she thundered towards the stage. Spotting Geraldine, she shouted, "Look out, they are right behind me. I held them off as long as I could."

Sure enough, two men appeared behind her with tranquiliser guns. Geraldine addressed the audience, ad-libbing like a trooper. "Look," she cried, "this brave fellow has tried to stop the Armada alone."

"Oooooooohh," said the audience.

Geraldine added, "Before escaping to warn us."

"Aaaaahh," said the audience.

Geraldine turned to Cuthbert and hissed, "Quick, lend me your knife."

Cuthbert stared. "What knife ...?"

Geraldine snatched the blade out of the wall and slashed Arkle's remaining buckles. They stood together mid-stage and Geraldine announced, "We go to a better place- For England." She kicked the right plank and they dropped from view. There was a crash because no one asked for mattresses to be laid ready.

Spontaneous applause broke out as the rest of the cast gaped.

The men from the asylum advanced. The twins glared at them. The men scowled back. The twins inched the cannon around. The men sneered. The twins produced a match. The men hesitated. The twins did not. Just as the cannon roared, Henry kicked the same plank and the men fell through the same trapdoor. At least there was something to land on this time.

"To London?" suggested Cuthbert weakly. The cast obediently cried "To London" and all rushed off in different directions.

The curtains closed. Cuthbert dropped his script and bent to pick it up. Straightening, he banged his head on a knife handle. "Oh. Geraldine must have put it back," he mumbled, rubbing his head. Above, Ronald cursed again.

Another hole had appeared in the wall and the T.V. crew shouted "Thank you" as they pushed a microphone through it. The crowd went wild. This was better than the circus when the lion had attacked Blind-Pugh from behind.

Cuthbert dodged under the curtains in time to see the hedgerows fly upwards knocking Percy flat on his face. He looked as if he was trying to swim out to the Armada alone.

The wooden panelling was lowered and, in a corner, Henry was kissing Queen Elizabeth.

Cuthbert stared at his script. He didn't know why he bothered, this lot made it up as they went along.

Ronald had decided to come down and finish the job himself and he was skinning down a rope with a knife between his teeth. This was the same rope taking the hedgerows home and so after a lot of effort he ended up back where he had started.

The curtains swished open again. Queen Elizabeth sat in splendour in an oak-panelled throne room. Henry entered and bowed with a flourish. He kissed her hand and they gazed into each other's eyes.

The air seemed to crackle between them. The audience sat up. These two had chemistry.

Touches lingered and eyes caressed. The messenger from Portsmouth hadn't arrived yet for some reason and the love-birds happily ad-libbed to pass the time. The front row loosened their collars.

Percy ran in too fast, skidded and crashed into the side of the throne. Shoving his feather back in his hat, he was soon back in his costume.

The Queen glared at him and snapped, "Where the devil have you been?"

This wasn't in the script and Percy panicked, "Gardening," he said.

Henry covered his eyes.

"Gardening?" roared the Queen. "Gardening?"

Percy panicked again, "Not gardening." he tried.

"Not gardening?" screamed the Queen in fury. "Not gardening."

Percy was speechless with fright. This was a beheading offence.

The trapdoor creaked open slightly and Geraldine's eyes appeared under the lid. Her disembodied voice narrated, "Knot gardens were all the rage in Elizabethan England."

The trapdoor creaked again as it closed. Percy was looking everywhere for the ghostly voice and the front row tittered, "Well, was he gardening or knot?"

The trapdoor slammed back on its hinges.

Geraldine snarled, "Have you lot seen those sausages outside?"

The front row nodded mutely.

"Well, if you don't shut up, you'll be joining them."

They shut up. The trapdoor closed.

Percy was racking his brains for the right line as Margery turned to him and hissed, "Well?" with a sound like a razor through silk.

Percy doffed his cap and the feather fell off again, "Madam," he spluttered, "the spanners are conglomerating and attacking our lizard."

"What the devil are you blathering about, man?" screamed the Queen of England in her pre-execution voice.

Henry interrupted smoothly. "Your Majesty," he began, "I believe that this common foot soldier is trying to say that the Spaniards are congregating off the Lizard Point, ready to attack."

Percy nodded furiously like someone whose neck was loose enough already.

Elizabeth softened slightly as she turned to Henry. "Where is Drake?"

"Bowling, your Majesty," replied Henry.

The Queen turned to Percy, "Frobisher?" she asked, dangerously calm.

Percy was still smarting, "Sailing in Norfolk with some broads," he snapped.

The Queen shot to her feet and pointed to the exit. "Get back immediately and warn the fleet. I will address them myself."

Percy gaped. "But it's miles ..." Wilting under the combined glares of the Queen and her minister, he bowed and shuffled off muttering, "Common foot soldier. As if they would have special soldiers for feet. That's cobblers."

The Queen paced up and down in consternation. Wringing her hands she said, "Where will I find a hero in time to save my beloved England?"

The curtains closed.

Backstage, the panelling flew upwards and the dockside returned. The crowd assembled.

The curtains opened.

Queen Elizabeth strode into the crowd with Henry by her side. "Where is my fleet?" she demanded.

"Coming now, Miss," said Percy, keeping out of the way.

The golden figurehead appeared and the audience gasped as a ship hove into view. The milkman stood heroically with one hand on the rigging and a foot on the cannon. His tight breeches strained and his muscles bulged beneath the gossamer shirt.

His red sash held a brace of pistols. The crowd sighed. Leaping over the gunwale, he landed with panther-like agility.

Bowing to the Queen, he prepared to catch her as she swooned at the sight of him and pleaded with him to save her England. He uttered his longest line. "Your majesty, I am Captain Cuthbert."

The Queen ignored him. "Is this the best we can do? How many guns do you carry? How many culverins?"

Cuthbert flicked frantically through the script until a knife pinned all the pages together.

The Queen stalked over to the ship and snapped, "Is that Torredo worm in the timbers?"

Turning to the milkman, she snarled, "Well? Speak up, man. What was it, Captain Cloth-ears?"

The milkman could only gape. He had spent hours practising the 'Swooning maiden' with a pillow, but at the moment he was somewhere behind the figurehead in the Oscar nominations. In desperation he struck a heroic pose on the dock-side, only to double up as the Queen elbowed him out of the way.

"Look at those sails," she demanded, "call that a repair? I may only have the body of a feeble woman, but I know good stitching when I see it."

The milkman was signalling to Cuthbert for help, but Cuthbert was looking suspiciously towards the crow's nest for Ronald. The Queen was storming back towards him, so the milkman leapt out of the way and clung onto the figurehead.

One of the twins inside said, "Hello, handsome," and the milkman yelped before disappearing under the cardboard waves.

Percy was dispatched to the local inns to recruit sailors and he ran into the wings gratefully.

Henry knelt before his Queen and took her hand, "In your presence, I may be only a whisper, Majesty, but a whisper can blow out a candle. The whisper may become a breeze, the breeze may power an inferno. I will take command of your fleet and together we will sweep the Spaniards from the seas forever."

The audience sighed, the women felt their spines melt and many hearts beat a little faster.

The men wondered where Henry got his cod-piece.

The curtains closed and the audience was on its feet. The sound of clapping energised the whole cast. Geraldine came out of the trapdoor where she had been prompting Margery and they hugged.

"Queen Elizabeth-one," shouted Geraldine.

"Captain Cuthbert-nil," screamed the women in chorus. The cast obliged with many curtain calls and gradually left Henry and Margery centre stage. They were too busy kissing to notice.

Cuthbert was called out for a special mention, but no-one could think of anything so he wandered off again.

Percy was outside. He sat on the tractor as he prepared to switch it off and gazed at the sunset. Just then the twins knocked the jack out from under the driving wheels and Percy was heading for the sundown.

Ronald was sulking. No-one had lowered the crow's nest and he had run out of knives.

The badger had enjoyed the performance, but every time he tried to clap, he fell off the tractor seat.

Henry was outside talking to his old press colleagues. "Sorry, gentlemen," he announced, "this was just an adolescent fantasy done for a school project years ago. It involved old paper and tea-bags. My fiancée and I joined in to support a good cause."

He smiled fondly across at Margery, before adding impishly, "The real news, gentlemen, is that you have just given to charity." The press pack groaned.

Margery tucked her arm into Cuthbert's and said, "You know, Henry is going to enrol the twins in his old boarding school. He says it will hone their skills and prepare them for Government."

She kissed Cuthbert on the cheek and went over to join Henry.

Cuthbert sighed. He had felt at one with both the valley and the theatre tradition tonight. Cuthbert stretched and yawned. He would release the two asylum workers after Geraldine and Arkle had a long enough head start and he might even rescue Ronald eventually.

Gathering up the scrolls that had started all this off, he smiled at the thought of his teacher saying, "These will never amount to anything, lad. Who do you think you are, Shakespeare?"

Cuthbert tucked the scrolls under his arm. There was no point putting them back at the Mill.

He would use the secret panel in his bedroom where all the other old scrolls were.

THE END

About the Author

Patrick Barrett is a sixty year old ex-miner from Mansfield in Nottinghamshire. He is married to Paula and between them, they have several children. 'Shakespeare's Cuthbert' is his first book, though he has been writing comedy for several years.

His aims as a writer are 'to be successful and make people laugh by providing them with an escape from the harshness of real life'.

His other abiding interest is in antiques.

* 9 7 8 1 9 0 7 9 5 4 5 0 4 *